JIMMY ADAMOWSKI: TELEPORTER

DAVID J WINTERS

{Subgenre:Publishers}

ALSO BY DAVID J. WINTERS

Nurse-and-union-leader *turned* homicide-detective, Eminence Gray, uses her gifts of empathy and emotional labor to catch the most vicious of West Brandon's killers. Em's ability to maintain this skillset will be put to the ultimate test when the highest-profile murder case her department has ever faced falls right into her lap. Add to Em's troubles a corrupt executive from her union days, back and up to old tricks, and it might just be Eminence Gray requiring a little *bedside manner...* or a lot.

Roger Jech doesn't have any superpowers, but he has a super ability: harm him, harm yourself in equal measure. Hit him with a right hook, your jaw breaks. Shoot him in the head, your brains blow out the back of you. Drop him in a war zone, your enemies kill themselves killing him. Jech's a weapon to the wrong people and a savior to the right, but before he can become the former, he must learn to harness his gift before it becomes his curse.

Shale City has seen better days. First, the dam burst, flooding out the town's iron mine. Then, local officials shut down the shipping and courier services, the only thing keeping Shale City hanging on... It was all the mayor of Shale could do to fight off the more 'legitimate' of sleazeballs trying to destroy her city, but now it seems as though some other kind of sleazeball force is encroaching upon her town, set on putting the final nail in its coffin...

For the Adamowskis

1

***

ON THE WATERFRONT

When life's got you anchored at the heals, *further down's* where you visit before there's any rising for any surface. Finding peace isn't like the flipping of a switch.

So, for now...

It's a man on a couch. Drinking. Heavily. He's watching a movie. *Watchmen*. He's watching, lounging, glancing out a window over his left shoulder whenever the mood should strike which it never does. It's not desire, it's compulsion. One of the mildest sort yet enough to drive him to do it.

It's a nice view. Nice as a matter of conformity and conformity's justification: unchecked tradition: a bigotry of forgotten utility. Not so nice a view by any other standard, aesthetics for example.

It's the ocean.

Aesthetics of an ocean view are unremarkable, sure. Price on the other hand...

He's looking out the window once more, more and more, movie be damned.

"Water seeks its own level."

Ocean is this guy's interlocutor right now.

What's that mean? In the sense of water *as* water. I know it means, pardon the idiom for idiom here, *birds of a feather*. Know that much. Free the poetry, means water likes, what? To be flat? What possible purchase ya got? You're an element whose sole overriding ambition is its own lack of feature. A plumb blandness?

People *do* pay a premium to live adjacent the soup, he thinks.

He near-finishes his drink.

He rises to his feet, starts pacing the hardwood from the living room to the kitchen by way of dining room. He's wearing black track pants and a Winnipeg Jets jersey. The old one, from before they were the Coyotes then the Jets again. Not the new one with the logo that makes it look like the Jet's having missionary-style intercourse with the maple leaf. He's got his four-point-five-ounce rocks glass in hand, nursing the last ounce of bourbon in it. He stops to look out the dining room window to the balcony out front. He's staring through the kind of glass that provides a hermetic seal even when on sliders. Thick. Not cheap. Worth it? Everything's temperate enough around here. Windows are clear enough. Sees that water through that west-facing wall of them. Again.

He needs more booze though a little pacing and pontificating will serve his satisfactions too. He paces his way to the kitchen, sipping. Back and forth. Back and forth. He gets about a foot closer every four loops or so. As he loops he rehearses arguments he'll never have with people he'll never meet and this appears to quell something in him.

"The ponds and the lakes—I mean, they're great in all their bucollia but it's all periphery. Trees, sands... People, places, and beached whales... All on the other side and the... the... *other* sides. Water's like the celebrity boyfriend standing off to the side of the red carpet... holding the purse... of geology. *What about when them waters glisten like a mirror? Isn't that a sight?* That's the entirety of the wet showing us everything but itself to get attention for itself. Nature's foil. Facile. The ultimate hanger-on. *Can't you see all the wonderful things I surround myself with, aren't I that too?*"

No, he thinks, opening the cabinet. And what are you hiding in there and I don't mean the purse? What you got down there? Shit's scary. Oh it saves lives, sure, sustains life in the right measure at the right purity, sure, yet that don't make it pretty. People die in it too. Get eaten in it. But really only in the movies. But it saves lives if you swallow it but you wanna live in a hospital parking lot? Then why next the water for that? You don't.

He inspects the liquor cupboard, squinting. He leans back, kinda deliberating. Sucks down the last half-ounce of bourbon in the rocks glass. Purses his lips and sips it up like a straw so he knows it's there. Half-ounce would sit in his maw like a raindrop in a bathtub otherwise. He wants to feel his booze before he *feels* his booze. Grabs another glass full now? Nah, grabs another bottle. Bourbon's all gone so he'll try the Irish whiskey. After that it's a couple light beers and Kahlua from a bottle in such a state of disuse the liqueur's glued the cap to the bottle-top threads.

My father was a watchmaker. He abandoned it when Einstein discovered that time is relative... says the TV.

Yeah, sure, he thinks. No one in town'd have a use for a device you could look at any time a day and make a world of accurate predictions about your and others' states of affairs just because... What? Thing don't tick in a black hole? He grabs the bottle of Irish Whiskey.

A symbolic clock is as nourishing to the intellect as a photograph of oxygen to a drowning man...

"Yeah but that *pichure* represents something real. Real and what would save the guy's life. Is the symbol of danger representative of something real too? Danger imminent? Cuz that's what she wants to know you pompous idiot! She ain't asking whether or not a token instance of the symbol's the life of the party! You drive offa cliffs because the *Bridge is Out* sign lacks nourishment too?" He puts his forehead against the cupboard door. "Calm down yer no better Jimmy boy."

He lands on the couch, flops. Bottle's in one hand, rocks glass is in the other. Couch creaks at the impact. *Be careful Jimmy.* He pours whiskey three-quarters up the glass. Two beers worth he reckons. He gulps down two of the three. Gulps the last immediately after. Refills. Why even use the glass? He likes it. Makes him feel like he's in a western. He wishes he could have a cigarette but this little adventure isn't about stimulation.

Some Time.

Bottle's half deprived of its spirits.

He's slurring his speech. Slurring it at the TV.

"Gimme a goddamn break! He can't really *sthee* the future! Off the hop he's not literally *seeing* cuz if his mind were awash with nothing but imaginings of every event of his life it would be a sloppy collage of meaningless phenomena. Like looking through the holes in a picture of your third birthday to see through the holes of your second to get at the picture of your first.

"His whole timespan must be given in something like a life history, a theory, like a collection of life events *azzsth* propositions. Maybe they're images like future memories or something but they're still just representations. Audio-visual propositions. Have to be like he's reading it from some sort of *book of the mind*—maybe a picture book of the mind—but that's where Dr. Manhattan's a dummy cuz if he thinks the proposition 'Dr. Manhattan will come to know the proposition *Laurie and Dan have been sleeping together* is true at some time ahead of time *now*' he *beliefths* a proposition that is either true or false though if *true* a proposition providing sufficient information for him to know *Laurie is sleeping with Dan* at *this* time and not the future. The proposition is made false then and his premonition is therefore wrong. If the proposition is *falsh* to begin with, then Dr. Manhattan believes a false proposition and is not seeing his future adequately. If we accept a non-classical semantics, where there is some intermediate truth-value representing a proposition that is neither determinable as true or false, then we have indeterminacy and Dr. Manhattan still can't see his future.

"And what happens if he opens his *history of Dr. Manhattan* mind book to the section representing the exact moment he's opened the book? Mirrors facing each other and there's no bottom. No meaning. Can't see shit and his mirror book would have to be infinite in size for all that meaninglessness. Meaningless information is still information and there's not enough storage space in the universe for that! Fuckin movie! *Determinishm's* bullshit."

He realizes things have started spinning on him. Realizes he'll have no realization of any of this tomorrow morning. He has to work to keep his eyes open too. Literally put in the effort, reverse Clockwork Orange style. Has to work to keep from vomiting as well.

Time for bed.

⌐Ǝ

Ǝ

Jimmy's in the king of the master bedroom. Instantly. One foot goes off the mattress and sits flat on the floor. The spinning eases.

ii

Jimmy's stone. A blackout. Nothing moving except his diaphragm and his uvula causing loud sustained snores. Eyes under those lids of his are the stillest thing about him. Then...

A *THUMP!*

"Knew it!"

It's a *Man's* voice. He's stumbling through the front door in the dark.

"Shhh!"

It's a *Woman's shhh*. She's following the Man in.

He taps at an alarm system control panel next the door. "I told you it was off." Says this like he's won some sort of bet.

"Shhh!"

"Why are you shushing me?"

"Stop! Don't move!" She says. Man obliges the command despite knowing less about the intent of it than the *shhh!* Woman leans forward over the threshold bobbing and weaving her head like her ears are leading the rest of her. "You hear that?"

"No—"

"It's a buzzing," she says.

It's Jimmy's snoring.

"It's noth—" He stifles himself a second. Listens. Then... "Holy shit! It's a buzzing... Quiet!" We'd see the Woman frown if she weren't standing in the dark. Man's not done with the imperatives. "Turn on your flashlight."

"I don't gotta flashlight."

"On your phone!" He starts climbing the stairs like any cat burglar would. A cat burglar in a Blake Edwards movie...

Stairs lead from the foyer up to a ground floor that's not a ground floor at all really. The house was built to face that gawd-awful ocean and all of the ocean around here sloshes up against a hill. A coastal graben, more precisely. It's more like a *ground wall*, the floor a cantilever.

"You're not still going in?" the Woman says hushed though piercing. "There could be somebody up there!"

BOOM! Bedroom door's kicked open, rousting Jimmy. Lights

flip on. Jimmy looks into the glare. Man and Woman do the same for that matter.

"Who the hell are you?" shouts the Man, squinting at the bed. "I got a gun!"

"What gun?" asks the Woman.

"*Shhhh…it!* I'm kinda wingin it here hon!"

They're no cat burglars! They're *Husband* and *Wife* most likely. They're home early.

"You're home early," Jimmy yawns.

"It smells like the inside of a beer can in here," the Wife sniffs out. Jimmy's drunkenness *has* waned, demanding he tie one on, yet the hooch is still metabolizing away from him in a vapor that if it smoked it'd waft.

"We were offered a promotional fare but it required taking an earlier flight," The Husband explains.

"A discount? You're millionaires!" Jimmy chides gesturing all around the room as though the room alone implies millionairedom.

"Not in this economy," Husband rebuts.

Jimmy props himself up on one elbow. Gets comfortable. "A number's a number man."

"In nominal terms. However, in real terms… Hey! Who are you? I have a gun!"

"You don't have a gun," Jimmy says assuredly, rolling onto his back. He clasps his hands together behind head, relaxing. The wisps of his armpit hairs, hanging free due the tank top he's wearing, feather at the pillows.

"He's using the good linen…" The Wife says concerned.

Then…

¬∃

Jimmy's blipped away! Disappeared! Sheets and all!

"He *took* our good linen!"

DING! BEEP! BEEP! BOOP!

Man rushes away down the hall, to the laundry room. Bedding's in the wash! He rushes back to his Wife still at the door, astonished.

"Hon, you know what just happened? We've been Ported!"

She smiles a *you really think so?* gaping smile. Then...

Ǝ

Jimmy's back, standing next the cushioned armchair kitty-cornered the bed.

"The Teleporter!" the couple say in unison.

Jimmy grins. Tips the brim of an invisible hat. He takes hold of the backpack he's left on the armchair and...

¬Ǝ

Gone again. Wad of cash's on the chair in place of the pack.

2

SAN MARZANO

Jimmy's vomiting in the middle of the Atacama. Thought he was going to sleep this one off. Best laid plans.

He's dry heaving steadily now so he must be done.

A beat.

Then...

He wipes his chin on his bare wrist and grabs his pack. He starts rooting through it. Finds his small flashlight in a side-pocket first. Pocket's conspicuous enough to be accessible even in the dark. He pops it on issuing a whopping three-watt challenge to the dark of the moonless desert night. Pops it into his mouth to have his hands free.

"Shit shit!" He roots a little more vigorously. Stops. Pulls out the twist-on top of a featureless aluminum canister. "Shit!" Rooting recommences. He pulls out a wad of old photographs, square. Not polaroid's, older. He lays each of the wad onto the sand making a two-by-two grid—puts a little pebble on top of each photo as he goes. He takes the light out his mouth and examines them up close. They're all of a little yellow house in a little green farmyard. He scoops them up and puts them back into a pile. He roots again. Brings out the container part of the aluminum canister. Keeps digging. One last thing. Got it! It's a larger piece of paper folded over twice to match the area of the photographs. He unfolds it. A sonogram of an infant at three months. He refolds. Puts the sonogram and the four photos back into the container.

A fox howl.

A couple more chirp back.

Shouldn't be a threat. Shouldn't be in this region either. Gotta be hungry. He stuffs the canister into the pack.

He's back on the coast, hiding in the bushes outside the house he'd been squatting in no less than a half-hour ago.

"He was really quite considerate."

"A-after we caught him."

"Booze was gone but he paid for it. Put the bottles in the recycling even."

"Listen folks," says the responding officer, "I know it's real easy to get enamored with this guy, this 'teleporter'. He slip you anything?" *Cop* starts moving his pen light left to right in front of the Wife's face.

"Like what?" she says, then... "Hey!"

Eyes track. Cop's still not convinced of any sobriety. "Visits from this guy," he says, "this conman, they're almost like a rite of passage for some people, especially in these places where ya think that big gate'll keep everyone except him out so you're real lax about your alarm systems. Maybe intentionally so..."

"What are you saying?" the Wife asks, catching the innuendo.

"However," the Cop redirects, "he *is* breaking the law."

"And we don't want to charge him with any offense," the Husband insists.

"None at all," the Wife concurs.

"Listen," Cop says, confused. "That's not up to you, but—"

"But in the movies the Cops always ask *do you wish to press charges?*."

"That's in the movies. And it's *press* charges. Like, *press us police to charge him...* Citizens don't get to lay any charges."

"Well," says the Wife in all irrelevant confidence, "we do not wish to press any charges."

"That's fine because we have no one around to charge." Cop realizes something. "Look, if you don't care one way or the other that the guy broke in, why even call the police?"

"Well," says the Husband like it's the most obvious answer in the world, "so there'll be a public record of our being Ported."

Wife nods.

Cop frowns like he's tired of doing so so often in this neighborhood. "Maybe we should frame the report for you..." he mumbles.

"What was that?"

"You can expect a copy of the incident report by mail within the week."

Superfluous Cop pulls away in his prowler and Jimmy comes out of the bushes. He starts walking down the middle of the empty subdivision road. His eyes are closed. He's navigating just fine despite this. He stops. Turns to a house five up and across the street from the Husband and Wife's.

We're in that house now. Not in it really: 'observing' it. This is a part of Jimmy's gift. He *Gifts* himself a glimpse of the world before beaming into it. For safety's sake of course. Don't want to beam into the path of a speeding car or some live wires.

Foyer's dark though there's some feature.

Garage is empty.

Back in the foyer, alarm panel says *System Ready*.

Master bedroom's dark but, again, there's enough feature to see the bed is flat. Kids' rooms are definitely empty as photo-sensitive night lights are on indicating as much. Master bedroom could have people in it but what kind of self-respecting horned-up married couple sleeps when the kids are away? These people are on vacation.

Jimmy opens his eyes. Lets his senses tell him anything about the consolation digs The Gift may have missed. He shrugs. He pulls his pack tightest over his shoulders.

¬Ⅎ

We see the light of the opening fridge brightening through the kitchen window.

ii

Week later.

It's a farmers market. It's nowhere near the ocean. It's West Brandon, Amerika. Jimmy doesn't live here. He's not domiciled anywhere, technically speaking. Why would he be? Guy can beam anywhere a guy can beam safely and bedrooms are generally safe last he checked. He doesn't make them any less safe either. Hell, Jimmy's a lottery to those homeowners. Give the middle-upper class a thrill why doncha? He *does* spend most of his time in West Brandon. Seems to be where the action is.

He's selling the freshest of Mediterranean-grown San Marzano tomatoes. Strange, considering their rarity. Doubly strange considering, nine times out of ten, when they're eaten in Amerika they're eaten stewed out the can. He's selling them cheap as can be too. Whole show's like a magic trick. He's got a produce stand with a counter made of three bound wooden crates tipped on their ends. There's an eighth-inch chipboard rectangle for signage propped up by broomsticks. At the rear of the stand is a broom-closet-sized box made of the same chipboard. Closet has a thin cloth curtain on a snapped broomstick rod for a door. Process is this: Jimmy takes an order, goes behind that curtain a few seconds, then brings out a wooden basket of thin latticed pine strips containing the desired measure of San Marzanos.

Folksy.

How's he doing this? the people think.

The people marvel. Line up for blocks too. They near-crowd-out other sellers in the Canadian Tire parking lot the sellers sell in but the sellers don't mind. Shoppers there for Jimmy's tomaters aren't there *just* for Jimmy's tomaters. They won't pass over a nice bundle of zucchinis or jar of cran-berry ketchup if they see such things. He brings in the foot traffic.

A man with a poppy at his left lapel is putting in an order.

"How much you want?" Jimmy asks.

"I'll take *oh* four pounds."

"Don't know pounds. Gimme volume."

"Don't know pounds?" *Poppy Man's* confused.

"Don't got a scale. Use your hands." Jimmy mimes a series of *once caught a fish this big* hand motions, bigger-to-smaller in opposing wavering palms.

"Ok..." Poppy obliges as Jimmy churns his hands at him. The poppy shopper holds his hands about an inch and a half apart.

Jimmy frowns. "Well that's never six pounds. That's a single tomato."

"Oh no, my gesture means a single tomato's width, make no mistake. Only, I want that single-tomato-wide pile to be six feet high."

"Six feet!"

"You said volume. That's height. That's three dimensions."

"Make your palm-width the height!"

"I can't stretch my arms the width of four pounds of tomatoes one palm high. I'm not over six feet tall."

"What's *your* height got to do with anything?"

"Arm span is as wide as a body is tall if you're of standard human proportion. I'd need over six feet of body for over six feet of arms to span the width of the tomatoes I want."

Jimmy's head's now jittering in some sort of teeth-grinding confused frustration.

Poppy notices. "Best I can do for four pounds is span the width of a pile of tomatoes one tomato wide and six feet high."

"You can do two-by-three in a circle."

"Can do three tomatoes by two in a parallelogram but I won't. I'm not scaring away a bear. And if I were, I'd do it with more dignity than a drunk forest ranger counting fruit like a constipated bird!"

Jimmy notices the waiting customers are starting to jitter the same. "Just make a baby rocking motion or something!" he orders. "Make the baby the size of the pile you want."

"What's the volumetric conversion for four pounds of baby to four pounds of tomato?"

"If I knew that I wouldn't need the pantomime!"

"Just get me three dozen."

Jimmy retreats into the closet. Closes the curtain.

¬∃

A beat.

∃

He returns with the *baby-basket-of-tomatoes-thiiiis-big* basket of tomatoes but...

Poppy man is gone. Jimmy dumps the fruit. He grabs both hands onto his crate counter corners and leans forward. Looks around. Poppy's nowhere.

Sir...

Jimmy feels the slight elevation and sharp corners of something under his left palm.

Excuse me...

He picks it up. It's folded paper. He half unfolds it.

I'd like...

It's a note. Guy drop it by accident? He flips it and *Jimmy*'s written on the other side. No accident. He unfolds more. Barely has time to read,

Figurace meets Prez: 11/10 730pm

When...

"Sir!"

Jimmy snaps out of it. Stuffs the note into his pocket and attends to the customer next in line.

"I'd like a six-month-old's worth." The customer is rocking an invisible six-month-old in her arms.

"Absolutely! Apologies for the distraction." He's about to re-enter the closet when...

"Jimmy Adamowski!"

He turns to face the inquiring shout. A bunch of suits are approaching. They're pushing their way through the crowd of shoppers.

"Federal agents! Don't move!" They've drawn tasers.

Jimmy doesn't think. Bolts through the curtain with so much force the whole closet bursts apart outward.

¬ꓱ

Chipboard sides lay on the ground like unfolded cubes of one side curtain. Jimmy's gone and the collapsed closet is completely empty. No tomatoes, baskets, anything. One of the feds kicks the curtain away as though hoping to catch Jimmy under it. Says *shit!* as though hoping to catch Jimmy under it.

Our government, ladies and gentlemen.

Jimmy's definitely gone. Another agent has sidled up through the crowd next to kicker. He shakes his head, frowning, reconfirming Jimmy's escape in this lament. Nothing more for these feds to do other than something wildly inefficient. Like, take a two-hour lunch to buy a sub sandwich for one-hundred-fifty bucks...

ꓱ

Jimmy's among the Marzano vines. He's hunkering down, dropping his gloves into the top of a stack of small wooden storage baskets—those pine-strip boxes he was using for his sales. Folksy. Hold about a one-month's worth each. Next item to drop are his pruning scissors. He's patting around in the dirt for them when...

He hears a voice!

Now another!

They're Italian voices, Napolitano. Jimmy rises out of his squat just high enough to peer over the nightshade bushes. He sees who must be the proprietor of this grow-op with a likely *Hand* both moving toward at about fifty yards out. Jimmy starts rooting for those scissors a little frantic now. *Root root root* when he realizes he can just leave them. *Damn it Jimmy boy!* But the *Farmer* and Hand are on him.

The pair are one row over and groping for the vines. They're pulling them over just enough to get a clear view of Jimmy when...

¬∃

Jimmy's gone again! Baskets too!

But...

There's a good ten-ounce chunk of raw gold in his place. Gold sits next to the scissors incidentally.

Farmer picks up the scissors as Hand picks up the gold. They examine their respective items. Farmer looks perturbed by the would-be thief's tool as Hand just beams. Farmer moves on to examining the *as-it-turns-out* carefully pruned tomato plants. He's gradually glancing over the stems in the direction of the Hand's hand. Second he sets eyes upon that chunk he comes to his senses. Snatches the gold away and slams the scissors down in its place. Farmer, laboriously, lifts the mass closer to his eye.

Lightest heavy-lifting he's ever done.
He beams.

3

THE LEGEND CONTINUES

Another night another 'night'.

Another movie. Another liquor cupboard. *Sin City*. Crown Royal. At least, he thinks it is. It's in a crystal decanter but it's a brown liquor and it plays at the sickly sweetness of a rye without quite committing to the role. That's what makes it palatable for him. Everything else in the cupboard is fortified, syrupy, where the fancy decanters don't help the fact there's no way he'll ever keep any of it down. He pours more whiskey into the rocks glass. Same one he had last night. Travels with it apparently.

Drinks again.

Stares out the wall of glass *again*.

I love hitmen. No matter what you do to them, you don't feel bad...

Out the glass wall is Lake Okanagan. A nice lake because there's hardly any of it at all. A thin strip of water surrounded by desert mountains. Mountains are low and rolling too, not just walls of rock make you feel in a pit. Water's calm tonight. Cooperative. Reflects the mountains.

Jimmy gulps, lowers, pours, raises, gulps. He's still looking out the window.

Fine coat like that and you're bleeding all over it...

He side glances over to the TV. Then back to the wall of glass.

"Decent movie. Decent view."

Jimmy's out cold but not blackout cold. We see his eyes twitching under closed lids.

Is he dreaming of torturers? Because the sleep looks torturous. He's Gifting in those dreams. Gifting the thing he fears most, we can only assume, from all the tossing and terror'd shouting.

It is just that:

He sees half the world as it is, half the phantasmagoria of his REM sleep when this happens. **There's a mountain-top. Cold, snowy, blustery. It's Everest. The peak.**

He zooms into it.

The Widow's **there, standing balancing on the peak, hardly exerting any effort at all to do it. Peak's more needle-like in dream. She beckons.**

He wakes shivering in the snow in nothing but the boxers and tank top he went to bed in. He's gasping in the thin air. His bed is firn, abrasive in addition to achingly cold.

How long has he been here? Feels like hours though

he'd be dead. Feels like hours because even minutes at twenty-five below centigrade dilate to hours. Jimmy's panicked but...

¬ヨ

ヨ

By luck he's managed to send himself back to the night's bed. He's not warming. He wraps himself in the comforter and lifts his feet up onto the mattress, crosses them under himself and the blanket. He grabs the crystal decanter of sherry off the nightstand. Knocks the rocks glass off in the process—hits the click flooring below. It doesn't shatter just chips, a wedge of it gone to the bottom of the cup. He starts chugging from the decanter.

Could almost look a contrived sort of classy, his drinking out of this affectation. Would indeed be a quirky and unique affect if not for Jimmy's cold-induced shakes. Would look like *something* if not for the sloppy nature with which he drinks. He's shaking, sure, but those vessels weren't designed to get your lips around. Not like the mouth of a Jameson bottle. They've got some strange glassy chunk of a lip around the top, measuring about a half-inch of depth all around.

It's all he's got and so he drinks from it, clumsily, fancily. He shivers waiting for the booze to get his pilot lit. He starts to sob. Can't control it.

"W-Where to next time Jimmy! Bottom of the f-fucking ocean!" He looks up like he's pleading. "I can't do this any more!" he cries.

He vomits.

His pack! he realizes. It's gone! Where the fuck was he up on that mountain? He left it there! He starts to Gift. Goes to the peak.

It's there! Right where he woke. The top of goddamn Mount Everest!

Damnit Jimmy boy!

He's about to make a move despite the smothering height up there and despite the unrelieving cold down here, when...

A hand reaches down. Takes the pack. Jimmy backs up a little. Hand's of a man most likely judging by the stature. Figure's hidden otherwise, wearing a thick woolly robe with fur in places, gloves and a toque of sorts with ear flaps. He's got long-johns over his pants—under too, presumably. All what you'd expect in a cold like this. Curiously, there's a hem of blaze orange fabric hanging a few inches out the bottom of the wool robe.

Jimmy shakes from more than the cold now. Refrains from the drink. Needs his wits not dead sleep. He watches, shivering.

Figure takes the pack. Doesn't look into it. Just leaves. Makes sense, it's cold as hell.

Figure's indeed of a man. He's taken Jimmy's pack to some sort of temple of many levels. Like from *Game of Death*. He's a man out of those winter clothes, blaze orange hem was the bottom of a robe. It flows now. He sets the pack down at the center of the large hall at the temple's ground floor. He leaves.

Jimmy's almost convulsing but...

¬⅃

⅃

He takes the pack in hand then promptly collapses from the hypothermia. He can't move. Can't Gift. Can't get his wits enough to beam away to anywhere. Then...

A hand extends from out a sleeve of blaze orange, distancing itself from cuff as a hand tends to do when reaching. Hand takes Jimmy by the shoulder.

Strange. There's a warmth.

4

NOTHING VENTURED
NOTHING GAINED

W e're just leaving the Everest temple. Jimmy goes in nothing but the robe the monastery men had given him. It's fine. *Fine* linen-wise but *fine* comfort-wise. Fine because he's about to beam away, yes, but he's still feeling that warmth in addition. That unearthly warmth.

¬∃

ii

Back in West Brandon.

Jimmy sits on a toilet in a public washroom of the West Brandon East Shoppers Mall. He likes the privacy these stalls give him. The mall's near a vestige yet there are still enough shoppers the complex is profitable. No call for the wall of men's room stalls though. Never more than three of the dozen and a half ever occupied. Hence the privacy. No one ever in a mad-clench knocking on Jimmy's door. *Sorry for knockin at yer front door pally but I got somethin knocking at my backdoor! Almost through?* Mall's near a vestige. If they made *Dawn of the Dead* today Ken Foree'd have to speculate over what the zombies *weren't* doing: *Some kind of instinct. Memory... Of what they used to NOT do. This was an important place TO AVOID in their lives.*

"When there's no more room in hell," Jimmy mutters, "the dead will stay home and buy by drop-ship."

He's *just* sitting by the way. Pants are on. It's like an office for him and he's working late. Should be home in the night's accommodations by now, watching *Highlander 2* or something similarly underrated.

He's Gifting himself a look around the world. Trying to find a new business venture. Selling those tomatoes was the closest thing to a straight job Jimmy's ever had and he was exposed for his scruples. There were the Feds, he thinks, but also the weirdo with the Poppy.

"Poppy with them suits—"

He stifles, remembers. He reaches into his pocket and takes out that note. He scans the letters and numerals. He fixates on the one term whose denotation he can't figure.

"What the hell is a *figurace*?" He pronounces it 'figg-er-iss'. Like *licorice* but with an 'F' to start and an *ssss* in place of the *shhh* to finish. Make sense? He looks to his *FatButt*™ wearable fitness tracker on his left wrist. Taps at it. Screen lights up. Says,

Nov 10

6:42

0 steps

He swipes his finger right and the interface one screen over slides into view. He taps the *Alarms* app. Sets a reminder for seven-twenty-eight pee-em

"What else ya got to do..."

"What was that?" asks a voice two stalls over. Someone's come into the can while Jimmy was distracted.

"*Huhp?* N-Nothing," Jimmy defuses, badly. Tries again, "Just... Just constipated. For days!" Oh boy. "Trying to justify all the sitting to myself."

"Thought you said you were constipated?"

"*Sitting.*"

Silence a second from Jimmy's neighbor, then...

"That's how hemorrhoids happen buddy. Be careful."

"Will do."

"Tell you what you do. Eat yourself a handful of dried apricots. Dried. Drink something with aspartame in it. Works every time just don't make plans."

"Will do."

Well hell, might as well mention—since we've entered the *unabashedly scatological* section of this tale—Jimmy has no real need to worry about constipation. Jimmy defecates the normal way, sure, though frequently he just beams *over there* taking everything but his feces with him. Just teleports right away from his own shit. Can do the same with his shoes. Can do the same with a lot of things. But mostly his shits. Lotta Jimmy-Cakes left sittin on the floors of the deserts of the world he visits. I digress...

*FLUSH

Poo Samaritan leaves the cubicle. Jimmy hears some water run a few seconds then some footsteps moving out toward the exit. He gets back to business.

He starts looking around the world for something worth a small fortune he can sell. Safely. Must be a precious antique or work of fine art. Something with a plausible story of acquisition. *Found this at an auction sale online... A yard sale... Estate sale... Friend's grandma just dumped it at the curb...*

It's gotta be an artifact and it's gotta be something bad people bought by fair means with bad money. Something they don't deserve yet haven't deprived anyone of. Something they'll never report as stolen. Jimmy's go-to is the Picasso lithograph. There're hundreds of originals and thousands of reproductions. Tom Wolfe told him that. Told it to Bill Buckley Jr. really, but Jimmy heard. Listened to it. But, there're hundreds of those things where even the reproductions go for thousands. More good news: most are owned by drug dealers at this point. Not even on their walls. Stored under the stairs. Bought to launder money. The perfect quarry for a teleporter. Jimmy's foil.

Why not just find more gold like the chunk he used to pay the tomato farmer? every single one of you must be wondering. He tried that. Worked well at first. Gold's easy to Gift-out. Just find a region known to hold it—silver or platinum too for that matter... Gems... Anything precious of the earth— and have a look around where it's too remote for people or their contrivances to tread. Then *BOOM!* Jimmy's got his hands on a handful of precious everything! Beam in, beam *it* out. Problem wasn't the acquisition or the movement but the dealing. It brought the bureaucrats out of the woodwork. *Natural Resources Amerika* opened a case on Jimmy before he could move a second ounce. Damn you Ottawa! Even if he'd found the materials on land he owned—and this is worth understanding if you think you're gonna get rich digging around your acreage, everyone—he may have owned the surface and what sits on it, but the Amerika East government owns everything underneath. *Own* like the guy with the gun to your head owns what's in your wallet. From Ottawa to Wilmington and everything in between, the government takes whatever of the subsurface ain't basement and sometimes some of that. Damn you Ottawa!

Arts and antiquities will have to do.

Jimmy closes his eyes. Gifts himself a look into a cartel compound.

Mansion's ninety-percent concrete with wood façade added to make it appear like a hacienda. Jimmy moves through the entrance passing by a scale model of the head of the Statue of Liberty. As you do in these sorts of places. He moves around—and occasionally *through*—the occupants at the front receiving area. It looks like an accounting firm. Basically is. There are a few armed guards and some kids and moms moving about. Money men otherwise.

Jimmy's spinning around trying to get the lay of things when he turns into the face of a glaring guard.

HYAHH!

Thought the rent-a-muscle could see him for a second. Nah. Guy's not looking at Jimmy just through. He's watching a kid kicking a football up against a massive pedestal with a vase on it. Pedestal's made of more of that concrete so the ball don't budge it yet the vase still vibrates. If kid knocks that vase over, it's the guard's ass. If guard tries disciplining the kid and gets caught, it's the guard's ass. Guy's not having much fun. Still beats riding on the boss' car bombs?

Jimmy'd like to know more about the deliberations of the average cartel heavy and how he goes from *I'll do this for a politician or pampered celeb* to *I'll do this for a brutal black market tyrant*, but Jimmy's on a mission and the joke answer is *the* answer, that is, *because the cartel heavy has integrity.*

On with the mission...

He's not heading for the proverbial stairs under which the proverbial Picasso lithographs are proverbially stored. He's been here before. What he's searching for is—

FatButt™'s vibrating. 7:28's flashing on it.

Eyes open. Jimmy hits the little check to turn the alarm off.

In for a penny Jimmy? He shrugs.

Eyes close.

He Gifts himself a peek right into the Oval Office.

He's done this before too. Far less eventful than you'd think. Only real scheming Jimmy's ever witnessed *The Prez* engaging in involves dreaming up ways to fool *The People* into turning a blind eye to all the scheming intended to fool them into turning a blind-eye. Other ten percent of the time Prez' just putting up a tough-talking front to the civil servants desperate to maintain their cherished bland status quo. Civil servants he'll inevitably capitulate to.

Prez sure does try to come across as tough though. Always talking about doing push-ups no one's ever seen him do. Always *threatening* to do push-ups really. Can you threaten people with push-ups? Because that's what he sounds like he thinks he's doing.

When *not* conducting himself in a way meant to let others know a geriatric flurry of unprovoked calisthenics is on the table, Prez walks around looking real confident for someone who shouldn't. And, ya know, it really is the person who shouldn't look this way ending up the only person who looks this way. Like tattooing *I'm With Stupid* on your forehead to hide your lobotomy scars. He looks about thirty pounds overweight. Has a comb-over. Bellows a weird marble-mouthed southern drawl when he talks.

"*Getch* the hell over here junior!" He barks this at the *PM.*

PM is there too. Looks like a walking *kinda*-talking Stretch Armstrong... With brown hair... With all the fluid drained out. When he speaks, his weakness of voice causes people to think air must be leaking from something.

Prez continues bossing him. Some things never change, thinks Jimmy. Prez is reaching across his chest and over his right shoulder to pound on the top of his chair's backrest. Gesture hastens the PM to his usual post. PM stands to the right of our sitting Prez now, left hand on the top right corner of the backrest. Diligent toadiness.

Assistant to Prez and PM enters. "Senator Fletcher will be a few minutes late," she says with a hint of a pouty smile as though trying to ameliorate a Prez who's about to—

Eyes open just before the inevitable tirade. Jimmy's got a few minutes *at least* to keep searching for that rent check. He sets a timer on his watch for three minutes.

Eyes close.

He's back moving around the cartel mansion. Reconnoiter's done. The usual goons and accountants are about, family otherwise. The usual. Dealers are gone on business. Good. Now for those lithographs... He's not looking for any *under-the-stairs* lithographs, remember, and that's because the stairs are made of solid concrete. Can't build a closet into that. He knows what to look for and he knows where to look. He Gifts into the basement. It's dark though he sees a locked chest in silhouette. It's about the right size to hold a number of printings off the stone.

He can't turn the lights on and he can't open the chest. That's not how The Gift works. There's no manipulation or alteration of the environment. What he can do is move around like the space marine in *DOOM* with the no-clipping cheat on. That's about it yet that's a lot. You could say Jimmy's master bedroom has a *walk-in world* but, as we've seen, he's no homeowner. You could call him *The Invigilator of the Universe* though we don't yet know if the universe is the extent of his Gift. He's never Gifted himself a glimpse of anything outside Earth's atmosphere. If he Gifts there, he can beam there *and* he don't wanna beam there *so* he don't Gift there despite his dreams betraying him in this. He can warp too. That is, he can jump from location to location in an instant, like teleporting in his Gifting. Virtua-teleporting? He can't turn on the lights but he's ninety-nine percent sure that crate holds the—

FatButt™ timer goes off.

"You're talking World War Four!" Prez bellows.

"Five," *Senator Fletcher* corrects. "We're due."

"Won't do it."

"We gave you Four."

"And I gave you Three! Not my fault you thought this was some sort of *quid pro quo* deal all the way down!"

"I've got it to committee."

Prez grimaces a little. "Listen you, I'm *Commander in Chief* got it? That ain't some honorific, boyo. You go ahead and declare your war and I'll *command-in-chief* our men right into permanent R&R."

"You gave us Three!" Fletcher implores.

"Went after my grandkids. Plotters were hiding in the goddamn bushes! Fuck em and the coalition they were hiding behind!"

Fletcher's aide starts pecking away on his phone, exercised as Fletcher continues bargaining. "We're due. People are losing faith."

"Not in me!" Prez beams at PM, prideful as anything. "What are our numbers junior?"

"Um..." is the PM's contribution.

"See!" Prez boasts.

"There are other ways..." Fletcher intimates.

"And what's that?"

"The people."

"Ha! Think the people'll push for this if you, what, blow up one of our embassy's somewhere? Kick a dog and say The Russians did it? People are in an *everything is a conspiracy* phase. They'll sniff out your scheme like nothing. Wouldn't trust ya even if ya weren't lyin to em. *Tactics* Fletch! Gotta go to war to get em to rah rah for ya then you get em in the *nothing is a conspiracy trust everything* phase then you can fool em. Need the war first boyo."

"Then give it to us."

"Told ya, people won't buy it."

"Needing to start a war to start a war..."

"I know, paradox. We need a natural calamity maybe. Something we can't contrive so easy but can pretend to be able to solve so easy. Record droughts. A pandemic or the like. Then they'll be so scared they'll put their faith in the bark of a dog with enough promise in his eye."

"Still think a war will do it."

"Ah, you're just being silly now. Be another Vietnam."

"Still—"

Prez puts a shushing hand up, attends to the senator's personal aide. "What say you Liberace? Don't you want to talk some sense into your boss?"

The aide looks up from his phone. "I-it's *Figurace*, sir—"

Jimmy's eyes pop open. *Fih-Gurr-Ah-Chee* he mouths in realization.

"I-I happen to agree," Figurace says.

"Ha!" Prez barks. "Choosing them for their obedience eh Fletch?"

Jimmy's on Figurace from here. He's looking over the shoulder of the aide, who's back on his phone. Teleporter can't drown out all the polit-speak and formality completely.

You see that movie 'Airforce One', Fletch? How accurate do you think it was?

Aide's just scrolling through his calendar. Swiping to the right bringing up the next day. Days are broken into hours constituting the portion of the interface that's visible. Multi-colored blocks span across the hours...

Who you guys thinking of invading anyway? Seems like something I should know.

...The blocks represent events. The colors, presumably, represent types of events. The span of any one block represents the beginning-to-end timespan of the event. Looks like bureaucracy Tetris. A dance card for authoritarians with two far-left feet.

I think I'm gonna get into bow-hunting. Got the arms for it.

Jimmy's seeing nothing out of the ordinary over the guy's shoulder. He's just about to hang it up when...

Aide minimizes the calendar app and brings up a texting window. Recipient is just some email address whose handle consists entirely of numbers. Aide texts,

> See if the party planners are available for November 16th. Too short notice?

There's an immediate response.

> See if the party planners are available for November 16th. Too short notice?

Now Jimmy's *definitely* hanging it up.

Eyes open.

What the hell was that about? *Figurace meets Prez: Plans Party*. Stop the goddamn presses Redford and Bernstein!

"Poppy Man must be some Natural Resources guy couldn't make a case against me. Feds with grudges wasting my time. Good luck finding me now dinkholeberries!" Jimmy gets a pang of something. It's in his gut. Not anything he'd need to lift the seat for, more an intuition. "Figurace sure got a weird look when the Prez started talking about his family though. Almost happy about—"

"Who you talking to in there?"

"Constipated!"

Time to go. Time to pay the rent. He lifts his legs up and crosses them on top of the toilet lid. He leans forward and opens the stall door and closes it on himself again. Does this so they'll think he's left and no one will know he just vanished away. Pure genius. Legs are a little tingly. Then...

¬∃

iii

Jimmy walks out of the pawn shop and into the crowd of the busy sidewalk. He's counting a stack of bills like it's a movie and we have to show him doing this in order to inform the audience that he's just sold something for a massive payout even though counting a giant wad of cash is really dangerous in a neighborhood like this. Jimmy doesn't have to worry of course. He uses his cash-free hand to pull the hood of the sweater he's wearing over his head to fade into a crowd already indifferent to all things around them but his cash. Once Jimmy pockets that cash he'll be gone before he's gone. He does just that. Then...

¬Ǝ

5
***
PARTY PLANNERS

nother night another 'night'. Another house, once again littoral. No hooch this time. No entertainment.

Jimmy's sitting criss-cross applesauce on the living room floor like a kindergartener. He tried the lotus position only it strained his knees. He tried the hardwood only it twinged his coccyx. He's on one of the couch cushions. His hands rest in the hollow between his diverging inner-thighs. Hands sit palms up, left hand nestled on top of the right, spooning. His mind is empty. Gift is quieted. It's workin—

7:28pm!

Shit! The alarm he set for Figurace the other day! Must have set it to *Every Day*.

He hits the check on his watch, stops the alarm. Opens the settings and turns it off. Does all this quick and in agitation, like he's losing something. He is. His calm. He puts his hands back into that upward-spooning position but his mind's eye's full. Phenomena abound. He's not Gifting, he's imagining.

Naturally, Figurace keeps popping into his head. Specifi-

37

cally, Figurace with that excited look he got hearing about Prez' grandkids. Jimmy's thinking about that weird email handle. He can't remember the string of numbers verbatim though he can remember it was *some* random string.

"Don't do it, boy."

He tries a last desperate attempt at not quieting his mind... Forget it. Just focuses on getting any political sycophants out of it. No good either.

He Gifts a gander into Senator Fletcher's office. He's been here before. Been to most places the higher-ups frequent.

Nothing. Office is empty. Good. Only way to find Figurace is through the Senator and Senator's gone. Jimmy's done. No point hanging around a single minute mo—

Eyes open.

"No..."

Close.

A poppy's on the desk. Jimmy warps to it. It sits on a note reading,

You know he's got an office on this floor. He's
Personal Aide to the Senator! Have a look around.
(Get rid of this note while you're at it).

Eyes open.

¬Ǝ/Ǝ

Jimmy crumbles up the note, pockets the poppy.

Eyes close.

Fletcher's office suite consists of a massive rotunda. His office is the largest and sits at twelve o'clock of the hooping structure. All other offices are smaller and circle around the rotunda converging on a main entrance at six

o'clock. How important is a personal aide? Eleven o'clock important? One? Jimmy thinks neither though what difference does it make? He starts moving clockwise. Warping his way around the hours—office to office.

First is occupied by someone Jimmy doesn't recognize. Probably important by virtue of proximity but who cares? *Chief of staff* maybe? If Senators have such a thing? Guy's got his head down, reading. Boring. Jimmy warps on. Two o'clock, empty. Three o'clock, empty. Four o'clock, cleaners. Five o'clock, Figurace!

Fig's office or not, he's at the desk. Sitting across from him is a man with moderate male-pattern baldness and a massive gnarly mustache as though grown in consolation of his shiny head getting shinier.

"Relax," says *Baldy*. "You're acting like we're being bugged."

"With Fletcher's paranoia..."

"Yeah, but who ya think he'd have do the bugging?" Baldy smirks.

Figurace chuckles. Focuses the index finger of his right hand into a hard point on the desk surface. Talks like the digit is where the crux of the conversation sits. "He'd thank us for this if he'd only consider the ends."

Jimmy feels queasy.

"Tell him about the ends," Baldy assures, "and he'll demand to know the means. We need deniability here."

Figurace nods. "And we can trust these guys?"

"No, and that's the point. They're wacko ideologues. Deniability, Figgy. These guys fight abstractions. Get em on the stand they won't point the finger at a Senator's aide they'll point the finger at 'power structures'. At groups of people never people."

"Jesus, if even one of them gets a shot off..."

"Gotta be the real deal. Secret service will know otherwise."

"Plastic explosives?"

"Trust me. Two birds. I look legit to the muscle *and* I rein in our guys. Last thing these fuckers want is to hurt themselves. They'll hurt a college kid reading a Thomas Sowell monograph, sure—not a guy who can hurt em back. Can't mob up on a bomb. Can't intimidate plastique with a bike lock in a sack."

Figurace looks unconvinced. Baldy notices.

"Trust me, Figgy. Fletch wants a war, after what we do to Prezzy's dearest, Prez'll give him that war for starters!" Baldy laughs like the implications of this are immaterial —like any and all conscience. Jimmy's breathing heavy hearing all this. Feels faint in addition to nauseated. Baldy feels nothing. Laughs out what follows, cruelly, "Sink a continent or two by the time we're done! Purr-Puh-Tuity Figgy!"

Eyes open.

He can't get out of that damn crisscross position fast enough. He can't get to the bathroom before... He's vomiting again, but... He hasn't touched a drop. What's wrong with him? Vomit splashes directionally as he staggers to a toilet no longer needed. He goes back down to his knees. The crisscrossing has put his legs to sleep though that's not it.

He grabs at his temples.

Give him that war...

Perpetuity...

Images of innocents walking among live Bouncing Betty's in a battlefield-*cum*-demilitarized-meadow flash. It's not The Gift. It's a memory of it. He tries his damnedest to shut it out. He can't. If it were your neighborhood it would be your neighbors walking among the ordnance of a battlefield of an unending million-mile-away war assholes like Figurace and Baldy want to reinvigorate. That they regard as though out of a movie. Children walk, as...

BOOM!

He bolts back upright. Eyes well. More memories flood in. More memories of past Giftings of what happens when fuckers like Fletcher, Figurace, and Baldy do what they do: fight their wars by flip of switch from up on a hill where they're not to experience so much as a scratch. Invader or invadee, this is always the way for people like them. Kept little sub-statesmen with their RISK boards and their Monopoly money paying real people to bludgeon real people. Whatever their plan, it will lead to more of this while they, the switch-flippers, luxuriate billions of years away.

Now The Gift is uncontrollable. Memories of the torture, the dismemberments, the shootings, the bombings: replaced by a live mental feed of such. It's the site of an ongoing invasion. Any you please. They all look the same but-for texture.

Jimmy stumbles down the hall.

A mother holds a three-year-old in arms, begging, crouching into a squatting fetal position to shield the little one.

A zealotous monster holds a baby in his arms. He's shielding *himself* with the child at his chest. Taunting with it. Begging the enemy to send him to his heaven though not before the baby.

Amerika-backed soldiers shoot them all to bits ending everything but their own callow desire for self-preservation in an instant. Almost everything. Almost in-instant. Vestiges of the infant cries linger in tiny gurgling gasps.

This isn't a memory.

This. Is. Happening. Right. Now.

Head butts smashing into the drywall. Stumble or demons do this? He bellows. He reaches into the wall. Not *through* like he did with his head. Different part of the wall, a recessed wine and booze rack. He pulls out a single malt scotch from one of those *this-is-useless-and-only-serves-to-indicate-something-expensive* decorative cardboard tubes. He crunches the cardboard in his fist, pulls out the bottle. He gnaws at the plastic wrapped at the cork, shreds it, pops the top, pours the contents down his throat and not in the sense of the poets. Bottle's inverted the whole of a ten-ounce pour.

He curls up onto the floor, cradling the bottle.

Rate of scotch intake is maximal yet The Gift remains.

More dead at the hands of the callow soldiers. They've lost a man too.

Jimmy follows them. He wishes he could stop.

The Callow **are cutting through a dilapidated school. Jimmy warps around the structure. It's empty so far save for the soldiers. Empty room after empty...** *Zealots!* **Three. Gonna get caught by surprise? No. They're waiting for these soldiers in the northwestern-most classroom while all but two soldiers come up the center hall. Other two move through the classrooms to either side the hall, assessing. Each room has an adjoining door to the next at the far corner so the two can stay in the classrooms as they move.**

Three zealots with AK-47s are no match for a unit consisting of... Looks like fourteen soldiers... But...

He sees it. They're wired. It's a suicide mission for these guys.

Jimmy shakes his head. Drinks. His eyes are open. The Gift is loud and clear nonetheless.

"It's what they signed up for. Both these sacks of rabid dogs' shits. They're all murderers anyway. They're—" He smashes the bottle! *Oh please! Jesus!*

School's got a crawlspace. Children are down there. Parents. Elderly too. Zealots do it so the Callow won't blow the place from the sky. Callow do it anyway but you know this.

Crawlspace dwellers are silent. Huddled. Appear apathetic. Have they given up? Is it coercion? The same courage of ideology as the Zealots?

"They're children for Christ's sake what's it matter the motivation?" Jimmy yells this to no one. He pulls himself up out of his half-drunken fetal position. Up along the wall. Reaches into that smashed drywall for leverage. Kinda works though he tears more of it away as he rises cuz at first he's pulling out not down.

He's up and moving swift to the kitchen.

Not like this...

Anymore...

PLEASE! GOD!

The kitchen wall has one of those magnetic blocks holding an assortment of knives.

The Callow soldiers are moving lightly and slowly. They've moved up two classrooms in the time since Jimmy discovered the innocents in the crawlspace. Callow are three rooms away from the bomber Zealots.

He grabs a chef's knife.

"Can't..."

Callow are two doors down...

Strange. Jimmy's back to memory now. Image at mind's eye. Image is of a man, pinned by collapsed metal. It's an industrial setting. There's fire all around. There's Jimmy, standing, looking at the man. The man pleads for Jimmy to free him. Jimmy doesn't.

He tries lifting the knife. Hesitates. It's *will* that's the cause, not the *flesh*. He manages to get the blade to neck. Immediately drops it again in hesitation.

"Won't."

Tries once more. Knife's back to his throat. He keeps it at this height, steady. He's fully committed to what it is he's committed to.

One door down...

He looks up in that pleading expression of his, knife at his Adam's apple.

"I CAN'T LIVE LIKE THIS ANYMORE!!!!"

Then...

¬∃

∃

Jimmy's behind the Zealot furthest back of the other two. His arm is around the Zealot's neck, knife poised. In a flash, before the bomber notices a body's encroached on him though not before he's noticed the faint smell of vomit Jimmy carries... *SNIP!*

¬∃/∃

SNIP!

¬∃/∃

SNIP!

¬∃

Now for the Callow just inching up to that door...

Callow soldier taking point moves across the entrance

threshold simultaneous to the callow assessor moving through the adjoining corner doorway. Zealots see both at once as they depress their detonators. Callow use the last few microseconds they have left to betray a look of panic, as...

BOOM?

No!

It's...

Ǝ/¬Ǝ, Ǝ/¬Ǝ, Ǝ/¬Ǝ, Ǝ/¬Ǝ, Ǝ/¬Ǝ, Ǝ/¬Ǝ, Ǝ/¬Ǝ, Ǝ/¬Ǝ, Ǝ/¬Ǝ, Ǝ/¬Ǝ, Ǝ/¬Ǝ, Ǝ/¬Ǝ, Ǝ/¬Ǝ, Ǝ/¬Ǝ

Callow are gone! Guns and other equipment sit on the floor.

Then...

Ǝ/¬Ǝ, Ǝ/¬Ǝ, Ǝ/¬Ǝ

Defused bomb vests are gone from the confused Zealots. Remember the *SNIP!*?

Then...

Ǝ/¬Ǝ, Ǝ/¬Ǝ, Ǝ/¬Ǝ

Zealots are gone too!

"You're not gonna believe this Sarge!"

The detention officer has come bounding up the precinct stairs heading toward his desk sergeant.

"What is it Mooney?" *Sarge* says this in a tone suggesting *Mooney's* crying wolf again.

"It's... It's the holding cells... It's probably best if you just come see."

Mooney bolts back downstairs.

What Mooney, Sarge, and a few other staff observe are the contents of two of the precinct's four holding cells. One is filled with the Callow soldiers *sans* ordnance. The other cell holds the three zealots *sans* bomb vests. Captives are all surprisingly cordial for men who just a few minutes ago were slaughtering each other on orders of anyone but themselves. They just stand looking confused.

"How the hell Mooney!"

"I tell ya Sarge, they just started showin up. Outta nowhere. One after another just poppin into them cells like popcorn kernels popping in a pan! Outta nowhere!"

"That's not how popcorn works Mooney."

"You know what I mean boss."

"That's not how anything works."

"You know what I mean? Doncha boss?"

"No I don't Mooney. If this is some sort of practical joke..." Sarge moves closer to the cell with the Callow soldiers. "Har-d-har fellas but this is trespassing, even if Mooney here put you up to it." Sarge's thumb jerks back over his right shoulder in Mooney's direction. "Well! Speak up!"

"Oh they don't speak English," Mooney explains. "Or, at least, what they were speaking before you came in, it certainly wasn't English."

Sarge walks over to the only other occupant of any other cell. *A Mugger*, a regular. "What about you? What'd you see?"

"I gotta right to remain silent," Mugger says, assured.

"And I gotta right to recommend more than a suspended sentence to the DA."

"Whoa man!"

"Spill it muggy!"

"Alright alright!" Mugger makes a *c'mere* finger bend at

the Sarge. Sarge moves in for the aside. Mugger leans even closer as though to whisper. Then... "It was Mooney!" he says full volume. "Snuck em in to fuck with ya!"

"Hey!" Mooney protests.

ii

The incident has already sparked diplomacy concerns across NATO countries, says the television. This, despite the fact the bulk of abductees serve as armed forces members of allied nations. Though the President is scheduled to address the public tomorrow morning, he has already Twooted that the Amerikan government in no way played any role in the abduction and detention. We will have more on this story as it develops. This is Simone Simmons, reporting.

It's only the end of the eleven o'clock news hour yet news travels fast.

Jimmy's back in the night's accommodations. He's not paying any more attention to the media tales of his exploits. He's still a little drunk, sure, but he's determined to make the most of his cleared conscience. Gonna keep it clear.

Gonna clear the hallway of vomit too? Fix the wall?

"Blow the whistle now..." He says to himself. "There's nothing incriminating. Baldy's all about deniability after all. Let it go past the crisis-point, we can't put the genie back in the bottle. It'll mean war. Gotta stop em at the crisis-point but what's the crisis-point?"

He closes his eyes.

Figurace's asleep in the bed at the corner of the living room of his studio apartment. He's not alone. Prostitute? Of course Figurace is. Poor girl. Make him clap his hands when you go to the bathroom dear. Figgy's phone is on

vibrate on the nightstand. It's gone off twice in this Gifting alone.

"Don't you do it Jimmy boy... Don't you—"

¬Ǝ

Ǝ

He grabs the phone off of Figurace's nightstand.

¬Ǝ

Ǝ

Damnit! Phone's locked. Of course it is superspy!

¬Ǝ

Ǝ

Jimmy's back at Figurace's. He holds the phone up to the aide's face and hits the power button. Girl *SNORKS!* Rolls over. Phone lights up. Jimmy pulls Fig's eyes open real quick and real abrupt, two finger V-over-brow-style. Facial recognition initializes. Lets go of those lids as Figurace furrows his brow in a still sleeping annoyance when...

¬Ǝ

彐

Jimmy starts swiping, tapping, and scrolling through Figurace's message app. He starts by looking for Baldy's weird email handle. Got it. He scrolls to the last message hoping to hit pay-dirt. Message reads:

24602@OVERLOOK.COM

Ha ha! Pervert!

Redundant, Jimmy thinks.
Previous message reads:

Igore those, thought it was my browser

24602@OVERLOOK.COM

Ha ha! Pervert!

Message before that reads:

Mary Poppins nude

Igore those, thought it was my browser

24602@OVERLOOK.COM

Ha ha! Pervert!

Before that:

Mary Poppins nud

Mary Poppins nude

Igore those, thought it was my browser

24602@OVERLOOK.COM

Ha ha! Pervert!

Then:

Party planned: 11/18/24 304 Whitmore Avenue East.

East.

See you there.

Mary Poppins nud

Mary Poppins nude

Igore those, thought it was my browser

24602@OVERLOOK.COM

Ha ha! Pervert!

"Gotcha."

¬Ⴈ

Ⴈ

Jimmy's setting the phone back on the nightstand when...
SWOOSH!

He reaches out grabbing the glass of water he almost knocked over onto Figurace. Close one! He looks at that glass of water curiously a second. Looks at Figurace. Looks at Figurace's girl.

He dumps the entire of the glass' contents onto Figgy's crotch.

"Explain that to her ya toddler!"

¬Ⴈ/Ⴈ

iii

Jimmy sleeps like a baby this night. A sobered baby.

6
———

PARTY CRASHERS' PARTY CRASHED

Crisis-point.

It's a wedding reception. Uneventful up to this point just a few before the crisis.

Stop it now and nothing's incriminating. Nobody takes any kind of a fall. Means war. Don't stop it in time and people get hurt and it still means war.

Jimmy waits, cautious.

He waits at the back corner of the reception hall, in coveralls with an embroidered patch over the left breast pocket reading 'Ernie'. Coveralls are a little loose-fitting. He's got a ridiculous polyester mustache spirit-gummed between his upper lip and nostrils. It tickles both its borders. Looks extra ridiculous because all Jimmy could find at the novelty store was a waxed-handled handlebar mustache he cut the waxed handles off of. Stache's ends flatten at perfect right-angles like a cannon shot the thing through a bread slicer set to Texas Toast. Looks like the elevator doors are closing on it.

51

Jimmy's got a hat too, a gray plastic-adjustable-strapped ball cap. On the back of his coveralls, spanning the shoulders, is a much larger patch with KCCH embroidered on it.

He has this on his back so he can best pass for a janitor right where he stands: the Kairn Center Concert Hall. Fanciest ball room in West Brandon. Most of Amerika's political elite are here. Here for the governor of Laurentia's daughter's wedding. Entertainment industry A-listers are here too. Athletes. Billionaires of all stripes. Fletcher's here, Figurace at his side. Everyone except the Prez and PM are in attendance. No Prez, though his nephew's present. Nephew's the target of the party crashers.

Jimmy'd blend right in if it weren't for the fact none of these snobs want a janitor around despite wanting things immaculate as hell. Think they're gonna clean up their own messes? But that's a job for the caterers. Caterers wear those dress shirts and bow-ties just one tier above *dickey* on the sophistication scale. Politicians and A-listers like them just fine as their whole lives are about facades anyway. Athletes and billionaires find the virtual-dickeys a bit pathetic as, despite their superciliousness, they have to get results to make it in their world. They recognize and abhor inauthenticity when they see it.

Ah, but ol Jimmy'd blend right in if it weren't for the crowd's snobbery and his stupid mustache and, I almost forgot, his threadbare wooden push broom that predates the invention of itself. And then there's that stupid mustache worth mentioning twice...

He stands in the back corner of the ball room not blending in though not doing enough harm to prick up anyone's nose. He notices how easily the caterers blend in with such simplistic garb. He also considers how much easier finding that disguise would have been...

"Idiot!" he mutters to himself. "Spend all this time planning and you didn't think to dress like a chimp—"

"You talking to me?" A woman in a white shirt, black vest, and clip-on bow-tie has sidled up to him.

"*Huhp!*" His fake mustache shifts back and forth like a flapper's skirt during a flapper dance all-a-sudden. "No!"

Woman appears the kind of offended her half-smile is meant to belie. "How insistent. Am I *so* not worth talking to?"

Jimmy flushes. "No. You're fine... I'm sure."

"*I'm sure.*" She dumps some teacups and saucers into the bus pans of the bus pan cart Jimmy stands behind.

"You just caught me off guard's all."

"Ah."

They pause a second to observe the toasts taking place. Toasts are glorified speeches really. Seem to've been going on immemorial thanks to all the muckety-mucks around.

Let me tell you a funny story about the bride, says the current speaker. *Back in '94 when the bride's father and I were just junior senators, my proposed public health reforms...*

Jimmy and Woman look pretend nauseated at each other. Simultaneity of the response provokes a smile in them.

...Needless to say, it was my foresight...

Jimmy's head falls in theatrical exasperation. Woman pats him on the shoulder as though to comfort him, adding to the theater.

...And thanks to my initiative...

She breaks the silence, "You next?"

"What's that?"

"Your turn." She points at the lectern monopolized by the speaker. A senator of something or other.

Jimmy chuckles. "I don't know these people."

"None of these people *know* these people. Just talk about yourself. Seems the custom."

...And with my proposed lunch programs, thousands of hungry children...

"Obviously the patent self-concern is all I'm lacking." Jimmy tugs on his coveralls.

"*The eccentric tech millionaire-turned-billionaire investor.* Father of the bride'll think you're his best donor. Come on. Dare ya."

"What are you twelve?"

"I look like one of *them* to you?" She swoops her arm across all the elected in the room. "I work for a living buster."

His lips purse, left side of them rises. Half-smirk happens under an unmoving mustache by the way. Nose moves the thing, lips don't. Curious. "Make it worth my while," he offers.

"Name it."

"Make it *really* worth my while." He takes out a notepad and a pen from his overalls pocket, hands it to her. "Write me my options. I'm lazy."

She scoffs. Takes the stationary. Starts writing.

Girl's really doing it, Jimmy thinks.

Writes more, until...

He tips the pad away from her view. "Wait, won't work. Can't talk about myself. All I ever do is sleep until I'm ready to tackle another day of doing nothing else in particular."

"Tell them what you do in your sleep then," she says with an eyebrow.

She being coy? Jimmy thinks this in a manner he don't realize is hopeful yet... "Don't know what I do in my sleep," he says. "Can never stay awake long enough to find out..."

Rest of the clip-on tuxedo crew start to move to the periphery of the banquet hall.

"That's bad," she scoffs. Playful.

"Best I got." His eyes twitch and dart above a fading smile of good humor. He's itemizing the looming caterers. He counts about fifteen? One's in a coat, just one, a tux jacket to be precise, baggy but-for the bulges in front. "Excuse me."

"Where are you going?"

He turns away from her. "To take out the trash."

"No."

He feels a blunt pressure at his lower-back. Like a hard finger pointing pushing. Just then, he catches a glimpse of the man with the poppy. Man's standing at the hall exit wearing that poppy of his pinned to a pair of coveralls identical to Jimmy's. Man tilts his head, swoops his arm in a *these are the guys* gesture across the caterers. They're not converging just yet though definitely looming. Jimmy's attention goes back to Poppy. Gone! Uncann—

Rigid digit pushes deeper into Jimmy's back.

It's a hollow steel tube, can see the rifling inside it and all.

¬Ǝ

He vanishes from out front of her. She's stunned a second. Gun in her hand inches forward as much as the pressure she's applying to a recently removed Jimmy entails.

Ǝ

There's a presence at *her* back now, for just a second, like arms reaching around her searching. A tension's on the gun.

Gun jostles.

¬Ǝ/Ǝ/¬Ǝ

Gun blinks in and out of existence. She marvels.

Then...

Ǝ/¬Ǝ, Ǝ/¬Ǝ, Ǝ/¬Ǝ...

Same eerie presence is felt by all of the clip-on brigade. Like ultra-swift hands reaching, feeling, caressing... Jostling... All in a blur. Then...

Teleporter pops up in front of that caterer with the tux jacket. Catches him just stepping away from the wall left of the hall entrance.

"Conspicuous, that coat." Jimmy says this extending a finger to the coat man's chest. Gesture halts the man despite no real pressure. Must have decided to entertain Jimmy a second.

"Like that mustache a yours?" man observes.

Speaking of conspicuous mustaches...

Baldy—despite his caterer disguise *plus* blazer, wig, fake beard, and tinted glasses—can't hide the muskrat on his face.

"Yours too," Jimmy says. "How's Fletcher gonna maintain deniability with everybody pointing at the bald aide with insecurity for an upper lip?" Baldy's eyes widen. "I mean..." Jimmy continues. "You're not as close to Fletch as Figgy, yet if they get to you they get to Figgy so they get to the senat—"

Baldy shoves Jimmy backward toppling him to the floor. A couple bow-tied henchmen drag our hero out the back ballroom door with minimal commotion. All in attendance are too busy waiting for their turn to speak to notice. Goons pin Jimmy in place. Their knees go to his chest, guns to his temples. Before anyone else in attendance can continue not reacting, Baldy, The Woman, and the remaining peripheral caterers move toward the center mass of banquet tables. They move because of the Jimmy-caused haste yet they move according to plan. Baldy unbuttons the tux jacket revealing the C4, six bricks of them, Velcro-strapped in columns of three at either side of a black zip-up utility vest.

There're some different colored wires leading out of two holes of a black metal chunk in Baldy's hand.

Baldy puts thumb to a red plastic groove protecting a toggle switch. He moves toward a ballroom table of interest. All other caterers pull their handguns. All but The Woman already *gun-up*.

'Shut the fuck up Bob!" Baldy shouts to the filibustering toasting senator. "No one wants to hear any more about the shit other people've done that you take credit for!"

Bob looks up from the lectern shocked. Hasn't seen any of the guns or explosives yet.

Well I never—

"Shut it!" Baldy lifts his chunky detonator up to the crowd. "Nobody move. This is live!" He tugs at the collar of the bomb vest with his free hand. "Uh uh!" He spins around catching the attention of the various bodyguards and secret service-people inching toward him. They stop. He picks up Prez' nephew, wraps his arm around Nephew's neck and pulls him away from the table knocking neph's chair over as they go. Security remains still as the caterers swarm in to disarm them.

Meanwhile, Jimmy's still pinned, guns at his temples.

"Wanna get out of this alive fellas, do as I say." Jimmy says this in all assurance. Caterer gunmen look at each other then back to Jimmy, scoff. "He's using you," Jimmy insists. "*They're* using you. Mustache, Figurace, Fletcher even. Hell, I don't know."

Gunmen don't scoff at this. They don't appear concerned either. One warns, "Say another word—"

"*WAMN*[1]."

---

1. WAMN: With Any Means Necessary. A militant protest group fighting 'fascists' (flower children, Buddhists, John Stuart Mill, etc.). Mostly just

Gunmen shut up.

Jimmy goes on. "I know his plan. You know enough of it too. He leaves with *nepote* in there while you stay with the remaining hostages, awaiting his call and the all-clear. Only, he won't be calling. He'll be gone. Gone and safe and eventually the secret servicemen, the paramilitary guys—you're thinking not the ones in there but their friends but it'll be them—they'll open up on you. Blow you to pieces. I'm sure you *WAMN* guys aren't smart enough to check for hold-outs? Those guys are trained to disarm Green Berets. Half of them *are* Green Berets."

Gunmen look to each other. Look transforms from blankness to confusion.

"That ain't the plan!" they say in unison.

"Darn," Jimmy kinda-laments. "Oh well. Just needed to bide enough time. Crisis point, fellas." Then...

¬∃

Jimmy's gone, much to the gunmen's compounded confusion.

⛩

"Don't make me tell ya again Bob!" Baldy warns as Bob shuts up again and almost certainly not for good. "Alright ladies and gentlemen, your imperialist genocides have gone on for long enough—"

"*White-supremacist cis-hetero-normative* genocides!" shouts one of the caterers from the back in all of her middle-aged first-year fervor.

---

aggressively annoying but will not hesitate to resort to violence when no one's looking (like the DA). Have become uncharacteristically organized and well-funded as of late. Next to impossible to investigate. Impossible to prosecute. WAMN members are all between the ages of forty and sixty.

"Shut! It!" Baldy says through grit teeth. He cinches up Nephew's collar with his free hand and starts dragging him toward the door. "You and your president—and your bonehead of a prime minister for that matter—better end all your global occupations and proxy wars—"

Except for Bulgaria!

And the other 'Garias!

End all imperialist wars except in nations whose flags we have in our bios!

"*SHHYUTT!*" Baldy's having a hard time composing himself amidst the weird hypocrisies. "If you ever want to see this brat alive again—"

Ǝ/¬Ǝ

POOF!

Baldy's wig, beard, and tinted glasses are gone. Crowd gasps. Fletcher gasps loudest of anyone. Baldy doesn't notice the missing apparel though he does notice the agitated attendees. He looks to Figurace. Figurace's white as a sheet and silent. Fletcher turns to Figgy with a glare that almost could—and maybe should—burn right through his aide's head. Figgy looks forward at nothing a thousand yards away, doesn't flinch.

All others in attendance remain focused on Baldy. There's a recognition emerging in certain of them.

Hey! I know that mustache. Guy's an aide, works at Fletcher's office!

Crowd turns to Fletcher as Baldy lets go of Nephew. Fletcher's turn to not flinch... Keeps staring those daggers at Figurace.

Yeah, name's Diddy or something...

Baldy-*cum*-Diddy-*cum*-Something staggers backward. He's touching at his bare cheeks and balding head with his detonator-free hand. "No..." he mutters. Caterers hold their guns closer to the ribs of the security guys despite every-thing falling apart.

Fletcher rises to his feet. Looks to Baldy. Looks back to Figurace. "You are fired!" Figurace's head sinks.

Yeah... It's Diddy for sure!

Baldy spins to bolt for the back door when...

Ǝ

Jimmy's at his front, shoving him. The thug aide doesn't fall due his forward momentum but he does stumble a few steps backward.

¬Ǝ/Ǝ

"You..." Jimmy shouts as he pushes Baldy from behind now.

¬Ǝ/Ǝ

"Shouldn't..." Jimmy pushes him from the front again.

¬Ǝ/Ǝ

"Push..." Behind!

¬Ǝ/Ǝ

"People..." Front!

¬Ǝ/Ǝ

"Around!" Behind!

This all happens to Baldy so fast it just looks like he's flailing, trying to put out an invisible fire.

¬Ǝ

Then...

Ǝ

Jimmy's back at his front, holding him by the collar of his vest. Guy's dazed from The Teleporter's jostling. Tele-porter reaches out to the detonator still in the villain's hand, flips the red plastic cover upward. Toggle's in the open air.

¬Ǝ/Ǝ

Jimmy pops up behind. Speaks over Baldy's shoulder.

"What are you waiting for?" But the pseudo-terrorist only startles. He's trembling.

¬Ǝ/Ǝ

Front again. "Do it!"

Trembling comes to a concentration at Baldy's face. He shakes a *no no* out of himself. Vibrates a *no no*?

¬Ǝ/Ǝ

Over the shoulder. "Blow the place!"

¬Ǝ/Ǝ

Got him by the collar once more. "Thing never was live was it?" Jimmy takes the detonator from Baldy's hand and rips its wires out the vest. Throws it into the crowd. He pulls the aide up extra close for a face-to-face. "What about mine asshole?" He's got a detonator of his own in-hand. Little red light is on and everything. Aide knows exactly what that means.

Jimmy steps away taking the detonator with him. Wires pull taut. He flips the red chunk upward and all the caterers point their guns at him and start pulling their triggers. All but The Woman. She hesitates. She hesitates until she hears the *CLICK! CLICK! CLICKING!* of the guns Jimmy'd unloaded. She joins in with some *CLICKING!* of her own.

"Who'd'a thought." Jimmy chides. "Can't trust a bunch of suburbanite revolutionaries to tell the weight of an unloaded pistol." He puts thumb to toggle switch. "But you can feel the weight of all that plastique, can't you?"

Baldy looks terrified in his catatonia-otherwise.

Caterers all run for the door. A few are stopped by security. One of the guards has got hold of The Woman. Security hold onto the caterers they've caught and do little else. They're not sure what to make of the janitor that's got Baldy by the toggle switch. *What's this guy gonna do?*

Well...

First...

Jimmy grins at the aide. "You may not be getting your war," he scoffs, "but you're sure as shit getting the collateral damage."

Second...

He depresses the detonator button—

"*BOOM!*"

He shouts this into Baldy's face. Baldy shrieks. Shudders. Breaks out of the catatonia and back into the shaky shock. Second faux detonator falls to the floor. Jimmy backs away, hands go up as secret servicemen and paramilitary swarm toward he and the shrieking shuddering aide. Just as they're about to put hands on Jimmy...

¬Ǝ

He vanishes. Hundreds of pistol rounds and those six clumps of C4 fall to the ground from where he teleported away. *THUD!* go the clumps. *JINGLE! JANGLE!* go the shells. The Woman's head tilts at this as one of the guards puts her in zip-ties.

ii

She sits in an interrogation room all her own. The rest of the Party Planners are still in holding. She doesn't like this one bit. It means—

"Well well well," says the lead investigator coming through the door, "look who's attracted herself the attention of the *eff-bee-eye!* "

Special Agent *Hank McRae's* back there behind the lead. He walks through the door held open for him. The Woman eyes McRae up and down. Says nothing.

Agent waves the Lead off. "I'll take it from here, detective."

Lead looks to McRae. Looks to McRae's clenched right fist to be precise. Looks to The Woman. He rolls his eyes like he *gets it* like a by-gone valley girl gets something judging by that eye roll. He leaves, closing the door.

Soon as the door clicks shut... "What the hell do you think you're doing?" She pounds her fists onto the scuffed metal surface in front of her to punctuate the query. McRae sits. "Council's on its way," she warns. "Fletcher's office hired them personally!"

"Give it up, Rip."

"I can still work em Hank. But not if they see me talking to you."

"It's over."

"Two years and you say it's over!"

"Because it is Bart! Libby flipped on Figurace the second he got his wits back. Started screaming *Figgy did it! Was Figgy!* Claimed he'd even snuck recording devices into the aide's office to document everything. Also claims to be on *our* payroll. I pray that's not true. It's over agent."

"Fletcher?"

"Ignoramus like them all. Right under his nose. If he were a CEO shit might roll uphill." She tears off the clip-on at this. Done in disgust? Maybe it's just a camel's straw of annoyance? Only of those straws she has any control over? McRae notices regardless of the motivation. "The People hate decision-makers whose decisions they can take or leave. Love the ones who don't give em any choice but you know that." *Bart* don't disagree. McRae goes on. "Director's already passed down his edicts from on high. Another fungible fed. *Why bust just Fletch if he's part and parcel with the rest?*"

"Can't have em falling like dominoes..."

McRae nods, appears more disgusted with himself less

the broader state of affairs. Then... "Forget him." He brightens in the slightest. "Fletcher's already in disgrace thanks to the kids at the wedding." He takes out his phone, starts streaming a vertical brick of a twenty-two second video. Kids call them *NikNaks* or something. It's an edit of Fletcher firing Figurace,

Yer F-F-F-Fired! Fuh... Fuh fuh fuh fired!

It's basically a Max Headroom rip-off these kids will get complete credit for originating.

Bart's not entertained. "So this ends at Figurace?"

"*Figurace used Libby for his connections*—and morality quite frankly... or lack thereof—*and Libby went to work.* That's it. Tell me about the vigilante."

"Ha! Two years with those wackos. An inch away from the money and this guy just strolls in... 'Strolls'... Just shows up and... Took the bullets right out of my gun Hank!"

"You did fine Rip. *WAMN*'s moorless. A bumbledunk affinity group again. Worst we'll see of them from now on is the odd milkshake pelting."

"There'll be more moneymen."

McRae waves his left hand across the table. Lifts up his right hand still in a fist but loosening. Tosses her a key. "Tell me about the vigilante." He's a little more insistent this time.

"Wanna know why I dialed him?" She starts taking the shackles off. "Guy didn't fit. And his costume was too ridicu- lous to mean another agency. Ridiculous guy coming across serious? Fed. Serious guy coming across ridiculous? Had to get a read on him."

"Tell. Me. About. *The.* Vigilante."

"Come on Hank..."

"First you see him, then you don't, Bart?"

She raises an eyebrow. "You know *WAMN* testimony's unreliable."

"Haven't talked to a single one of em."

"NikNaks are edited..." She looks imploringly. He doesn't budge. She frowns. "I'm not saying anything that puts me in a rubber room. They love to do that to us outta-covers. Where's the badge?" She rubs at her freed wrists.

Once again McRae doesn't budge, though this time out of some sort of contrition.

"Hank!"

"About that..."

"You promised me."

"It's been two years Rip."

"I saw you put it in that lockbox stays under your ass. Protocol."

"Listen sister!"

"...All due respect boss."

"With all due respect... It isn't in that lockbox anymore. Don't know how else to say it." Hint of contrition grows in those last couple words. "I didn't touch that locker till this morning."

"It's fine. Just brass."

"I'll track it down," he says like he knows it ain't *fine*. "It's more my ass than yours." He offers this a little meek.

Bart stands. "Covering your ass is work too boss." She moves toward the door, smirks wry. "I heard you used to be some sort of investigator." She kisses him on the forehead like he's her grandpa all-a-sudden. Takes off.

Tension broken, McRae spins transforming from contrite patriarch to hard-ass superior. Spins to catch Bart but the interview door's already closed.

She hears his booming voice as she walks briskly down the hall.

Goddamnit!

It's like he's in her ear despite being ten yards back and on the other side of a wall.

Nine eh-em debrief in my office agent! Or it'll be your skinny little ass this time!

She cracks a hint of a smile.

iii

She's home. Hasn't been home in a long time but it's still home. Her mom's been making sure of that. She walks over the threshold, observing, mostly sniffing. Isn't that the way? Isn't it curious how this particular sense modality is most trusted when it comes to confirming a head of the manner's home n' hosed, done n' dusted, and everything's right in the corner penthouse?

Place is a little musty though mom's Pine-Sol masks it. What'd you expect for an apartment unoccupied for, what, twenty-six months? Everything's as she left it. Spartan but-for the comfortable furniture. Everything about the furniture looks overstuffed. She doesn't compromise on that. Bare surfaces otherwise. Dustless thanks to mom. Only thing she really missed about the place was her recliner.

"What's this? A care package?"

She's eyed something sitting on the seat of the chair. Was it mom's intuition telling her her girl's coming home? Because someone's left something for her. Right where she couldn't miss it. Bart clicks on the lamp beside. Illumination brings with it an odd dissonance. It's something alright, though not anything of mom's doing.

It's her badge. It's sitting on those coveralls with *Ernie*

66

over the breast pocket. Beside the badge is the notepad on which she managed to write three-and-a-half *make-it-worth-my-while* offers. List goes:

> *1. Pay ya $50.*
> *2. Listen to your life's story.*
> *3. ~~Listen to my life's story.~~ (Masochist?)*
> *4. Walk up to one of the tables and eat*
> *an egg* r

She's stone at this. What's she thinking?

7

DEBRIEF

"**R**ipley Jeanette Bartholomew!" he says swinging her around in the bear hug he's got her in. "I never want to let you go! I can't believe it's been two years."

Bart's visiting Agent Bart. Some relation... Lots. The father, the daughter. *Agent Bart* is what we'll call him. *Lee* is what he calls her. He's a former field agent of *CSIS*[1]. Now he teaches counterterrorism courses for them at West Brandon District.

He finally relents. lets her go, sets her down in his desk chair.

"I saw you last week!" she chuckles.

"Yeah but that was in a '*consultancy*' capacity." He slumps himself into the left of his office's two guest chairs. "I felt like Jason Robards in that parking garage."

"Hal Holbrook. And it was right here."

"Not the same! I have Lee the civilian before me now

---

1. Pronounced, despite all good sense, *SEE-SISS*

68

and that makes all the difference. You have no idea how hard all this was on your mother…"

"She was right here with you!"

"Yeah only she thought it'd be more… Martin Balsamy."

"Hal Holbrooky. Cloak and Dagger?"

"Got to wear her trench coat at least."

"Took her forty-six years the civilian wife to learn the blandness of the job."

Papa's smile falters in the slightest. Rip notices. She listens. He notices her listening. "There *was* a difference though baby girl. For both of us."

"I know," she relents.

"Ah!" He gets back to boisterous. Kicks his feet up on the table. "But you're home and this consultancy nonsense is over with."

"Hmmm…"

"*Hmmm?*"

"Not quite?" she says. Dad's ears twitch. Rip drops the intimation. "Need your help one last time."

He does a criss-crossy motion with his hands. Lets each index finger take turns pointing at himself then his daughter "You want we should switch spots maybe?"

"Offices even. The agency shrink's?"

"What ya got Lee girl?" he says this in pro mode. Agent *not* daddy.

"Ever come across anything involving sleight of hand?"

"Bunco stuff mostly. Though I've crossed paths with the odd trickster in my interagency days with the fraud squad."

"Vanishing acts?"

"Wallets and pocketbooks."

"No people?" she asks. Dad looks quizzical. Not judgmental just quizzical. Rip pushes her luck. "Remember that story you used to tell me about Houdini?"

"*Rosabelle Believe*?"

"Yeah, that codeword to convince his wife of an afterlife."

"Or better, refute it. Treated the absence of any *Rosabelle Believe* as as good a proof of *no* afterlife."

"Yeah but what if that skepticism was just a front?"

"How you mean?"

"What if he *doth protested too much* to throw people off the fact he really could tap into the supernatural? Like, disappear?"

"He *could* disappear."

"Really disappear."

Dad leans back in his chair. "What'd you see Lee?"

She takes out her phone. Starts playing a video.

Yer F-F-Fired!

"Watch to the very end," she says.

"Think I've never seen a NikNak before?"

Fuh-Fuh-Fuh Fired!

"You watch em?"

"Your nephew, *that damn grandson of mine*, has me watch em. Whatever happened to the days of making grandpa play Nintendo?"

"Grandpas make the kids play Nintendo now... Look!"

Video's winding down.

Yer Fired!

Video's cut to Jimmy in the last second. The last shouting of *Fired!* perfectly coincides with him vanishing, leaving the bullets and C4.

Agent Bart looks unimpressed if not probative. "Clever edit?" he asks.

"What if I told you I saw what you just saw, unadulterated, from ten feet away?"

"Closest I've come to this..." Dad grasps for something

relevant, more to preserve his daughter's sanity than anything else. "Heard reports of farmers claiming hippy cultists've moved into the neighborhood. Swear these hippies flash in and out of existence as part of some sort of ritualistic practice." Dad's head lowers a little. "Company assumes a natural gas accumulation in the area…"

"And this guy don't flash."

"Right. What's McRae think?"

"Saw the video. Heard testimony of no one reliable. He's pushing me for details."

"Tell him everything."

"What?" Rip's a little aback.

"Won't be any shrinks involved. He hates the job too much to do it by the book. He's your greatest asset. Trust me, I know government boys."

iii

"What in the hell of this office ain't you telling me agent? Gotta be real twisted if you're afraid to talk after the tale of The Invisible Man!"

My two dads? No! As hinted, McRae's real fatherly when his agents are in the shit of things. However, once they're back-to-bureaucracy, Hank McRae's a real Frank McRae in *48 Hours*.

"Not invisible, *vanishing*."

"What was that?" he asks and she exasperates a little uneasy air at him. She takes something out of her pocket. The badge. Tosses it onto his desk. "Where'd you get that!" boss demands. And it is a demand. Phrased like a question though it's elliptical for *tell me where you got that!* He spins to the locked safe behind his chair.

"Came to my place." She's stopped him on the third digit of the combination.

He spins back in discernment. "And you shot him where he stood and so case closed?"

"Wasn't home. But how else could he get to you? Me? Your safe? My apartment?" McRae goes back to working the combination dial. Bart's eyes narrow a third at this. "Not gonna call for an FFE?" She leans right in her chair to see around her superior's bulky frame, to get a better look at what he's up to. "Any signs of tampering you would have seen... Boss?"

McRae spins back to face her, a file in his hand. "Listen little sister, you tell anyone about this it'll be..."

She reaches for the file, scanning much of the folder-cover before it even leaves McRae's hand. He releases it.

Written on the *File Title* line of the manilla is,

Joint (Bureau/ Natural Resources Amerika): J. Adamowski

She folds the document from the top right corner letting a few random pages flip away. The word *disappear* or some synonym is spotted in each flip suggesting the concept referred to plenty. She stops on a mugshot of Jimmy, half-fading away. Jimmy enjoying himself? *Only known photograph...* memo says. *Only confirmed engagement...*

"...My ass." she says, astounded.

"Mine too sister."

iii

Bart's enjoying herself, laughing. She shouldn't be. She can't help it. She's in her easy chair looking through the rest of the *Natural Resources Amerika* file on our hero.

"Christ Jimmy! Moving a pound of raw Russian platinum at a pawn dealer's in..." She runs her index finger down a length of the page. "...Winnipeg Manitoba!" She skims on, reading certain of the more entertaining or informative passages aloud, like, "*Last seen in Krasnoyarsk region, Siberia, March 14th approximately 10:45pm... Apprehended at Sherbrook Buy and Sell, Winnipeg, March 14th approximately 9:55am.* Bad timing Jimmy." Her nose twitches. An intuition's knocking. Now a second of pensiveness. "Wait a sec..." She takes out her phone. "Sirli! What's the time difference between Manitoba Canada and Krasnoyarsk Siberia?"

"*According to the Coordinated Universal Time system, there is a thirteen-hour difference, with Krasnoyarsk being ahead of Manitoba.*"

"Thanks Sirli."

"*You're welcome! If there is anything I can help with feel free to ask and, did you know, in addition to initializing our conversations by saying 'hey, Sirli', you can——*"

"Shut up Sirli."

"*Hmmmph!*"

Bart does some math in her head. Frowns. She's tired. She does some math on her phone. Ha!

"That's some serious bad timing Jimmy."

Apprehended just ten minutes after leaving Russia on your watch. They tracking you all over the world? she wonders, or are canuck cops all expert metallurgists enforcing outdated Amerikan mineral laws? They hang around pawn shops all day too?

She skims more...

"Ah, this might explain something..."

The passage of interest reads,

It is becoming excessively difficult to maintain cooperation between the NRA and the various local law enforcement agencies required to surveil, pursue, and—if needed—apprehend the subject: Adamowski. Police in areas where Adamowski remains active simply refuse to apprehend him as, per Adamowski's MO, upon reporting the subject in custody, Adamowski 'just beams away', 'vanishes', etc. Flight usually occurs from within the arresting officer's assigned vehicle where this officer is then made to face formal reprimand for allowing a suspect to escape his/her custody.

Reportedly, Jimmy once fled the same officer's custody eight times in a single night. In the span of three hours to be precise.

PFFNRRRK! Bart chortles some wine out her nose? Not quite, though it sure feels like it's back there. A pickling of the *retro-nasal space*. Reads on,

Here are some illuminating excerpts from the arresting officer's debrief:

"I'd get back out on the road and there he'd be, sometimes just a block from the precinct house. Just waiting. Let me put the cuffs on without incident, put him in the cruiser, then I'd radio it in [INAUDIBLE SHUDDERING] and then [INAUDIBLE SHUDDERING]..."

"By the fourth escape it was just a pride thing. I was gonna get this fucker if I did anything else, you know?"

"Fuckin Jimmy Adamowski!"

[INAUDIBLE SHUDDERING]

(From Follow-up interview:)

"But then, the next day, there's this fruit basket on my doorstep. Had an assortment of, like, eighty-or-so kraft beers in it. Had a little note with it, said, 'I hereby confirm Jimmy Adamowski washed bottles for an entire eight-hour shift in return for this sampler.' Was the owner of the brewery wrote it. Jimmy earned the thing fair and square. Gave it to me. I couldn't keep it of course, but... What the hell? Fuckin Jimmy Adamowski right?"

[WITH LOOK OF AFFECTION] "Fuckin Jimmy Adamowski..."

Adamowski's motive, most likely, was to send the message: there will be annoying consequences for anyone who pursues him but that, otherwise, he really means no harm. (Tactic seems to have worked.)

Bart pours herself another glass. Has a weird smile on her face. Drunk?

UPDATE: We have been warned by local law enforcement to cease issuing subpoenas to officers believed to have engaged with Adamowski in any way relevant to our case, but who refuse to complete any formal reporting on said engagement. We are told we have no jurisdiction to do so (EDIT: this is apparently correct on further consultation with Human Resources); that any legal intervention would be 'useless anyway' as 'their cops' would (and this is apparently the common sentiment) 'rather do jail time than face the embarrassment of explaining any encounter with Jimmy Ada-Fuckin-Mowski,' where officers often added, 'And he's really not that bad a guy anyway'.

Don't these officers care at all about the mineral rights legislation of foreign nations?

We have had no choice but to deputize our lonelier and more insecure of agents in order that someone (anyone) be willing and able to forcefully apply our precious mineral laws. Officiousness-over-integrity is what is needed here and these agents tend to be lonely and insecure due their alienating officiousness or, become officious in an effort to vindictively lord rules over anyone they feel responsible for their lonely alienation. Not surprisingly, preliminary assessments have revealed that recruitment will not so much be a matter of determining who at this government bureaucracy is sufficiently petty and small, but who at this government bureaucracy is maximally petty and small.

UPDATE: Turns out everyone at this government bureaucracy is maximally petty and small. Selection will likely come down to who I would most want to have a beer with, but everybody's so awesome around here it's near impossible to choose...

Truly an embarrassment of riches.

We're coming for you, Jimmy Adamowski!

UPDATE: Turns out surrounding yourself with nit-picky unflinching authoritarians high off their own fumes has its drawbacks. The Adamowski case has been officially tabled and I am facing resignation or prosecution. 'My choice' I was told by the smirking conniving team members who reported me for failing to include the T-S47 slip in my formal request for government overreach. Those guys really screwed me.

I miss them already!

> *— NATHANIEL 'NATE' ROCK, INTERIM*
> *POLICY PROCESSOR, MINING AND*
> *MINERALS, NRA*

She gulps down the last ounce of wine. Flips quickly

past the copious addenda included by NRA. Seems to be nothing else illuminating in the f—

Scratch that, what's this? A short paragraph surrounded by a rectangle of asterisks. Obviously eye-catching. Reads,

It has become alarmingly clear that—with the subject Adamowski anticipating our every move, even leaving confidential Natural Resources of Amerika documents at his last known locations, documents that only NRA agents have access to, documents we keep behind lock and key (within three-factor-locking TRTL-30X6 safes), seemingly to taunt us—Adamowski must be surveilling us in addition to us surveilling him. He is almost certainly using his expert skills of breaking and entering to do this as well as his skills of evasion.

A flash of that badge comes to mind. Jimmy's coveralls too. The notepad.

Adamowski must be surveilling us...

She feels a little queasy at this. On the verge. Feels like all matter behind her has just silently instantly burst away leaving only an endless expanse of grasping groping accessibility. Feels like that expanse is behind her and *only* behind her. Like an open door. Like even if she jumps out of her easy chair and spins to see the chair and the cinder block wall behind it, she's only shifted the void. As though the expanse has gobbled up her apartment wall and picture window because it's now behind her precisely because it's behind her because that's where the void stays. *Behind* so all the ghoulies and beasties of the capital-W world may approach at her back unencumbered. She feels that fearful anxiety anyone would, caught running a scenario of vulnerability late at night, in the dark, in the place a person ought feel this vulnerability the least.

Yes, even undercover cops experience this from time to time.

She does jump out of her seat though she doesn't spin. She moves to turn on more light than what the forty-watt lamp next her chair provides. She realizes the implausibility of her fears and this brings a levity that calms her. She holds onto a little of the spook in her spine anyway as it's fun. It's why we watch horror movies. Still, she wonders as she moves around her apartment on some sort of a mission... You knew about me? she thinks, my investigation? Like you knew about them? Are you here right now? Watching listening? She moves into her bedroom trying not to let her bearing betray her intentions.

She gets to her closet and swiftly slides the mirrored doors open. Nothing. She peeks around the space left between the wall and the door she'd opened. Nothing. She's exhilarated. Is this rational? If rational, is this how she should feel?

She whips wide the shower curtain.

Does the same to the coat closet door in the hallway.

The fridge door even.

Nothing.

Nothing.

Nothing.

She's sitting thinking on her couch now, facing the apartment door. All the lights are on and the apartment door is wide open. *All* the doors are open and she's put a floor-mounted mirror across from where she sits so she can see as much of what's behind her as possible.

A neighbor walks by and looks in. Neighbor's confused at the sight at first, then surprised to see Bart just sitting there staring in her direction, right through her.

"So sorry," she says shaking Bart outta the deliberations.

Bart waves her off. "On a case Livia."

Livia goes...

Bart's losing her drive. Chemicals and *Candyman Candyman Candyman* induced thrills are wearing off. She yawns.

"Not yet. What have I missed."

She reaches for those files, jostling her badge. She hesitates. There's another intuition though it's blind just yet. But that badge evoked it. What's the intuition's meaning? Its proposition? She picks up the brass. Feels the weight. Eyes the grooves and pitting converging into text and image. An image of McRae locking it into the safe behind his desk is of mind. Now the whole of the lovable hard-ass's office too. You think Bart's apartment is Spartan, this guy's office is a Buddhist's wet dream. McRae could teach em a thing or two about renunciation. Could teach—

"Son of a bitch!"

The proposition's arrived.

You knew all about this.

She waves the badge in the air. "You knew. There was nowhere for you to hide in that glorified file cabinet yet you knew exactly where to go to swipe what you needed to get my attention. And what about the others? You're spying on some pretty big names. By teleportation? How? How is it you never *send* yourself into anything other than the perfect context in which to overhear? Intervene? Never pop in next to Secret Service? A paramilitary garroting? Libby was a bad dude and you worked him like a toddler works gramma. You steal from drug dealers yet you've never *beamed* your way right into a cartel shootout? Hell, never in front of a moving bus? Unless... Of course..." Agent puts down the badge. She looks up at nothing giving it her undivided attention. "You can *see* can't you? That's the only way a guy who can do what you do—as many times as you've done it—has avoided jumping into certain death."

"You can see me? You've been watching me? You *have* been watching me."

She gets up. Starts turning off lights. Closes the door. Turns the deadbolt. Unease has returned and not just at her back.

"Well Jimmy..."

Only light left on is the bathroom's. She exhales sharp in confirmation of her course.

"Well... I hope you're a gentleman."

She doesn't say this coy though such a quirk of intentionality is certainly on the table. She doesn't say this concerned, though that tone would fit too. She doesn't say it in intimation, though she may be testing Jimmy for virtue, more. She just gets up and goes into her bathroom not shutting her door because he'll see right through it. She just drops her robe revealing her nudity, turns on the tub faucet.

Jimmy rears back. Jostles his head in all directions like it's some strange calisthenics. Tries to shake away The Gift.

Bit of side-boob as Bart feels the running water for temperature.

He shakes his head again. Baps at his temples in alternating jabs trying to hammer the sleazy theater out his head. Puts his hands in that weird spoony position and crashes down onto the floor, crisscross.

Aum...

8

PROCEDURAL FORMALITIES

Now you see him, now you don't. Some are calling him the 'Houdini Hero', the man who foiled the plot to kidnap the President's nephew. Though others aren't so approving...

I t's reporter *Simone Simmons* talking in narration. The video of Jimmy disappearing plays in the background.

But who is he? Who is he as a matter of identity but, also, who is he to take it upon himself to intervene in matters involving life and death?

The video cuts to canned interviews of randos wanting to talk to the camera.

"I mean, he saved the president's brat of a nephew but who gives a shit... Can I say that on TV? That shit about how awful the president's nephew is? I don't want to get sued for slander... Oh, it's only slander if it's not true? Well... He saved that asshole of a nephew but he also stopped those guys from fooling the presi-

dent into another war... again. I mean, who wants that? So yeah, I'd say he's a hero."

Another interviewee,

"No, absolutely not! We have police for these sorts of things. You can't just go around stopping guns from firing and bombs from exploding. Someone could get hurt!"

Another,

"Wish he'd make my boss disappear..."

Now back to Simmons in studio.

And so there you have it. The identity of our janitorial justice seeker may still be a mystery but the one thing that isn't: his polarizing effect on the public. More on this as it develops. This is Simone Simmons, Reporting.

Story's over so Jimmy tunes out the tube. He doesn't want to listen to stories about himself at the best of times. However, he heard this Simone Simmons could be a real bulldog. Maybe he should...

Simmons is walking to her car in the underground garage of her station when...

"Simone." It's a whisper from out of the shadows.

She spins, squints into those shadows. "It's pronounced *Simon.*"

"Sorry." Jimmy emerges into the light. "You want The Teleporter's story, I'll give it to you. But you gotta tell it straight."

Simmons leans her back against her car a second. No deliberation. "No."

"What?"

"Nah. Last time I told the tale of a guy like you I got a husband and two kids for my trouble. Love em to pieces and spending any time at all with a hero like you means life love and death but especially death. Lot of death. I got a family to think about."

"Rumor has it your husband's the Masked Fla—"

"I hate that name."

"Still, guy's a hero."

"*Vigilante.*"

"Touché. You're already telling my story."

"Fluff. A perfect mix of every kind of useless opinion."

"You took an oath."

"Reporters don't take oaths."

"Your integrity then. What happened to you?"

"Same thing that'll happen to you if I do this all over again. Life and death happened to me Jimmy." He flinches funny at the sound of his name out of Simmons' mouth. "Don't worry," she winks. "I won't tell em who you are but that also means I won't tell em who you are. You're on your own as far as PR goes."

"Even if it means your reputation?"

"What reputation?" she chuckles. "I gotta get out of the network game anyway. I'll go freelance if I want my rep back. Start a YouTube." She's unlocking her car door now. She's trailing off too, talking to herself more than Jimmy.

"Finally get away from this *vigilante beat* bullshit." Door's open. "Bye Jimmy."

Door slams. Car rolls.

She's gone.

And that solves that.

ii

"Let's make a deal," Bart says.

Says it to Jimmy. Says it to no one as far as proximity is concerned. *Maybe* no one as far as any real knowledge of Jimmy Gifting is concerned. He *is* Gifting a look at her of course. She's sitting in her easy chair, speaking out into the ether as though her audience.

"The deal is premised on a benefit of the doubt. I'm going to assume everything I've read about you is true and you *are* a gentleman.

"You know I'm investigating you. You're going to be watching out of self-preservation. Fine. That's fine. However, my personal life, especially family, is off-limits. You want to observe me in the wild, you observe me right here in this chair. Not in the kitchen, not on the toilet, in the laundry room, doing yoga just inches beside this very chair.

"Right. here."

She's angling her finger downward at the right arm of her easy chair. She makes her point and picks up a little whiteboard and a dry-erase marker.

"Now," she continues, "I don't know if you're listening so I'm going to write all this out on this little board. In fact, anything I need to tell you that isn't me saying it on the job or in this chair will be on this little board. This is

85

just for me and you and it will sit on this chair whenever I'm not."

She starts writing.

iii

Procedural Element #1

"I'm not talking to any more government people," The Widow says.

"You've talked to us already?"

"You mineral people," she says through the crack of the closing door.

"Natural Resources?"

A beat. Then... "Yes," is heard at the other side of the door now closed.

"That's not me," Bart says. "Different agency."

"Still government."

"I just want to—"

Door comes back open—just a crack. "You want to lock him up. He saved lives. My husband's! We're lucky to have a man with his gifts and you want to take him away!" Door closes.

Bart persists. "If you know of his gifts you know we can't lock him up. Not for any longer than he wishes. I just want to know, myself. Is all there is to his Gift the good you see in him? Just knowledge. For me, but for you and him." Silence. Bart tries one thing more... "He can see. He's maybe watching us now? Ask him for permission."

The Widow turns to Jimmy, looks imploringly.

"They can't hurt me," he says. He peeks through the

window curtain next the door, sees it's just Bart out there but he already knows that. "It's you I'm worried about."

"I'll tell them whatever you want me to."

"Tell them the truth. Anything you wish as long as it's true. They can't hurt me. They won't hesitate to hurt you for any lies."

¬Ⅎ

He's gone. Some flowers and a stack of hundred-dollar bills are revealed on the kitchen table behind where he stood.

The whole refinery's gone up. Flames and explosions. Everyone alive to get out has gotten out. All but...

"Who's there?" *The Pinned Man* demands.

Jimmy emerges from around the corner.

"Get the hell outta here kid! Place is goin'!"

Jimmy hustles to the pipes and girders lying across the man's waist and legs. He tries to move them. They won't budge and he doesn't know what teleporting them out will do to the rest of the structure. Girders are warm from the fires burning. Getting warmer.

"Told ya to scram kid!"

Jimmy sits.

"I'm so sorry," he says, pained.

"Kid?"

"You shouldn't be alone."

They've been conversing for a short time. The Pinned Man isn't so much of a talker though he appreciates Jimmy there to witness any last testament. Guy's more a listener. Divined Jimmy's life's story that's for sure. What little of it there was… Divined the presence of The Gift that's for sure.

"I don't know what will happen…" Jimmy worries. "It could kill you."

"Christ Jimmy, look around!"

"I can move the girders maybe?"

"You tried. Even if the whole place doesn't come crashing down, then what, we walk out of here? I can't feel my legs." He looks down at the junk all around him's got him pinned. He shakes his head. Jimmy sees The Man's tears hit the steel. They don't sizzle but they do steam, evaporate in seconds. Man looks up. "Please."

Jimmy takes a deep resolving breath. Man's hands reach out. Jimmy takes them.

"Wait!" The Man shouts. "Take me to City General. It's closest to my place."

Jimmy nods.

"Jimmy, my wife."

Jimmy nods.

¬∃

"He got him out of there," The Widow says. "Like he promised. Right to *City* like he said he would." She blots under her eyes with a tissue. "They couldn't stop the bleeding. Jimmy blames himself. Thinks it was his Gift that did it. Thinks it hurts the people he moves. Well, I got to say goodbye to my Robert for it and he got to drift off in peace, his children with him when he went." She pauses to let out more of the grief Bart's reimposed upon her. Comes out in a long shuddered sigh. "T-That was all because of Jimmy."

She tries collecting herself. "He has more than a Gift, Agent Bartholomew. He is the gift."

She walks briskly to her car, selecting an entry from her phone's contacts: *Ma and Pa*. She sits in the driver's seat, closes the door but doesn't start the engine. Phone's ringing.

"I just wanted to hear your voices," she says, breaking. She weeps as soon as she ends the call.

Looks up in her tears. "I'm so sorry Jimmy."

Then, a text,

DAD

That's why I teach now baby girl. Couldn't take losing the people around me.

iv

Procedural Element #2

Bart interviews the Zealot. Guy refuses an interpreter. She doesn't speak his language either. She just gets in the room with him as he sits, waiting, shackled to the table. She confirms he's one of the Jimmy-ported terrorists. She stands. She turns and looks upward.

"See Jimmy, he's alive and well. Look at him. I know you've been searching for these guys ever since *DOD* snuck them back underground. Here's one. Alive and well. You didn't hurt anyone."

Zealot looks on in confusion. Looks up at, for all he can tell, a raving fed. Looks at what she's looking at. There ain't no camera up there.

v

Procedural Element #3

Bart interviews a Callow soldier this time.

"He's alive too Jimmy. I can find more of them if you'd like?"

Jimmy shakes his head. He isn't convinced though his eyes are welling.

He reaches out as though to stroke her cheek. To say his thanks. His hand goes right through her.

vi

Procedural Montage

Sequence #1

Jimmy lays on the couch in fetal position with the doofiest grin on his face. Eyes closed.

Bart is sitting in her chair, talking away animatedly, laughing.

Jimmy's grin widens.

Sequence #2

Jimmy's FatButt™ alarm vibrates: *7:00pm.*

Bart takes the whiteboard off her chair and sets it aside. Written on the board is,

90

Got a minute? 7pm?

She plops onto the chair, reclines, starts talking away animatedly again, laughing again.

Jimmy's got that grin *again...*

Sequence #3

Bart's in the shower.

Jimmy's meditating. *Aum...*

Sequence #4

Bart's in a meeting of special agents and Bureau brass. Someone in his sixties is droning on at a lectern pointing to a PowerPoint with the permanent slide heading,

Workplace Safety and Equity: A White&Contrite™ Bigot from an Accredited University Approach

(Or something like that)

Bart writes onto her notepad under the table,

Could be worse. Could be you spending hours Gifting Figurace watching Rule 34 porn...

She looks up at no one. Wry smile.

Jimmy laughs.

Sequence #5

Bart's in the shower.

Jimmy's meditating. *Aum*... But... One eye opens. It darts around. He starts bapping at his temples...

End of Montage.

vii

Bart's in her office. Colleague knocks. Pokes his head through a crack in the door.

"Got something for ya," he says.

"Yeah?" She looks receptive.

He leans in further and drops a folder onto her desk. "Your guy. Pawnbroker downtown was questioned by DEA last week."

"How's a drug angle involve my guy?"

"Pawnbroker got busted with a couple Picassos..." He says *Picassos* in intimation. "Couldn't hold the store owner on anything. Etchings—"

"Lithographs?"

"Yeah yeah... They weren't reported stolen and—bet they almost certainly were since they're *goddamn Picassos*—only cartel assholes can *one* afford em and *two* not give a shit when they vanish. Might want to talk to the shop owner. Your guy's MO's all over this."

Bart picks up the file, waves it. "Thanks."

Agent bows, ducks back out shutting the door.

She bends the corner of the folder letting a few of the pages flip. See's enough, apparently. She spins in her chair to the bins behind. Drops the documents in the shredder.

9

SNATCHING THE MOUSE TO SET THE TRAP TO CATCH THE CHEESE

There's been a reversal.

She doesn't really know how it happened. Came on gradually. Likely started with the Widow. Hell, could've started with that wedding. Point is, a lot more Jimmy files than less have been going into her shredder.

Piece of the Jimmy pie that ends up in the shredder is getting bigger thanks to Bart. So's the pie. There's more and more chatter about The Teleporter among feds-of-all-stripes and so it's just a matter of time.

They'll just keep coming, she says. *I can get you immunity. A deal. That means... They'll just keep coming.*

There's been a reversal.

ii

"No worries Jimmy," she says up at nothing. "We're still on for seven. Just gotta check on something. That lead we talked about."

Car pulls up to a large brick building. It's brick

judging by the peripheral spill of Bart's headlights anyway. Only source of light around here.

"Damn it!"

Eyes open.

Jimmy never checked the address. Would have if he knew it was some warehouse in the middle of nowhere. He only rode along with her, didn't warp by any established location, no coordinates. He leaves Bart a second.

Eyes close.

He's warping his way through the complex. Darkest place he's ever seen or is it just the blind of the apprehensions? Dark as dirt even outside his dissonance.

"Oh this isn't worth it Rip, not at all."

Isn't it?

Jimmy heard the briefing that brought her here—didn't understand it. Interdepartmental *this*, Residual leads *that*. She said this was big. A surprise. An address off a dead CI. He can't make out anything in this dark when… He's through a wall! Didn't see it. Just breezed on through. He's hovering over the river at the west of the complex. *What are you hiding down there?*

Meanwhile, Bart's got her flashlight out of her rude bag and's popping it on.

She shines it around the only door up the only walkway at the periphery. She knocks with her forearm cuz the door's solid steel.

"You alone?"

"Yeah," she whispers. Looks over her shoulder and upward like Jimmy's watching but…

"Son of a bitch!" He catches himself wasting time over that bilge. He warps to the front of the warehouse. She's going in.

"Don't!"

BOOM! Lights are on everywhere. He's blinded by the glare even in The Gift. It's just yellow factory sunlight and indistinct shapes. It's blobs of what are most likely people and what he could swear is a shower stall on wheels, rolling.

"Make any of those moves of yours Teleporter..." It's a man's voice. Amerikan. Nondescript dialect. "...We kill her."

Jimmy's blinking profusely. Trying to get to the form in the shape. All he's doing is...

Mixing...

The...

Gift...

With...

The...

Real.

He can see now. Warehouse is an empty room but-for Bart, a guy next to her, and men at the edges. Men point scoped carbines. All wear tactical gear easily afforded by any fed but also, cartel? Then there's the guy beside, must have been the one doing the talking. He's suited. Again, could be a fed, could be cartel. Just a matter of how ruthless he is. Should Jimmy give him the benefit of the doubt? Assume him cartel?

You probably noticed he's Gifting and hasn't made a move. *Suit Talker* wasn't lying when he said he'd kill Bart if Jimmy acts. At least, he wasn't lying about the potential. All those gunmen's guns are pointed at her. She stands in a cage at the center of the room. That was the rolling blob that looked like a stall: a cage on castors. She walked right into it through that door. They've bound her hands and gagged her. Her eyes are puffy. She's had tears. None flow currently.

It's an empty room but-for Suit Talker, his men, their guns, Bart, and that cage.

Jimmy has no reason to doubt the requisite skill in here but what's that matter? Even if these goons were holdin short-shootin .22s in clubbed hands, too many would get a fatal shot off before he could disarm them all.

Suit Talker starts talking again. "I know you know what's happening. Somehow. I know you've been watching. You've got forty-five seconds to meet my associates at the following location." He holds up a placard with coordinates on it. "That's forty-five seconds to figure out *where* this is. We know how quick your commute is."

He arrives.

It's an ad hoc interrogation room. He knows it's ad hoc because the table at its center folds. Chairs don't. Never do because folding chairs are too flimsy to withstand the things done to the people sat in them in these rooms. There's a window of course, playing at being a mirror. He's been in a lot of these places though always on his own terms, either Gifting or messing with people messing with him. Not now. He feels a tightening. A sentiment of forewarning separate the circumstances—new, as though of the body. In his body, sure, that's where he and the feeling meet acquaintance and yet the feeling is telling him to... Watch... His...

But...

Two balaclava'd men enter the room, one holding a syringe. Syringe contents glow.

Jimmy moves the slightest slice of an inch when...

"Told ya Jimmy." Suit Talker moves closer to Bart. "*Dead!*" Several of the red dots of the laser sights on Bart converge to her left chest and forehead.

Jimmy relents.

Balaclava One drives Jimmy into a chair next the table, pulls the top of Jimmy's head over to the left. Right side of the neck is revealed for the needle. Jimmy breathes heavy through his nose, eyes are closed and Gifting. *Balaclava Two* buries the needle into Jimmy's carotid. Jimmy spits a spattering of saliva through the puffing valve effect of his otherwise sealed lips. Two plunges the glowing contents through needle into artery.

Bart's eyes are closed to the laser sighting all over her. A solemn tear roles down her cheek.

Second the plunge seal hits the bottom of the barrel, Balaclava goons relent. Let Jimmy go and back away.

"What'd you give me?"

Balaclava men leave the room. Jimmy Gifts himself a look inside himself. He can do that by the way. **Little machines zip through his veins. Give off the appearance of tiny robotic wood-ticks. Has no clue what they are.**

Two suits enter now.

Bart's still holding on. They've taken their sights off her for the time being.

"What's in me?"

Suits ignore this at present. *Suit One* pulls out a chair and sits facing Jimmy at the other side of the folding table. *Suit Two* moves to stand behind the captive.

"What is it?" Jimmy asks, meek.

"Just something to keep you social," whispers Suit Two over Jimmy's shoulder.

"Maybe a fast-acting poison where only we have the antidote," Suit One suggests. He looks probative at Jimmy.

"Maybe a couple of explosives," offers Suit Two. "'Bout the size of a pinhead. Just big enough to open up your ass."

Suit One leans back in his chair, ready to level with Jimmy. "It's whatever we need it to be to keep you from leaving without saying goodbye," he assures.

"Who the hell are you guys?"

Suit Two moves around the table to join his rising partner. Both stand, pull out their badges peacock proud. They hold em out and say in unison,

"United States Customs."

"What?" Jimmy derides at the absurdity, levity overtaking him despite it all.

"You heard us," they say a little deflated.

"Customs!" Jimmy shouts. "You gotta be shidding me. You assholes were Customs all along?" Suits look at each other confused. Jimmy goes on. "You kidnap a friend of mine! A federal agent! For what? To stop me selling produce?

Suit Two gets Jimmy's disrespect. Gets petty. Gets governmental. "Watching her Jimmy?" He whips a finger at the mirrored window.

Suit Talker puts a hand on Bart's cage. He looks up, speaks into the ether as Bart had so many times past. Speaks to Jimmy. "Name's Custy. Head of Customs."

Custy, Jimmy mouths like even though now is definitely not the time, that's the stupidest thing he's ever heard.

"You watching her?"

Abundance of stupidity or absurdity or no, those words in that tone with his pal in those bonds in that distress remind him. Reshake him. Make him feel like his ribs have shrunk to the size of a softball. It's a burning vomitus tight.

"Good." Custy jostles Bart's cage a little then reaches downward. He's slow about it.

Jimmy's Gifting this with a clarity he never thought possible. He reaches out.

Bart looks up, all around, then focuses. Focuses right on Jimmy, imploring him as Custy smirks on. Then...

She moves her hands that were never bound to begin with to the gag. She removes it.

"I'm sorry Jimmy." Says it still looking into his eyes. She says it in the kind of complete lack of betrayal of any emotion impossible to pull off without near-destroying oneself.

Custy opens the cage door.

Bart walks away.

Jimmy goes hot. *Always thought you may not feel the same. Always hoped yours only possibly less by intensity, by degree, not of a different substance! I never thought: you intended to hurt me. I wanted to die for you now I want to die...* He can't read this meaning into his confused feelings and yet that's the proposition of it. In all his confused sick pain he tries to maintain composure. He's tensing up like he's about to disappear himself because he is.

"Uh-uh," warns Suit One. "Want we cause you to combust internally?"

"Or freeze solid with the snap of a finger," adds Suit Two moving back around the table. Back behind Jimmy.

Jimmy relaxes in posture only. "What the fuck ever

happened to *do you have any items to declare*?" he says in loose agitation.

"Oh but you were real scared when you thought we were what? Terrorists? CIA?" Suit One asks. "Fuckin CIA," he says like he's talking about the hockey team one town over. "Don't fucking tell us you thought we were a bunch of black-baggin spooks Jimmy!"

"You move a lot of goods Jimmy boy," Suit Two interjects. Says this leaning into Jimmy's ear once more. "Goods you gotta clear with us."

"*Have any alcohol tobacco or firearms on ya*?" Jimmy mocks.

"Not funny dickle!" says Suit One.

"*Fruits or vegetables*?"

Suit Two grabs Jimmy by his collar and pins his face to the gritty surface of the polyethylene table. "Tell us what you can move!" He smooshes Jimmy's face a little more then lets him free. Makes a *pffft* sound letting him go like all's pathetic.

Jimmy slowly straightens. "What can I move? You to tears you do that again."

"What can you move ya fuck?"

"Tomatoes..."

"Everything!" the agent demands.

"Hey, if I could move *everything* who'd ever know it?" Teleporter says this a little defiant a little like a Catskills comedian. Stand-up act's what indicates the defiance.

"Huh?"

"Pointless!" Jimmy says. "Never register a change. Maybe I just moved the whole universe? Exactly four inches to the left of nothing? How would you ever know? It's like that philosophical problem of everything in existence doubling in size in an instant—"

"Tell me everything you can move!"

"Like to know myself..." *SMACK!* From Suit Two. "Things I can lift off the ground."

Then...

Custy enters. Jimmy looks at a loss, disappointed with himself. Hating himself.

"That's right Jimmy, right next door!" Head of Customs laughs.

"Where's the girl?" asks Suit Two moving back around the table like a tactic. Like his constant varying of proximity will put Jimmy at an ease needed for malleability then rip him out of it for capitulation.

"That's Agent Bartholomew to you!" Custy admonishes as he passes between the two agents converging. "Didn't want to stay for the proceedings." Jimmy's eyebrow raises a little. Then... "Ah, Jimmy," Custy says in some sort of mock concern, "we know you can watch us somehow, maybe even read the street signs, yet you're not a walking GPS are ya? Changed those signs, gave you the coordinates to plot into the map. A childish trick though it fooled you didn't it? She was right on the other side of that wall the whole time."

"That's not how it works," Jimmy relents. "I was... Stupid." *I didn't take my eyes off her long enough to look around s'more like it, eh? Six of one?*

"How's it work then Jimmy?"

He sighs. Never really understood a need to hide his powers from anyone until about a half hour ago. Then that necessity went out the window about a-half-a-minute-like-a-half-a-lifetime ago: indifference. "Like I can walk through walls. Like I can see and hear anything that doesn't have to be manipulated to see or hear. Like I'm over your shoulder."

"How do you get there?" asks Suit One, genuinely curious.

"Just get there. I don't know. I just close my eyes and go." He closes his eyes and goes. "See, like now. I'm outside the door." Jimmy speaks softly. "There's some nebbish standing there staring at Google Maps or something." Suit One looks as intrigued as ever. Suit Two looks incredulous. Custy just leans against the wall furthest from the door, against that mirror, arms crossed. "Go ahead, have a look," Jimmy whispers to Suit One.

Custy nods and Suit One tiptoes to the door. Pops it open, super quick. There *is* an agent on the other side. He *is* studying some sort of map on some sort of tablet. He *does* look like Woody Allen.

"Holy shit!" Suit One says grinning at Suit Two.

"Lucky guess," says Suit Two.

"Shut that off!" shouts Custy at the tech with the tablet. "Fuckin idiot."

"But—" says Tech.

"*Off!*"

Suit One shuts the door on the disheartened nebbish powering down his device.

Jimmy blips in and out of existence a second. No one notices except Custy—maybe. He squinted a little is all. It was very quick.

"So you're telling me..." says Suit One now really into all this. "...You can just close your eyes and *BAM!* You're in my house?"

"No. Only places I know the address of. That, or places I've been to." Jimmy points to Suit Two. "Like his house."

Suit One grins wider.

"Fuck you Jimmy," is Suit Two's contribution.

"Oh yeah," Jimmy insists, "I've been there. You got a spare bedroom you call a *study* but it's just a desk and a bunch of old Maxims and Golf Digests."

Suit Two goes stone.

"Yeah," Suit One chides, "but you can tell that just by looking at the illiterate!" He jostles Suit Two around at the shoulders.

"He's got his grandfather's pocket watch on the desk, encased in acrylic," Jimmy reinforces.

"How the fuck do you know where I live?" Suit Two demands, now fuming.

"Because," Jimmy says leaning back in his chair, "I had sex with your wife!"

Suit One laughs in all his enjoyment before catching himself.

Suit Two doesn't laugh. Now he wants to take Jimmy's head off in addition to know how the guy found his place. He's a font of emotions and aimless rage. "Fuck you!" is the best he can muster from all that.

"A lot of people been fuckin your wife," Jimmy insists. "Your boss is fuckin her right now!"

"Custy?" laughs Suit One.

"No, not Custy!" Jimmy says pointing to a Custy still just leaning and observing. "Your ASAC."

"Ricky?" Suit One says astonished. "No way!"

"Yes way—"

Suit Two lunges across the table getting into Jimmy's face. "Say another fuckin word Adamowski!"

"He's putting it to her as we speak!"

"Gonna mother-fuckin kill you!" Two grabs Jimmy by the throat as Custy and One pull him off.

Jimmy rubs at his neck. "What? I put your boss' ballsack in your wife's asshole?"

Suit Two's chest is heaving.

"I can prove it." Jimmy insists.

"Fucker, so help me…"

"I can. Just call her up."

"Shut! The! Fuck! Up!"

"Just call her up and she'll be all out of breath. From the bonin. Call her up and have him," Jimmy points to Suit One, "call Ricky's phone. You'll hear it ring. It's sitting on your nightstand after all."

"Oh! You gotta do it man!" Suit One says this like he's not gonna take *no* for an answer.

"Fuck no!" says Suit Two. "I trust my wife. I think…"

"Good god!" Jimmy shouts this with his eyes closed and his hands reaching out play-acting like he's a blind man reaching out in the dark. "You won't believe what he's doing to her with *his* penis and *your* bowling trophy!"

"Shut it you fuckin freak!"

"It ain't seven-tens he's splitting! I don't know bowling!"

"Mother fu—"

"Do it," says Custy.

"What?" says Suit Two.

"Call her," Custy says pointing at Jimmy. "I wanna see how good this guy is."

"Boss…"

"Do it!" boss reasserts. "And you, lil-chucklin-nuthin…" He's talking to Suit One. "…You call Ricky." No beat. "Do it!"

The two agents take out their phones.

"Speaker phone!" Custy adds.

Suit Two dials his wife as Jimmy pantomimes breathing heavy in orgasmic pleasure.

Phone rings… Rings a little more… Then…

Hey Babe, answers the woman on the other end of Suit Two's phone. She *is* huffing and puffing.

Suit One opens his mouth in some sort of slack-jawed elated grin. Mouths *holy shit!* to Jimmy.

Suit Two looks hit by a ton of bricks.

Custy gestures for Suit One to dial Ricky. Suit One does.

"W-What're ya doin hon. You sound tired."

Suit One snortles.

I've just been.. I... Why ya calling babe? Then... A phone is heard ringing in the background of Suit Two's call.

"Holy shit!"

What's that? says Suit Two's wife.

"Yeah, *what the hell is that?*" says Suit Two trying to hide the gut-rending rage.

It's... I-it's a phone...

"No shit, hon." Suit Two is bright red.

Says the caller's just 'Agency ID #42HB7'... she adds.

"That your ID?" Suit Two says in hush to Suit One.

"How the fuck should I know my phone code?" says Suit One in same hush.

"B-better answer it hon."

Ok. A beat. *Hello?*

HELLO... Hello... hello... hel... reverberates around the interview room as Suit Two's wife's voice booms through both phones' speakers. Then...

SMASH!

Two's thrown his phone against the wall over Jimmy's ducking head. He flies out the door. Then... His head pops back in. "This shit ain't over between us Adamowski!" *SLAM!* Then... Head pops back in again. "How big's his dick?"

"Tiny. Just an inch bigger than yours."

RRRRRRRR!!! SLAM!

"*Around!*" Jimmy yells through the door.

"Wow!" says Suit One marveling.

"Yeah, *wow*." says Custy noncommittal. He sits himself across from Jimmy. Looks him in the eye. "Ricky ain't fuckin anyone's wife. He's at a conference in Atlanta. Right now."

"I know," says Jimmy, smirking. "Saw it on the MEMO in *his* office." He's pointing to Suit One. "Didn't see it in the other guy's. Saw it untouched in the inbox on his door though. It's how I knew about Ricky and how I knew that touchy asshole of a partner of yours didn't."

"How?" says Suit One.

"*How* what?" asks Jimmy.

"All of it! Everything. How'd you do it all? Starting with our offices." Suit One says this like he's ready to sit at Jimmy's feet for the rest of his life gleaning all Teleporter wisdom in the world.

Jimmy obliges. The fuckin around is taking his mind off Bart's betrayal, anyway. "Offices were easy," he assures. "Saw your names when you flashed your badges. Knew where the Customs branch of West Brandon was so I *Gifted* there. Found your office numbers on the directory board at reception. Found your partner's home address on the mailing label of a Golf Digest in his office. Beamed down to Atlanta when no one was looking. Snatched Ricky's phone. Beamed back to West Brandon, left the phone on the nightstand, told you assholes to call it."

"Whoa!" Suit One's amazed at all this, but... "Hey! How'd you get Sally to be so out of breath?"

"Didn't. Saw her on the treadmill. That's why the whole idea."

"Oh ho *ho*! Yer diabolical man!"

Jimmy gives an *it was nothing* shrug.

"Yeah, *diabolical*," Custy says with that same lack of commitment. "*Smith!* Get in here."

Near instantly...

Woody-Allen-cum-Tech-Smith comes back in with the mapping app.

Custy looks to him. "Jimmy been anywhere in the last fifteen minutes?"

Tech responds with some apprehension. "You want I should..." He holds up the tablet.

"Yes! Turn the thing back on!"

Tech scrambles to get the device booted up. He taps and swipes a few times then... "Uh... H-here of course. Then... Our offices, the Ramada Atlanta, and some house in the burbs. In Vanwood. Whoa! He did this in just—"

"That'll be all Smith."

"Yes sir."

Smith's gone.

Fuckin arounds over. Jimmy looks to Custy like Custy can read the *how* all over his face.

Custy's read it just fine. "Jimmy oh Jimmy," he says, condescendingly. "How? Better question: *what are those little beasties swimming through your veins?*"

Jimmy's ears prick up.

Left of Custy's lips rise. Starts shaking his head. "Not bombs. Not poison. You're no use to us dead. Might as well tell ya since it makes no difference anyway... Nanotrackers. New technology. Nanobot trackers aren't so new, sure." A pregnant tick... "It's in their replication rate."

¬Ǝ/Ǝ

Jimmy's beamed exactly two feet to his left. Chair and all. Well, chair and all *except* those nanobots. They sit on the floor in a glowing puddle.

"Ha!" says Custy. "Thought you'd try that. That's the innovation. Nanos replicate far too fast for you to simply beam away from them all. Second any one of em detects anything below critical mass value they replicate back to that value. Takes just one to replicate to critical mass in point-five seconds. You'll never teleport fast enough!"

¬Ǝ/Ǝ

¬Ǝ/Ǝ

¬Ǝ/Ǝ

¬Ǝ/Ǝ

Four new puddles on the floor, only...

The bots are already back to critical mass.

"Don't break your back there Jimmy!" Custy chuckles.

Jimmy throws his chair against the wall. Doesn't break, just thuds. Real stalwart for the tortures. Custy rises to his feet. Suit One follows Custy's lead.

"You try it boy!" the crusty fed says, taunting Jimmy. "You try it and thirty agents bust in here and tear you to pieces!"

Jimmy's fire. His chest heaves.

"J-just calm down Jimmy. We didn't mean anything by—"

"Shut your mouth you damned fool!" Custy says to Suit One. He turns back to Jimmy. "You can't get away now. You like watching us? Now we watch you. We own you! Duty-free."

Teleporter just stands looming, emotions ablaze. What now?

Custy smirks a last time. "Oh you're free to leave any time. We'll be in touch."

¬Ǝ

"Where is he!" Custy bellows through the wall.

Smith reenters. "You're not gonna believe this boss."

"Where?"

"Top of Mount Everest."

"Smart boy."

10

OLD HABITS

...

10:05:25

27.9881° N, 86.9250° E

10:05:26

27.9881° N, 86.9250° E

10:05:27

27.9881° N, 86.9250° E

10:05:28

27.9881° N, 86.9250° E

...

Subject hasn't moved in 17 hours. Likely dead.

Nah. Metabolic functions cease, tracker functions cease too. He dies, they die.

The blaze orange looks like it wants to free itself of who it clothes. In desperation to fly. The winds at the south summit, gusts at kilometers per hour in triple digits, contrive this effect. There are several puddles of that green glowing fluid around him, their luminescence in varying degrees of intensity. He must have been trying for a while to shake those trackers. He just sits now. Palms spooning.

Curious: all appears temperate despite the pelting winds. He's completely comfortable. Not at ease, though comfortable.

Curious more, he's been here less than twenty-four hours yet he has a beard, a short beard but—

¬∃/∃

He's blinked in and out of existence. His beard is longer by at least a half-inch.

¬∃/∃

More beard.

He stands.

⁂

Subject's on the move!

Where?

Gimme a second...

Where!

Ha. Down the mountain a little.

ii

Little whiteboard sits on the easy chair. Says,

I'm sorry...

Jimmy's back at the south summit. He's in a meditative posture though he's Gifting.

It's his pack. To be precise, it's his pack in a locked evidence room at West Brandon Customs. It was seized the second he beamed away. Left hot. Left it in that goddamn interrogation room.

Wanted to help...

He shakes the image away.

As far as he's Gifted, all of the pack's contents are intact. Why does it just sit untouched? They know he can take it at any time. It's bai—

...Complete immunity in return for those trackers...

He shakes it away again.
Gotta be bait—

...You don't have to hide anymore.

Enough! echoes down the mountain.

He tries calming himself. His arms drift in that flowing blaze fabric. He gestures like fluid though there's rigid deliberation in every swing and thrust. Arms dip and weave and plunge then... He shoves both hands out! Palms up. He brings them back into his lap in that resting spoon of his.

"Alright, wanna help?"

¬Ǝ

Subject on the move!

Where!

Oh boy...

iii

She shuts and locks the door. She's sniffing again. Kinda the ritual. Don't know if she's sniffed this out, but... She knows something's amiss. Whiteboard's on the floor next the chair. She's armed though she doesn't grab for her gun. She moves for the board.

Looks at it. Message starts out,

Want to help?

...

BOOM! BOOM! BOOM!

It's a knocking at the door. She spins.

"Who is it?" she says wiping away the message.

"United States Customs! If you're OK say so through the door."

Door swings open. She sees the Customs guys holding tasers. They try to get a look into her place. They peek around her. She doesn't make it easy yet they glean it's just Bart on that side. As far as they can tell...

"Christ guys. If some home invader had a knife to my throat don't you think he could get me to say *OK*?"

Agents put their weapons away.

"Nothing funny happening ma'am?"

"Not this generation. Glad to see you guys anyway." Agents are confused. Bart explains. "Just wrapping up the Adamowski file. Custy's wanting all evidence at your place and my boss *doesn't want to get wrapped up in any 'interagency bullshit'* as he put it. Told me to dump all I have with you guys."

Agents look put-upon. Hands go out. "Where?"

"Pardon me, meant *you guys* as in *Customs*. I have to bring it to Custy directly. Chain of custody Custy... You know you know... Thought you could tell me if he's in today."

"Atlanta till Friday. Conference."

"Custy or Ricky?"

"Both. Important conference."

"Darn. Well, see ya Friday."

She closes the door on the agents now tilting to see into the ever-lessening gap. *SLAM!*

iv

She's at Customs less than an hour later wearing a pack looking conspicuously alike to Jimmy's. She's also got something under her arm.

"Bartholomew, Ripley, dropping off for the Adamowski

file." She holds up what was just under-arm. It's a long black cylinder.

"What's that?" asks the *Evidence Custodian*.

"Pure plutonium!"

Custodian's eyes widen.

Bart smiles. "Just keeping you on your toes. It's a binding fluid for aquatint etching."

Custodian's eyes go whatever shape means confusion.

"For lithog... For painting," Bart explains. "Real pricey. Adamowski was selling it cheap to arthouses."

Custodian's eyes go bureaucratic. "Ticket please."

"Ticket?"

"Can't take that without a signed lodging ticket."

"Well get Custy down here then!"

"Agent Custy isn't a regional employee. He only attends to branch—" but Custodian catches herself in her boiler-plate. Something's off. Looks like she's rebooting. "D-did you say *Custy*?"

"*Crusty Custy*. You got it."

Custodian's slack-jawed.

"Relax," Bart intercepts. "He's not my boss." She sets the cylinder down, leans onto the counter like she's relaxing. "Though, gotta say, he has been extra *Custy* about this Adamowski guy. Your boss thinks he can jump down even the *Eff-Bee-Eye*'s throat. Put him in a room with *my boss* though, all things equal, Custy'll lose a ball or two." She takes the cylinder back from the counter, holding it to her chest. "Whelp! I'll let Federal Branch know about all that red tape you're insisting on..." She leans her face closer to read the custodian's nameplate. "*S. Luxem*?"

Custodian lunges over the counter taking hold of the cylinder. "J-just. Give. Me. That!"

Bart's pulled nearly halfway over the counter before she

finds enough leverage to wrench the fluid back into her possession-true. "Whoa lady! Be careful with this." She holds up the cylinder. "Stuff's dangerous."

"You said it was safe."

"Said it wasn't plutonium. It's still incredibly volatile when out in the open. Very few chemicals can be mixed with this that don't result in... You don't want to know... Just don't spill any." She hands it back over.

Custodian brings the cylinder out from behind the reception booth and starts walking toward the evidence room.

Bart crosses her arms watching the custodian move away. Some sort of liquid squirts out her elbow and across the counter onto the custodian's desk. She's hiding a bottle in the crook of the left of those crossing arms. Looks like nasal spray. *Looks...*

Papers on the desk start to smoke as Bart catches up to the custodian.

There's an agent standing guard at the evidence room door.

Bart looks him up and down. "Adamowski show yet?"

"Not yet," says the guard.

"Supposed to tell me that?"

"*Fuhshhhit...*"

Custodian's punched in the door code and has entered the evidence room.

"You can't catch him you know," Bart assures the guard. "Surely you've been briefed?" Guard goes stone. Bart tries again. "He's probably watching you right now. That doesn't weird you out?" Stone. One more try. "Agent *Syess*?"

"What do you want?"

"So that lanyard wasn't issued to you by mistake... *Agent Syess, US Customs*. I know it and so does Adamowski thanks to you brandishing that for all to see. What else will he find out because of what you leave in the open? About you? Your family?" Stone crumbles. Guard puts the lanyard into his breast pocket. Bart smiles in a way sly. "What's the plan here agent? Come on, *quid pro quo*."

Guard sighs. "All I'm gonna say's this, it *is* about catching Adamowski... In the act."

She raises an eyebrow at this.

Custodian reemerges. She's about to pull the door closed when...

"Damn guys! You got a fire here!" Bart's pointing down the hall to the Custodian's office. A white-gray smoke billows out over the service counter.

The two Customs staffers run toward the fire. Bart slips into the evidence room.

v

Car pulls into the desolate lot.

Radio's crackling, *Sentencing is expected to be handed down today in the conspiracy trial of senatorial aide Kenneth Figurace—*

Cuts the engine.

She exits the car holding Jimmy's pack. She holds it out in her hand.

"Alright Jimmy, just as you said, right where you said. What now?"

Ǝ/¬Ǝ

Pack's gone. She stands alone and empty-handed.

"You gotta be kidding me!"

vi

Custy's meeting with all pertinent West Brandon Branch Customs officials. Tech's finishing briefing him, *ASAC Ricky*, and Suits One and Two on Jimmy's activity. All sit around a boardroom table that's bland, costs at least three times as much as any other table serving the relevant purpose, and serves less than that purpose. Standard *Fed Special*.

Suit One sits flanked by Ricky and Suit Two. He wears a doofy grin loving the awkward tension between his partner and his superior. Ricky and Two aren't on speaking terms see, not since Jimmy put the idea into Two's head that Ricky's been boning his wife. Why's Ricky sitting and stewing? Suit Two smashed Ricky's phone while demanding his wife tell him where Ricky was hiding. Did this after *he* smashed through his own bedroom door. 'This is his fuckin phone!' Suit Two shouted as he threw the thing into the ensuite toilet.

But you said it was smashed? you're thinking. Well, it slammed against the toilet tank first then dropped into the bowl in pieces. A real *Broke-n-Soak*.

Ricky and Two can sense One's reveling. They can't look over to confirm it however as that might cause unintentional eye contact between the two. So...

WHOMP!

They smack him at once.

"Ow!"

"Quit it the lot of ya!" barks Custy. "Finish!" he's churning his hand at Tech.

"Y-yes, as I was saying. It's a temple of some sort—"

"Who's in it besides Adamowski?"

"Don't know. Satellites show never more than a single person leaves at any one time."

"And?"

"Well, we can't tell if there are many people who all look the same, or a single person with no distinguishing features."

"Kinda temple?"

"Monastic. About all we can tell."

"How ya know?"

"Here…" Tech disseminates some photos. It's of the singular figure, birds-eye, blaze orange fabric's worn. Figure has no hair.

"Monks!"

"Most likely."

Custy nods. Takes control. "Alright, last known locations, done. Now we decide how we proceed with Adamowski. I like *Project Scorched Earth* personally, but I'll hear you guys out. Just as long as it hurts…"

Custy twirls his index finger in the air and points it to Ricky. Motion means *take it away* most likely. Ricky stands, his briefing documents at the ready, when…

"Oh wait," adds Custy. "Almost forgot. Headgear fellas." Custy looks up to nothing, smirks. "Wouldn't want ya listening in Jimmy."

All put on a strange contraption. It's a standard set of headphones connected to what looks like a choker worn by a nineties teenager. Choker's got two black checker-shaped objects attached to it. Choker checkers sit at either side of the men's adam's apples.

"Mouths closed. Speak like you're talking through your throats not your lips. Sensors will pick it up just fine."

Ricky starts talking in that weird way.

"Come on!" Jimmy shouts.

Eyes open.

He can't hear a damn thing.

vii

Really wanna help?

Bart scans around her place. She feels that unease she felt when she first realized, should he wish too, Jimmy could be lurking anywhere he'd fit. She's backed herself right into a corner without realizing. Still hasn't. She's hugging onto the whiteboard. She wipes it with her sleeve and starts writing. New message reads,

Fine. But this stays in my office from now on. Trespassing was never part of the agreement. We communicate there FNO.

viii

"There never was any *Project Scorched Earth*," she says in debrief, looking up at nothing, though this time from her office desk. "Custy's just trying to scare you. He really hates you. He really loves his job so he *really* hates anyone who finds a better deal and doesn't give the government its taste. But he *really* hates you.

"They don't know anything. Know about some temple but even if they had any jurisdiction to pounce, it's too remote anyway.

"Jimmy... I can't confirm this, but I think their plan is to lull you into a sense of their absence. Normalcy. They'll track you. Surveil you. Gather evidence of the extent of your powers. Then make a case for... Something no Customs agent has the authority to approve alone. Something drastic.

"Customs administrators are petty officious asses but it's beyond your embarrassing them that they have it in for you. They fear you on some level. Really Jimmy, in some sense we all do. I mean, what you can do... Even I... Yet there are those who'd rather stamp out that fear than make any compromise. There was a time..." She gives herself a moment. Looks like she's really thinking hard about what she's going to say next, how she's going to say it. "My source at Customs said you've been to my place twice since that night. We really need to talk about this Jimmy. About everything. Plea—"

Eyes open.

ix

Tech sits in a little dark room looking like an air traffic controller. He's tracking Jimmy of course, scanning all his maps and radar and everything else *video* in front of him that's dedicated entirely to spying on our Teleporter. Tech sits to the right of another Customs agent with far less machinery at his disposal: a pen and a notepad.

"On the move!" shouts Tech startling the agent next to him. Startles himself too. Jimmy hasn't moved in a while? "Back in Temple. Must be home for the night."

"Good," says the agent with the notepad. He rises. Tosses the pad onto the panel with the video equipment. "I'm getting a coffee for a shit. Want anything?"

"Not if you're gonna make it sound so appetizing..."

"You try living with a lazy bowel."

"Better than living with you."

BEEP! BEEP!

"On the move." Tech looks over his shoulder only to see his partner's gone. Gets back to business.

"Adamowski is...

∃

"*Here.*" A hand takes hold of Tech at the right trapezius.

"Make a move and I *move* you. Know what happens to a person when I do that?"

"No."

"Neither do I."

Tech shudders.

Jimmy continues. "How many watch me?"

"I-I'm primary—"

"Good!" Tech jumps at this. Jimmy nudges him to keep talking.

"I-I'm primary but there're other techs. Three three-hour shifts a week except me. I got four plus maintenance."

"Maintenance? That's what makes you *primary*?"

"Y-yeah."

"What are the chances that lofty little title of yours comes with just the shit work and no extra pay?"

"Pretty good." Tech chuckles. "T-there're the backers too."

"Backers?"

"Agents... Agents who listen and record. Keep tabs on me too. Like the guy who you woulda passed in the hall. Look..." Tech affects some sort of bargaining tone. "He'll be right back. You don't want him to catch—"

JOSTLE! Jimmy shakes Tech silent. "Don't pass people in any halls remember?"

"R-right. Forgot."

"Backers dumb?"

"Dumb?"

"Fool easy?"

"F-fool?"

"Can ya fool em? They dumb?"

"N-not so bright I guess."

"Honest man." Jimmy says this in some sort of satisfaction. Tech twists to glance over his shoulder despite Jimmy holding him. Jimmy lets him. Tech's got a look like he wants to know what *honest man* meant. Jimmy smirks. "I see everything remember?"

"Right…"

"Keep up! Because this last bit is important. I can see everything you're doing in here. I can see everything you're doing anywhere. You're my new pet, agent. My new pet agent. When you're in here you're not scanning me, get it?"

Agent's still.

Jimmy squeezes hardest.

Agent starts nodding vigorously.

"Say anything about this meeting. Do anything about this meeting. I *move* you." Jimmy eases the pressure.

Agent nods again.

"Put yourself in here as much as you can only don't betray yourself. Falsify the records. Don't betray yourself to *them*. Don't betray *me*."

Agent nods a last time.

¬∃

Jimmy's bought himself a little freedom.

11

WE NEED TO TALK

We need to talk...

It's sat written on that board the last three weeks. Jimmy's not been receptive. He's gone *dark* as they say in the agency. Twenty-two *dark days* as they say wherever *that's entertainment*. Twenty-two and counting.

Oh but he's been on the move.

He's been as active as ever though his absence tells her he doesn't need her. Not since she helped him blind the eye. Absence says he doesn't need any agency insider. Not *as* agency insider, anyway. Doesn't need anyone?

She's checking that board currently. She wonders if he's noticed her growing haste in moving to it, from office door, the last few days. Her expression? What's it look like? She's not going to take out a mirror though she's sure it isn't neutral.

He has noticed.

ii

Subject on the move...
Where?
Nowhere hot. Spruce Bluff Manitoba.
Where the hell is that?
Exactly.
He's not in Spruce Bluff...
He's coming out of another one of those pawn shops, *Jeneral Jane's Pawn*, Rugby, North Dakota. Got a wad of bills.

iii

We need to talk...

Has sat written on that board the last three weeks, but board hasn't sat in just one spot. Board's gone. Was it confiscated? Bart didn't move it.

It's not in McRae's ghost town of an office.

Bart didn't move it. She's been out of the office since last night and that's where—

Did Bart move it?

Must have. It's sitting on her easy chair, blank. Has she given up on him? He doesn't know if she's home. She's not in her chair and he made a promise.

Office is still empty.

So's the easy chair. Where'd—

It's a figure! Not Bart: a man, obscured. His back is to us. He's holding the board, writing. Turns just enough to reveal his message. Says the usual, only in this guy's scrawl. Says,

We need to talk...

He turns a little more to reveal just enough of himself to reveal everything in the world. The tip of the leftmost petal of that little pinned flower rotates into view. It's a poppy which means it's Poppy Man!

Jimmy's Gifting all this from the mountain top, calm as can be. Impassive as can be though the dam of his stoicism's about to burst. Where is she? He made a promise yet surely this warrants breaking it?

He's searching as expressionless as can be, as concerned as can be, when...

She's pulling into the office parking lot.

Jimmy moves his right hand from the top of the spoon to the bottom.

"Cozy little place..." Poppy Man says looking around the apartment.

Eyes open.

iv

Poppy Man's about to leave the hovel Jimmy's tracked

him to. Place looks dank though it's hard to tell without a sniff. Windows are all pasted over with tin foil. Only source of light currently is a small fluorescent bar hanging flickering over the sink. Place's open concept, likely real grimy. Who can confirm in this dim? Poppy reaches for a doorknob. A little help. A dining room table is revealed as hallway light enters through the narrow opening of the entryway. Only, the man hesitates, closes the door. No more table. No more help. He walks back to the kitchen counter.

He reaches into an open drawer. Takes out an object of a design just lustrous enough we can identify it in the fluorescent shine. A kitchen knife. He runs it through one of those notch sharpeners a couple times.

"Cozy little place," he says. Then... "Took your time. Don't know if you're here, but I know you're watching."

"Why you following her?" Jimmy emerges from the shadows of the hovel's worst.

Poppy drops the knife into the sink, turns to face him. "Wasn't. Was following you."

"No." Jimmy's got a look of denial less incredulity, the look of a man who's been a fool a fool a fool. Like these acts have been stacking up on him as of late—because they have—and Jimmy's had about enough of them—because he has. Like goddamnit the more he's discouraged by boneheaded-ness like this the more he fucks up all over agai—

"You're the only guy I know to catch him you let him hunt," Poppy says. He leans back against the counter. His eyes squint to better see Jimmy in the dim. "Got rid of the beard. Too bad. I liked it. Bet if I asked you nicely you could do your little magic trick and *BLIP!* a face like you fell into a year of Rogaine."

"How—"

"Got rid of the robe." Poppy squints on at the man indeed in just his track pants and Jets jersey. "Can see the utility in that, around these parts at least."

Jimmy tries again. "How—"

"I can help you you know."

Then...

A beam of laser light emits from the ceiling. Moves along Jimmy top-to-bottom, fast.

¬∃

Jimmy couldn't manage to port away before the end of the scan.

"They can't track you anymore," Poppy says this into the ether. "Go ahead, check."

Jimmy Gifts into himself.

Nanobots are dormant.

¬∃/∃

Bots sit in a glowing puddle on the south summit.

Gone. Every single one of them. He's clean.

¬∃

∃

He's back in Poppy's hovel. Poppy's holding some sort of Mason jar with a strange semi-translucent lid on it. Lid looks like it's made of a bottle-fly's thorax. A green LED blinks on it.

"Now," says Poppy, insistent, "we don't have much time. You expel the dormant bots and we store them in here." He shakes the jar. "This container can sustain a critical mass of them for up to a year. Put it wherever you want to throw the government off your trail."

Jimmy's shaking his head a little frantic. Goddamn plot sounds real good to him but... "I-I don't have em."

"What! Where'd you put them?"

"Everest!"

"Get them back!"

¬∃

Wait!

∃

Poppy hands Jimmy the jar. "Scoop em into this. Don't get too much snow in it."

¬∃/∃

He's back with the jar.

Poppy snatches it. Twists the lid. Glowing nano goo starts to fill the rest of the container. "Critical mass!" he says happy as anything. "It worked."

Jimmy's gone from stoic to frantic to relieved but what the hell's been happening here the last fifteen minutes!

Poppy notices the loss.

"Here." He hands Jimmy the jar. "Test it out."

¬∃

∃/¬∃

Jar sits on the south summit. Just the jar.

∃

He's back at Poppy's, Gifting.

Subject's on the move... South Summit.

¬∃/∃, ¬∃/∃

Jimmy's still at Poppy's but he's moved the jar to Spruce Bluff.

Eyes closed.

Subject's on the move... Spruce Bluff Manitoba.

Eyes open.

Jimmy grins. He's come a long way with his meditation though he can't help grinning now.

"Gotta keep it somewhere safe," Poppy reminds.

Jimmy realizes his face. Grin ceases. "It is," he assures. He didn't just drop the goofy grin for his training. "Who are you?"

"My name is Toll Lytrall. I'm like a life coach for vigilantes. Except I don't charge so I'm like a life coach who isn't a scoundrel so no life coach at all."

Jimmy shakes his head. "You're not Toll Lytrall. Toll Lytrall's dead."

"You know of my past?"

"Took *his* senior seminar on reverse causality."

"Don't remember you attending."

"I didn't."

"Ha! Of course not! Hope you got the most out of it." He sits at the table across from where Jimmy stands. "Think of me as Toll Lytrall 2.0 then."

"That's a weird way to put it."

"I'm a weird guy. Or, maybe, a normal guy in weird times." He gestures for Jimmy to sit. Jimmy doesn't. "However, I am Toll Lytrall. In the flesh." Jimmy's eyes narrow by half. Lytrall chuckles. "You can teleport but my faking my death is unbelievable?"

"Toll Lytrall was in his seventies when he died. What are

you, forty?"

"I think I can still play the *you're a teleporter* card here: you can teleport but my faking advanced age is unbelievable?" Jimmy don't budge. "Fine." Lytrall starts writing some coordinates on his palm. Holds them up at Jimmy. "Look here. On the workbench with nothing else on it."

It's a bag.

"It's a bag."

"Right, it's a bag Jimmy. Bring it over here." Jimmy don't budge. "Come on!" Lytrall says almost indignant. "If I were setting you up, you think I'd be this inefficient about it?" Jimmy don't— "Fine!" he relents. "I'll call a cab. See you tomorr—"

"Alright alright."

¬Ǝ/Ǝ

Jimmy's back with the bag. Lytrall takes it. Jimmy watches, on edge, ready to rock n' roll.

Lytrall pulls out some rubber chunks of something or other. Holds them in his hands. "Pardon the crudity of this. It should make the point." He smooshes the rubber bits all around his face pinning them down in all the right places. He looks up at Jimmy a much older man.

"Jesus Christ! Professor!"

"*Whatever a cause is, it stands to reason it must involve those circumstances such, should they not have arisen, the effect would not have arisen.*" He says this in a slightly lower slightly craggier voice.

Jimmy gets it. "*What* the hell are you?"

"I'll tell you sometime." He shakes his face and the old-man prosthetics start falling off into his hands. "Come see me at the location you got this." Pieces of his past drop into the bag Jimmy brought him. "This place is depressing me."

He stands, moves to the door and opens it, turns back. "Any time Jimmy."

v

Lytrall swings open the giant sliding door of a giant complex. It's really just a post-frame farm equipment shed on a homestead of his. Yeah yeah, *shed*'s a funny word for a building not quite the size of a Costco though close. Everything else is modest. A modest farmyard save for the former professor's technologies and the airplane hangar that houses them. And we're not just talking Mason jars and prosthetics.

Structure is completely dark inside save for a dull penumbra of pink creeping in from the yard light.

"I can vanish any time you know." Jimmy says this not in that penumbra: somewhere darker.

"That was quick. Curiosity get the better of you?"

"I can vanish you too," he threatens.

"I know. I've seen you at work." Lytrall flips a switch and the shed's lit enough to reveal our hero. The bay lights will take a couple minutes to reach full brightness.

"You don't seem so scared," Jimmy observes.

"I've done nothing wrong. They'll let me out of whatever cage you drop me in."

"Some other version of you."

"Same me."

"You don't know that."

"Not for certain, but I have a means of proof."

Jimmy's eyes flash with a curiosity he wished he'd stifled. Maybe the lights aren't so bright Lytrall missed it?

Professor smirks.

Jimmy goes stone.

"You like this place?" Prof asks.

"Farm go bust?" Jimmy says this walking past Lytrall and over to a workbench. He picks up another lid of one of those Mason Jars. "This don't look like a gas filter for a Massey Ferguson."

"It isn't at that. We should get this started."

"What's *this*?"

"The convincing. You don't yet trust."

"Convincing—"

"Why all the drinking, Teleporter?"

Bay lights are a little brighter.

Jimmy's eyes narrow another eighth, pupils dilate. "You another me? You a Gifter?"

"Nah, I'm another *another*. I'll tell you sometime."

"How do you know—"

"Tell me about the drinking Jimmy. How do I know? How'd I know about Figurace? How'd I know foiling his scheme best handled by a person of your abilities and not another's? *How'd I know you'd do it?* is the better question. I'm resourceful in my spy game."

"You wanna send yourself to the center of the sun in your sleep? That's why I drink. You ain't operating as ya do without some kind of power. Powers like mine."

"There're more convenient ways to quell your dreams. Prescription drugs. Lucid-dream conditioning. More. But you know that. You're right about the powers. Only, they're *abilities* strictly speaking."

"No."

"There are better ways."

"No."

"It's the suffering."

"No!"

"Sure. You used to be able to turn them off. The tortured,

calling out. Calling for someone like you. The most vulnerable of them even. The mothers... The children... In war zones. The working men buried, pinned... In cave-ins... Collapses. It never ceases. If you could just snatch them up... Take them away from their pain and yours. And yet you don't, do you?"

"Stop."

"Natural disasters. Man-made. Those stolen away, ransomed—ransomed if they're lucky. The desperate. The suicidal. Those tortured whose line is someone, anyone, stepping in to stop them. Catching them. Showing them they're not alone in this world but there're always too many but you never stopped to save a single one did you? So: They. Stay. Forever. Of. Mind."

"Stop!" He's doing that spoony hand thing.

"The voices never cease. You can turn them off in the day, maybe, through distraction. Maybe. Though never at rest. Not as you lay there at your most vulnerable... Robert Renda... His widow..."

"*STOP!*" Jimmy's chin goes to his sternum.

"That's why the perpetual stupor. The slurring and yammering."

Bay lights are at near full illumination.

Some tears. "Dreams."

"That's why the head in the clouds."

"Don't speak of it like that."

"Why not? The monks do. It's for balance not for running and hiding. It's for a calm for resolving your problems not burying them. But you know this."

Eyes clench saline. Floor's soup underfoot. "P—please..."

"You have two problems Jimmy."

"I got more than that."

"You have two problems where the first is your lack of complete control over where you send yourself. I can solve that in an instant." An eyebrow raises over red eye. "The second is: you can't move people. At least you think you can't. I can prove to you you can—that those moved will be none the worse for wear. But this, Jimmy, this I can't do in an instant. This will require a leap of faith."

"Think I'll trust you for your promises?"

"Quite frankly Jimmy, I don't care one way or the other whether you trust *me*. All I need by way of trust is a trust in *you* that your pain will end. You'll have a life. I know this hesitation of yours, this reticence, all your defiance and threats, just an act. You know you're a dead man dying looking for the easiest way to this *inevitability*.

"I don't need your trust in me. I just need your interest which I have, your curiosity. Got that too. *Maybe this guy will impose upon me this easier way?* Now I turn your hope on its head."

"What the fuck are you talking about?"

"You know exactly what I'm talking about. There is the inevitable, sure. There are three inevitabilities to be clear. Though of a pissant conditional nature, the condition of which is not absolute. You have three inevitabilities *if* you do nothing else. Three.

"The first, you keep living in that perpetual state of *extinction of the self* which means you're nothing more than a walking dead man with head in constant oblivion. Second, you go back to the booze and drink yourself to death but you live a little doing it. Third is you eat a bullet. You know this and you know one thing more: your three inevitabilities are as good as one. You're going back to the bottle sooner or later because at least then you have the pleasantries of its effect a few minutes a day *before* oblivion but you also know you'll go from booze to bullet sooner than later because the drink will make you slip and the slipping will let the tortured in. Their torture means your torture. Knowing it's coming is torture itself. You'll be tortured until it comes precisely for the fact it comes.

"*You can't do this anymore?* You're right. You know you're dead or dying or both only now you know that happens on a condition *not* guaranteed. You do nothing and you die. You do something and maybe you die but maybe you don't. Maybe you don't because you've quieted what needs quieting. There's one and only one way out of all this and that's the leap of faith I offer you.

"I don't have to convince you to trust me. I just have to convince you if you don't kill yourself to truly live you're dead anyway."

Lights are at full illumination now.

Jimmy's been taking it all in, pensive. He exhales from down deep. If it were ice it would be a plume. He lets fly with the following: "Never in my life have I heard such a raving convoluted conniving caring combination of words and never in my life have I been made to feel such a despair at the sound—if not any easy meaning—made. Don't like it. Not a bit. *Was* necessary for my wisening to what news there was in those words: *I'm dead anyway.* I'll grant that and I appreciate the wisdom but everything else is bad music. Needed the wisdom nonetheless. And something tells me if I don't oblige you, you'll just keep on talking. So, if my dilemma is killing myself in your silence or killing myself in your blather, I choose the former.

"Leap of faith?" Lytrall grins.

"Why not?"

12

I'M TOLL LYTRALL
AND I MAKE HEROES

"Here, put this on." Lytrall hands Jimmy a bulbous bulky SkiDoo helmet. It's covered in wires and through-hole LEDs.

Jimmy looks at it funny a second. Puts it on.

"Now you're invulnerable," Lytrall assures.

"You mean I gotta wear this thing everywhere I go?"

"Relax. Just watch."

Lytrall grabs a goose-neck pry-bar from the workbench. Rears back like he's gonna hit Jimmy in the gut with it.

"Whoa!"

"Fine..."

Jimmy's decked out in catcher's gear. Chest protector, mask, shin guards. Everything but the cup. Let's hope whatever the Professor has planned doesn't require one.

"Ready?" Lytrall practice swings that gooseneck a little too lusty...

"*Shwrrr—*" Jimmy pulls the mask from his face. It's a snug fit. "Sure." Where'd Lytrall get it anyway? Looks like it's from the fifties.

"OK!" Professor rears back with the gooseneck. Swings away.

BEEP! BEEP! BEEP!

¬∃/∃

There's a rumbling and muffled shouts coming from the rear corner of the facility.

"Whoops!" Lytrall rushes to the back corner. "Hang tight Jimmy. Try not to break anything!" Then...

¬∃/∃

No Rumbling. Shouts are silenced. Lytrall stops, observing, when...

"Where the hell was I?" Jimmy says from behind.

"*GYAHH!* Don't do that! You scar— Don't surprise me like that!"

"I Surprised *you*?"

"I forgot..."

"Forgot?"

"Slipped my mind..."

"Slipped?"

"*I forgot* to tell you I calibrated the harm detector to send you to a fixed location. Somewhere safe."

"*Safe?* It was scar— It was dark in there."

Lytrall waves his hands in a slight imploring manner, like they're windshield wipers. "Let me explain."

It's a big rectangular box, a little bigger than a fridge. It's painted in orange spray paint—a color similar to Jimmy's temple robes. It also has *Caution* tape crisscrossing all over it.

"That helmet you're wearing..." Jimmy's still got the Times Square New Years Ball on his head by the way. Lytrall's pointing at it like Jimmy may have forgotten where it is. "...That helmet has the ability to near-instantly detect risks of physical harm, harms indexed to severity, and assess expected overall harm."

"How *near* to instant?"

"Faster than any bullet can leave a gun."

Jimmy looks impressed if not convinced.

Lytrall notices, elaborates, "Any sufficient harm—and I don't mean a paper-cut or a playful bap on the shoulder or a stubbed toe—I mean any harm capable of incapacitating you or posing a risk of death greater than a two percent like-lihood, *any* sufficient risk of sufficient harm detected and the teleportation center of your brain—your pituitary gland—is activated. Then you're sent here." Lytrall puts a hand on the big orange box.

"What kind of tech is this?" Jimmy puts another hand on the big orange box.

"Cardboard,"

"That some sort of jargon term?"

"What, like inventor slang? Like how all of us technolo-gists call LAN cables *Net Noodles*? No. There's no such term as 'net noodle' and I can't imagine a technologist who would use such a term if there were. It's literal cardboard. It's the box my fridge came in."

"I was in a fridge box?"

"You were in a Jimmy box. Its function is to contain *you* from time to time."

"It was designed with a fridge in mind."

"It was designed with a range of appliances in mind. The factory that makes these sees fridges, freezers, and washer/dryer combos shipped in them, more... Modular sofas... Semi tractor transmissions—"

"Never me."

"The list of intended objects—containable—is open-ended. You haven't been ruled out."

"Haven't been ruled in either."

"A soup spoon in the arctic is a popsicle stick and yet, last I checked, the soup could care less."

"The soup's the fridge on this story. I'm the frozen soup but I'm not a frozen fridge."

"I can't believe I'm about to say you're right about anything you've just said and I won't. The whole point is, input and output determines function not intent. Design is irrelevant. Not only can you use a soup spoon to eat things other than soup, you're not even under any expectation to use the thing to ladle food into your face."

"But a salad fork—"

"The material is immaterial! The trick is in the preset coordinates the Danger Ranger™ sends to your brain."

Danger Ranger, Jimmy mouths to himself.

"*Because* Mr. Naval-Gazer, the helmet determines a *range* of risks *and* the name's clever. Anyway... There doesn't, technically, need be anything in this corner like there need not be anything special about any of the locations you teleport to. The only difference is the helmet sends you here. *You* don't send you here. Could just as feasibly be a dirt floor, but the box ensures something Jimmy-sized that'll keep people from standing where you could teleport right through them."

"What people?"

"I entertain."

"No you don't."

"How would you know?"

Eyes close.

"You have no coffee, tea, or alcohol of any kind in this whole homestead. Anyone who entertains more than two people more than twice a year would have this on offer as most expect some sort of stimulant or some sort of intoxicant in a social setting. You'd have leftovers."

Lytrall's discerning a second, figuring, squinting. Then... "I entertain."

"Nope. At best you entertain badly which is as good as not entertaining at all. However, I bet you don't even do that."

"Now you'll never know." He puts his gooseneck under his arm and mimes ripping something.

"What's that, an invitation?"

"You'll never know because you won't get one."

"I *do* know." Jimmy points to his head. Closes his eyes.

Lytrall stands silent a second.

Jimmy smirks.

Lytrall swings the gooseneck.

BEEP! BEEP!

¬Ǝ

Ǝ

"Hey!"

"Follow me."

The Professor walks Jimmy back to the workbench that lines the west side of the complex. Bench has tech of all kinds sitting on it—as well as recessed into it in places. They pass a large pile of shiny black cubes as they go. Jimmy gives the pile a curious look a second.

A massive terminal stands built into the part of the bench where they stop. It's one of many in the complex. However, this one appears special. Terminal features a couple of video screens and a lot of lights and buttons and analog controllers.

Professor puts his hands on the terminal like it's a pinball machine. Looks proud. Focuses on the terminal and not Jimmy as he talks. "Alright, this is the Danger Ranger Portable™."

"Portable!" Jimmy scoffs.

Lytrall spins at this, like he's in disbelief and has to look to see if Jimmy's got his tongue in his cheek or something.

Jimmy points down the way at the shiny black cubes they passed. "Thing's bigger than that pile of rocks."

Lytrall's doubly offended. "*Those* are no ordinary rocks! They're pure obsidian. They're used in building a black hole."

"Black hole? Not Black Hole™?"

"No."

Jimmy's eyes narrow not at all at this.

Lytrall grins. "I thought you'd never ask!"

"Didn't..."

"So I was right... A black hole is a geodesic chamber that creates a completely tangible, though virtual environment of any kind of your choosing. It's not something I can just tell the government about you see. Which I'd have to in order to patent it."

"A holodeck?" is Jimmy's contribution.

"A black hole has other... *Features*. Very dangerous in the wrong hands."

"So you're building an *ominous* version of a holodeck?"

"*Rebuilding...*"

Jimmy nods like he gets about half of all of this.

"One thing misunderstood at a time." Lytrall waves Jimmy's attention back to the large terminal. "This is just the Danger Ranger Station™. The brains of the Danger Ranger™. What I'm referring to as *portable* is the Danger Ranger Receiver™. A lighter-weight version of that helmet you're wearing. A computer chip. You can take that off by the way."

Jimmy starts removing the Ski-Doo helmet. "How light-weight?"

"This light." Professor holds out his palm.

Helmet pulls free. Jimmy lets the rim of it sit halo-like at the top of his head. He observes Lytrall's palm. "It's empty," he says.

"Exactly. But it's a virtual representation of the actual weight." Now he holds up a syringe. "Chip's in this."

Fluid in the syringe isn't glowing. Jimmy eyes it warily nonetheless. "Why's it in that?"

"Because Jimmy, it has to go into your brain."

"Uh huh..."

"There really are no health risks here..." Lytrall waits a second for any protest. Nothing from Jimmy, strangely enough. "No serious health risks. However, there *are* ethical, not to mention metaphysical ramifications in allowing machinery to override your free will—"

"Do it," Jimmy interrupts. "I'm already a slave to my own tortures."

Lytrall's a bit exercised by the lament. "How *first year* of you."

"What's that supposed to mean?"

"It means, if you still go around sounding like one of my

students right out of the burbs, just read Schopenhauer a first time, even after I fix you, then you must be the happiest person on earth."

"What's *that* supposed to mean?"

"It means: people tend to run from what causes them despair. Like you tried to do with the booze and the meditation. People don't greet it with open arms as though its effect some mark of distinction—worse, prestige—something that makes them interesting at parties. Only the people who've banked endless happiness and contentment, because they've banked near the same in opportunity and leisure, have the luxury of such boutique existentialisms. Fact that you're sounding so dire these days—instead of just your usual *looking* it—means you've never been so full of hope. That or you're a first-year snot. Last I checked, you don't carry a student card."

"Pfft! You check?"

"Not the way you check, ya peeping tom!"

"Ha!"

"There are ethical ramifications—"

"Do it." Jimmy moves closer to Lytrall, tips his head and folds his left ear at him.

"You sure?"

"If I don't like it I can always beam away from it."

"Not if the chip decides abandoning it constitutes suffi-cient harm..." is the whisper.

"What?"

"Nothing. You're absolutely sure?"

"Do it!"

Lytrall pulls out a fob and hits a button on it. A red light on the Danger Ranger™ terminal turns green. "There. You're on."

"On?"

"There never was any chip. Just needed to test your commitment. That helmet you had on determined your baseline net neuro-frequency. A pattern as unique as a fingerprint. Now you're in the system." He points to the terminal. Jimmy's blipping on a little radar screen in avatar form. A little green man to be precise. Above his avatar is written, *Aggregate Risk: ~0.01%.* It's in green too. "Teleportation center in your brain will initialize via the terminal."

"It work?"

Lytrall takes a swing.

¬∃/∃

Jimmy emerges from the fridge box.

¬∃/∃

"Guess so."

"You really can turn that off any time by the way." Professor moves to the terminal. "At the source..." He flicks a switch off and on. "Or with this." He tosses a second fob to Jimmy.

Jimmy catches it, looks. Has a single button and a little green LED next to an embossed *On*.

Lytrall flicks the terminal switch off and on again and Jimmy's fob LED blinks off and on in simultaneity. "Go ahead try," he says walking away from the terminal and toward Jimmy.

Jimmy hits the button. Green light goes off. "*This* work?"

Swing of the gooseneck...

THUMP! it goes into Jimmy's padding.

"*Ugh.* Guess so." He lifts himself out of the hunch, hits the button again, light is green. Puts the fob in a weird little pocket at the left breast of his jersey (looks like it's there just for the sake of the tale...).

Lytrall puts his hands on his hips. Appears to be itemizing in his head. *Up next?* "Now, would you like me to get the bullet-proof vest or do you want to test the effects of gunfire in the field."

"Field!"

"You should go play with this then."

¬Ⅎ

It's a bar. A couple of guys are squaring off less in a booze-filled rage, more in a booze-filled need to increase the limits of satisfaction booze can't, but a certain pain in your face and knuckles just might. Pair are currently engaged in that weird circling where you're not quite sure if they're psyching themselves up for a first blow or waiting for someone soberer to intervene.

"Gonna tear your ass up buddy!" taunts *Bigger Drunk*.

"Sounds sexual, Rock Hudson!" taunts *Smaller Drunk*.

"I shoulda said *your vagina!*"

"Then that's definitely sexual."

"I already got a girlfriend!"

"Well bend over!"

What the hell are these two assholes talking about?

But, just as either are about to throw a first punch...

"I wouldn't do that if I were you." Jimmy struts in between the pair and stares down Bigger Drunk. Bigger Drunk stares back confusedly. Then...

TAP! TAP! TAP! It's a tapping at Jimmy's shoulder. Smaller Drunk is trying to get his attention. "Look man, this is kinda a mutually agreed upon thing."

"You're not the victim here?" Jimmy asks over his shoulder.

"No." says the bigger drunk getting into Jimmy's face.

"A—and..." reasserts Smaller Drunk from behind. "I

take exception to you just *assuming* I was the one aggressed upon. Because why? I'm short? It was me who unplugged the jukebox!"

"*The jukebox*?" Jimmy asks, now confused himself.

"Yeah," says the ever-helpful Bigger Drunk. "Turn off a man's favorite song, it means it's time to rock."

"Well then..." Jimmy turns to face the Smaller Drunk. Complete rehearsal, "*I wouldn't do that if I were you.*"

"You and what army?"

"What?" Jimmy and Bigger Drunk say this in unison when...

Smaller Drunk shoves Jimmy!

Jimmy realizes the shove wasn't hard enough to register as a *sufficiently severe harm*. Has to improvise. "Now I know why they call you the *small* one," he goads.

Smaller Drunk rears back in more anger... "They call me that because of my *SIZE!*" He shoves on the *SIZE*. Shove hits the fob in Jimmy's pocket turning the little green LED light to little green nothing.

Closer, thinks Jimmy falling backward into Bigger Drunk, knocking him into his beer.

SMASH!

"Them's *time to rock* ruinations!" Bigger Drunk grabs Jimmy's shoulder to wrench him around.

Here we go... He lets the big man spin him. He has his eyes closed in anticipation when...

SMACK!

Punch connects sending our surprised Jimmy spinning tumbling onto his face. He lands on the bar floor and the fob goes flying sliding out his breast pocket.

"Mother pus-fucket!" he says as he catches sight of the lightless device. Thing's about ten feet up the floor and under the pool table. He starts a desperate crawl for it, but...

Drunks are kicking him in the ribs. He ups the intensity of his wriggling, as... Smaller Drunk grabs him by his ankles and pulls him back to one. "What the hell am I doing?" he says in the kind of realization fight-or-flight delays.

¬∃/∃

He's beamed under the pool table. Grabs the fob.

¬∃/∃

He's rematerialized between the drunks now chalking all the disappearing and reappearing up to the drink. Jimmy hits the fob back to the *On* position as big man and small man snap back into fighting mode.

Bigger takes a swing.

BEEP! BEEP!

¬∃

Swing and a miss and Biggie goes into a spin.

∃

Teleporter returns just in time for his aggressor to finish whirling. Biggie wobbles, trying to get his bearings. Dizziness is about to subside when...

BEEP! BEEP!

¬∃

CRACK!

A pool cue goes right through our disappearing Jimmy, breaking over Biggie's face!

"Ow!"

"Ah shit! Sorry man," says Smaller Drunk dropping the bottom half of the cue. He puts a consoling hand on Bigger Drunk's shoulder.

∃

"Weren't you two about to kill each other before I showed up?"

"Hey yeah!" Drunks say in unison as they start tearing into each other.

"Successful test," Jimmy says stepping out of the way of the two brawlers grappling past him on their way to the floor.

Jimmy's back in the lab, welts and all. He leans up against the workbench nursing a bruised rib.

"It didn't work?" Lytrall asks, concerned. He baps at the control terminal.

"Not when it's off," Jimmy says holding up the fob. "My fault."

Prof looks relieved. Completely relieved. Too relieved?

"Still rung my bell," Jimmy reminds.

"Bruises heal, or so I've heard. One last thing before the real test." Lytrall waves Jimmy closer to the terminal. Jimmy heads over, if a little labored thanks the beatdown. On the terminal is a list of locations below a graphic of the solar system. "Still worried about accidentally teleporting yourself into the Sun?"

"Every day."

"Not possible now. System locks you out of beaming to instant death. No sun. No outer space in general. No center of the earth. No bottom of the ocean. No ionosphere. These are locked out all day and night and other locations are locked out only in sleep. Like the Himalayas."

"How do we test this?"

"We don't, not directly." Professor taps a few keys on the terminal keyboard. "But I've just blocked your fridge box. Try beaming there."

Jimmy does. Terminal makes a *BALAINK!* sound and *Unauthorized Displacement* appears on screen.

"Perfect," Jimmy says.

Lytrall unlocks the box. "Not quite."

"What more could a teleporter ask for?"

"Not *for* you. You're going to start moving people Jimmy."

13

KNOW WHAT A PERSON
LIKE YOU NEEDS?

I t's a dinner of the Barts. Father and daughter. Ma couldn't make it—babysitting the grandkids—Rip's nieces and nephew.

Pa and Da are at a *Chicken Deluxe* franchise, a fried chicken restaurant of course. Rip's having a California roll and dad's having pastrami on rye. Franchise out and as long as you serve all that's required of the franchiser, you can serve whatever else you want, like what the people of this neighborhood want. Eclectic place cuz everyone wants everything, like the only combination of menu items Rip and her dad find acceptable at-once.

She's been dangling a piece of that California roll into her preferred mix of soy and sesame oil long enough it's damn near saturated. She seems lost in the thirsty crevices of that mealy soy sponge.

"Let any more of that juice into that bail the mice'll run out of it," papa jokes. "Thing's gonna taste like the Saskatchewan stretch of Highway One," he dads on.

It's not a patronizing smile. She appreciates him trying to broach the subject he knows is barely under the surface, if only by his patented obliqueness. These standing dinners are usually a lot more lively. *Usually*, though there have been dinners like these. More often lately. It's not a patronizing smile she smiles at him, but she certainly doesn't have her whole heart in it.

"Been doing your job again baby girl?"

"That obvious?"

"You look like every cop I know had to go by the book. If the devil wrote a bible it'd be that book."

"I thought it would help."

"You *convinced* yourself it would help."

"Yeah."

"You also look like me just before I stopped looking like me."

"Yeah?" She says this a little heartened.

"McRae tell you to do it?"

"Told me not to."

He nods approvingly, leans back in his seat. He's silent a second, looks at his baby girl a second.

"W—What?"

He grins. "Remember when you and your sister were little girls and you got the bright idea to take the training wheels off her bike?"

She chuckles. "Only because you love reminding me of it..."

"You said you did it because, and I quote, *it would make her a big girl and then she could stay up and watch MonsterVision with you.*"

"And I put her on that bike despite her protests and she rode right wobbly into the fence."

"And then what did you do?"

"I cried. I gave her a kiss on the cheek."

"Then?"

"I promised to be her *slave for a day*."

"You felt so bad you promised to be her slave for a day! *Then?*"

"She made me bequeath all my stuffed animals to her and she got my dessert in return for her fried cabbage *and* I seem to recall you and mom just letting it all happen!" She laughs this last bit out.

"Because it was like a sitcom!" papa guffaws, catching himself. "*Ahem*, because it was a learning lesson for the both of you. You cried over your stuffed animals all night and in the morning your little sister promised to be *your* slave for the day and you gave it right back to her even worse. Back and forth, back and forth this went until your mom and I sat the two of you down and asked either of you what you were so mad at each other about. So mad you felt you had to torture each other like this. What'd the two of you say?"

"*I forget.*"

"I forget!"

They laugh. Dad takes Rip by the hands.

"So you make sure to make amends baby girl. Only remember, it's measure for measure. You let that balance tip and this is all going to go up and down, up and down. Back and forth, back and forth. You make amends for now while remembering justice ain't a teeter-totter. While you're at this game of righting the wrongs borne of the book, keep this in mind: the best time to look for a job is when you already have one... Especially for lowdown feds like us." He tilts his head and slouches a little to get a look from some preferred angle. Old fed trick? Tries to suss out the level of contentment in his girl. She knows what he's doing. She squeezes his hands in hers. He leans back, contented. "Now," he says, "you go ahead and finish that salt lick and I'll take care of the tab."

He slides out of the booth and heads through the little archway to the front counter. Bart didn't even offer to pay. She ain't cheap. She's still lost. You can tell because she's back to dangling maki. She's heartened a little, make no mistake. Her dad's advice always shows her the light at the end of the tunnel but it's still a light *still* at the end of a long goddamn tunnel. She's in the dark unless she moves.

Half that piece of soaked roll falls off itself and lands with a *SPLAT!*

THUMP!

That *THUMP!* wasn't any sushi.

"Lose this?" Custy asks pointing to the pack Bart swapped out for Jimmy's. Landed in the mustard...

"I thought I smelled a bad deal. Don't you have a toll booth to man?"

"You know damn well that ain't what I... That ain't what we do."

"Close enough."

"Got you on closed-circuit stealing that."

"No you didn't. You're just playing a hunch. Hoping I'll bite. Watch a lot of detective movies on those phones ya coerce the pins of, border man?"

"Look inside asshole."

She pops the flap, gropes around. Feels like something laminated. It is. She understands the contents before that glossy piece of polyethylene is even halfway out. It's one of the documents she shredded, recomposed. A Jimmy note. A bunch of crooked paper strips in corporate amber though it's readable. *For the Receipt of R.J. Bartholomew.* No CCs.

"What do you want?" she asks.

"Jimmy Adamowski."

"Already had him. What'd you do with him?"

"Well he ain't in that bag. You're gonna help us f'ya don't want an inquiry into obstruction."

"It'll be a summary firing at most. I'm half out the door anyway."

"Not you girlie, the big fish. McRae." Custy picks up the laminated document. "All this happened on his watch."

She wants to snarl at this officious little prick and he deserves it. However, she holds that back. She doesn't hold everything back. Measure for measure Rip. Scare him back Rip. "You're taking a big risk trying to blackmail me in front of—"

SMASH! THUD! CRASH!

"Thought I smelled a bad deal!" Dad's back and cramming Custy into the booth. He's shoved him onto the bench and's pushing him along it by his sitting then scootching. Custy's pinned in place in no time. Only his head can move and boy is it moving—darting around frantically. "Goons aren't coming to the rescue," assures daddio. He tosses a couple tasers onto the table. Border man's about to shout when... Papa puts a hand to his mouth. Grabs one of the tasers and drives it into the captive's gut. Leaves it off to warn. "You're gonna keep your mouth shut or else I'm gonna reheat your dinner for you." Jams the taser further in for compliance. Custy eases. Hand comes off mouth. "Now, why you blackmailing my baby girl, scumbag?"

"I-I'm not—"

"Don't lie to me!"

"You're gonna be up on charges for this—"

Hand goes back as gag. "You're gonna be in a stalemate for this or'd you forget my connections?" Custy stops struggling. Hand off. Dad looks to daughter "What's this toll booth operator got on you Lee?"

"It's not a toll—"

"Close enough! What's he got baby?"

She hands her dad the document. He peruses, quick, gets it.

"Good girl," he says. He turns to Custy. "Taking a big chance comin after my girl in front of me." Prods with that taser. "Well!"

"Only place Adamowski isn't watching."

Rip raises an eyebrow at this.

"Yeah?" says dad. "Well that means I'm watching when he ain't. *Obsessional neuroses.*"

"Huh?"

"*Prone to obsessional neuroses.* That's what my psych profile says. That's just a nice way of saying I'm a real dogged son-of-a-bitch. Now I've got your scent. I'll take you down light-years ahead of Hank McRae if you keep on. Gonna back off border man?" Custy hesitates. Taser pincers near-taste his last meal. "Gonna back off!"

Custy nods.

"Good," says papa. "Now, I got to chatting with your friends outside so I didn't have a chance to pay for my daughter's and my dinner. Good thing because this one's on US Customs." He drops the bill in front of Custy and starts sliding out the booth. "Bit hefty, I know, but that's what happens when you bilk the proprietors of this fine establishment on the tuna." Dad turns to daughter, wry. "I'd say that's an irony worth paying sixty-two dollars for, my dear." He takes out a sawbuck and tosses it on the table next the bill. Leans in to Custy's ear, "Because I know your cheap ass ain't good for any gratuity..." He turns back to Lee, extends his hand. "Ready to roll?"

ii

You're going to start moving people Jimmy.

Jimmy twists on his torso to test the extent of the damage done to his ribs. He lets out a little wincey wheeze. Guess that's the extent but he's really just stalling.

You're. Going. To. Start. Moving. People. Jimmy.

It's a reasonable imperative. A goddamn quotidian one, more. A command issued not just every day but every Gift. There's been a little bitty voice deep down inside Jimmy that's become a massive asshole bullhorn that's been real insistent about all this. *Easier to snatch the innocent away from a bad situation than snatch a bad situation away from the innocent... Jimmy? ... Jimmy?* A damned reasonable imperative...

"You really need to start—"

"Told you," The Teleporter interrupts. "There's no way to guarantee it's safe."

"Those soldiers you teleported are alive and well."

"The terrorists?"

"Their deaths were a result of the state. Your teleporting didn't put those nooses around their necks. And yet, fourteen soldiers, none the worse for wear."

"They vanish when they go in. Annihilation."

"*When they go in.* What does that mean?"

"World Three."

"What does *that* mean?"

iii

Jimmy's in a light blue womb. He's not floating, not

standing, just kept. There're no surfaces though the effect of surface occurs wherever he wishes. Like at the feet of the fourteen soldiers *kept* at Jimmy's height in perfect stasis. You'd think they'd be spinning, looking like corpses, submerged. They're not. They're more like wax statues. And don't worry, they're very much alive though only Jimmy can move about in World Three. He drops the third bomb vest at solar plexus height and that's where he wants it to stay so that's where it stays. Vest sits kept with the other two.

¬⅂

⅂

He's back at the school. He's teleported to where the first Zealot stands. Jimmy's hands are on him from the jump. It's not even a millisecond in that school and...

¬⅂

⅂

He's back in the blue: World Three. He lets go of the Zealot statue. Zealot stands looking at Jimmy seeing nothing. As good as sleep but it won't feel like it when he comes out. Jimmy collects himself.

Eyes close.

Two Zealots remain in the school, perfectly still. It's not like World Three where humans are motionless due the incapacitating nature of the womb. Those Zealots out there are perfectly still because when Jimmy's in World

Three, time doesn't pass in World One: our world. Jimmy can stay in the womb till the last second of his life and in that second he reenters World One, only to keel over, it will be as though he never left at all but's aged decades instantaneously. He doesn't want to waste his life in here though it's often his best refuge. He doesn't want to waste any time about now as he'd only use it to rethink this entire mission.

Eyes open.

¬∃

∃

He leaves the second zealot for the keeping.

¬∃

∃

He leaves the third.

Now he needs to find a place to put these guys.

Eyes close.

"Sarge?"

"Ain't you got things better to do than bother me Mooney?"

iv

Lytrall looks intrigued—doesn't ask questions. Seems to intuit World Three's atemporal nature. Mechanics in general. He *is* deriving the missing pieces from the facts Jimmy's given.

"So time doesn't pass in your world. Explains the instant beards. You enter World Three every single time you teleport."

"Every time. The atemporal aspects are a little complicated, however—"

"No no. I understand."

"You do huh?"

"Remember how I told you about the Black Hole? The additional *feature*?" He points to the rocks. Jimmy nods. "Well, it and World Three have that feature in common." Lytrall waves his hand at this. He'd talk natural vs synthetic time displacement all day if you let him but there's the more pertinent topic to hand. "When you had those men in World Three, they were alive?"

"Yes, only, preserved Lepidoptera."

"And alive."

"I know what you're thinking but they're still annihilated when they go in. It's not like walking through a door."

"They come back just fine."

"How do I know they're not coming back perfect copies? Of a self I killed?"

"How do you know you're not coming back a perfect copy?"

There's an emerging scoff, its neck broke by deliberation. Realization proceeds... "Jesus!"

"Relax... Think about this, how do you know you're not a different version of *you* from when I started this sentence?"

"I have memories... A self... Continuity..."

"You have all that after teleporting too. You have *less* of that waking up in the morning."

"Jesus!"

"Ok!" Lytrall says, trying to calm Jimmy once and for all. "Let's prove you're you. Do you think all there is to life is the physical?"

"Physical?" Jimmy asks, breathing funny, doing that dipping, weaving, and plunging of his arms...

Lytrall shoves Jimmy's spooning hands downward, separating them. Looks at him serious. "Your sense of self. Your memories. Consciousness. You think all that's just a result of physics? Gray matter?" Jimmy's finding his calm though not fast enough for Lytrall's tastes. "The meat in your head Jimmy? Jimmy!"

Found a little of it. "Alright alright!" Deep breath. Dialectic? "Alright..." He whips his face back and forth a few times. Lips flap open and shut and into cheeks. *FLIB-BLELIBBLELIBBLE.* Wrings the panic out. Then... "Alright, you wanna hash this out?" *FLIBBLE* "All I know is this: I know you philosophers seem real hung up on the question. If you all can't resolve things even after three thousand years of trying, I'll defer to your incompetence. *I. Don't. Know.*"

"I'm flattered. How about this, would you say everything is physical or it isn't?"

"Who am I to falsify a tautology?"

"If life's not pure physicalism, there's something supernatural at work?"

"Like a soul?"

"Not necessarily, though something neither matter nor energy. Not constituted of the elements nor susceptible to natural forces."

"I guess there'd have to be on this assumption."

"And it constitutes *life* in part and it remains even after physical destruction?"

"On this assumption."

"Ok then. You're still you and the people you teleport are fine."

Jimmy's eyes squint and his lips go circular like he's making an inaudible *whuh* sound. Now comes the audible *whuh* sound, "*Whuh*-What? How do we go from talking definitions to QED in the span of a *sure*?"

"*How?* Jimmy. Our dilemma was *everything is physical or it isn't*. If it's just physical then the physical is sufficient for life because if it wasn't we'd need something extra, something nonphysical, then everything *wouldn't* be physical and we'd have a contradiction. Since the people you move are physically identical to who they were *going in*, you have everything sufficient not just for life, but *their* life. They're back." Jimmy makes that wincy *whuh* face again. Lytrall elaborates. "If they *weren't* back then something would be missing. Only, the whole of the physical *is* back so what's missing would be nonphysical which, as we've assumed, can't be the case. They're back.

"On the flip side, if not everything is physical, there's the supernatural, which can't be destroyed by your teleportation. Whatever that is is waiting for the people you move when they return or is taken with them. They show up with everything except that nonphysical component—to become reacquainted with it—or, they never left it to begin with. They're back.

"On both horns of the dilemma they're back. They're fine."

"What if I separate them from that non-physical component and they can't be reacquainted with it?"

"On this assumption, do temporal and spatial concerns constrain the supernatural?"

"I don't know."

"Either they do or they don't?"

"Sure."

"If they don't constrain the supernatural, there's no space so no separation. No problem. If they do, soul can call a cab! They're back."

"Fuck off!"

"They're fine!" Lytrall laughs.

"*A priori* they're fine. On paper. However, that don't cut it for me and there's no real way to check."

"Yes there is."

"How?"

"Take me to World Three."

14

WORLD THREE

In his right hand is a lighter. In his left hand is the rest of that arm.

"Light me up," he says jabbing that lighter insistently at Jimmy. "Why do you have that stupid look on your face?"

Jimmy's eyes are closed.

Bart's in the middle of another warning. She's in that easy chair of hers, slouching forward. Her face is flushed. There's an urgency.

"...W—wrong. Dead wrong. I don't know what he's up to but there never was any immunity." She leans back abrupt now, head at the back of her chair like the self-disgust's thinner up there? Thicker? Can't catch her? Can? Measure for measure girl. She implores regardless of what she owes, "You have no reason to believe me and I know I'm coming across just desperate enough I'd make anything up to flush you out, but... Believe me or don't Jimmy: Custy's gunning for you. Real desperate. You embarrassed him and worse, you import and export with zero regard for duties and tariffs. You're his white whale." She picks up the little whiteboard and erases the *we need to talk* from it. Looks up. "Listen, I'll be in this chair this time every day if you decide to reach out. Every day—"

"Jimmy!"

Eyes open.

"What?"

"Where were you?"

"Gifting."

"I know *that*. Why'd you have a look on your face like your parents just gave your puppy away?" Lytrall's eyes narrow by half at a now shrugging Jimmy. Widen again. "Anyway, here." He issues the lighter at Jimmy once more.

Jimmy takes it. Lytrall brings his extending left arm closer.

"What'll this prove?" Jimmy asks.

"It's a first step. Roll up your sleeve. Turn off the Danger Ranger™ too."

Jimmy puts the lighter in that weird little breast pocket also holding the fob, hits the button on it while he's in there. He starts rolling up the cuff of his right jersey sleeve...

"Left," Lytrall orders.

Jimmy frowns a little, switches sleeves. Rolls the cuff up to his elbow.

Professor moves closer, left arm still extended. "Light me."

Jimmy's seen enough. Not in the *alright I've seen enough! shut it all down!* kinda way. More in the *I've already been made privy to so many new tricks where not obliging the mad scientist now means returning to what's horrible anyway so why not just do as he says in perpetuity in for a penny in for a pound* kinda way. Jimmy takes the lighter out of his pocket and flicks it. He holds the flame under Lytrall's left forearm.

Is that burnt hair? It is, Jimmy's. Is that sizzling skin? It is, Jimmy's.

"Hell!" he shouts dropping the lighter. He grabs his singed left forearm. Rubs at it, delicately. He looks to The Professor whose forearm glows an eerie yellow.

Jimmy lunges. "You're on fire Doc!" He pats at the glare, affecting it not at all. The yellow eventually dissipates though not for Jimmy's actions. Revealed as it leaves is a flesh completely untouched by fire. Pristine.

Jimmy grabs onto Lytrall's arm like a trout. Eyes it closer.

Lytrall snatches it back. "Remember that!" He walks to his work bench, flicks a switch on what looks like a mini-fridge sitting atop it. Device reveals itself to be constituted of many parts. Those parts are separating now. A robotic arm emerges from somewhere deep inside the unfurling fridge and comes to a rest in a pose like it's ready to *Dylan! You son of a bitch!* someone. Thing's made of the same material as that Mason jar lid. Bottle-fly's thorax. Gotta be state of the art.

"Pardon the crudity of my AI," Lytrall laments. "We had some recent unfortunateness and I've had to rebuild." He opens a drawer under the fridge arm. Takes a nine-millimeter Glock out of it.

"What the hell?" Jimmy says still rubbing at his burns.

"Relax." Prof lays the Glock onto the workbench under the arm. Instantly the arm starts to move. It's now hovering its palm over the pistol like in anticipation of a duel. Real fluid about it.

"Jesus Chr—"

"Relax."

Lytrall walks away from the AI arm. He moves to about ten paces then...

He spins! Reaches for an imaginary gun at his hip only

the AI arm's quicker. Not that it would matter... AI picks up the Glock and *BANG! BANG! BANG!* Drives three slugs into The Professor's chest! Jimmy falls backward onto his ass in shock. Glowing beams of a familiar yellow light have erupted from where the bullets entered. Jimmy looks on in horror.

"Holy fuckin shit!"

"Relax," Lytrall says already moving back to Jimmy. His hand reaches down and he lifts The Teleporter up. The beams of yellow are receding into the holes that birthed them. Bright enough still that Jimmy holds his arm up to cut the glare.

Shine resorbed, the punctures begin to close aperture-like. Jimmy marvels at the integrity of it all. He's about to poke a finger into what he swears was seconds ago a bullet hole. Lytrall swats the finger away.

"I'm invulnerable. Can't be touched."

"No kidding?"

"That's not the half of it. Someone else tries to harm me, they harm themselves in equal measure. That's why your burn. Be careful not to bump into me or back over me with your car."

"No way."

"Look at your arm." He doesn't have to look. It's sore as hell and leathery. Lytrall continues. "Take me into World Three and if you kill me doing it you'll kill yourself."

"No way!"

"You're dead anyway."

"Not that. That little parlor trick with the lighter ain't sufficient for proof. Even if your harm is my harm, how do I know it works all the way up to death?"

"Well, I'm not going to let you kill yourself trying to find out."

"You were gonna let me take you to that womb."

"Because: *It. Wouldn't. Kill. Me.*"

Jimmy waves this conviction off, studies the room, thinking. Thinking... Catches something. Points to the AI arm and its smoking Glock. "Why don't you let *Frigidarme*™ finish himself off proving it?"

"Not how it works Jimmy. There's only the damage fed back if:

1. There's any damage to begin with,
2. The entity inflicting the damage is organic, and
3. The entity makes a choice to do something immediate where, if that something wasn't done, there wouldn't be damage."

"And the AI can't make choices..." Jimmy says this in realization.

"Actually, no. *Choice* is a part of the arm's AI function. It shot me as an act of its own will."

"Really had it in for you. Understandable."

"Funny, though definitely wrong. It may be able to choose but I can still limit its choices. Down to one choice in this case: shoot me."

"*What it lies in our power to do, it lies in our power to not do.*" Jimmy observes.

"Touché," Lytrall says turning to eye the arm suspiciously. Turns back, "Regardless, free will isn't the problem. It's the arm's inorganic aspect alone. Something about the field generated by a living organism. Nothing dead will—"

"Can't you just surround it in living tissue?"

"What do I look like, Frankenstein?"

"Yes."

"Alright Mr. Positivist, how exactly do you propose I—"

He goes still. Then... "Chia Pets!" He starts writing on a post-it.

"What's a Chia Pet?"

"What are you twelve?"

"Actually, I—"

"Here." He hands Jimmy the note. "Get these supplies."

"Just says *chia seeds*."

"Yeah, but get a lot of them."

¬∃

A second passes.

Then...

∃

"Hey," Jimmy says. "What if one of those shots from Army-man had ricocheted and hit me?"

"No time like the present to test the Danger Ranger™'s ability to handle bullets?"

PFFFT! Goes Jimmy, then...

¬∃

Goes Jimmy.

ii

Lytrall's stirring a canoe oar around a viscous goo in a ten-gallon bucket. Jimmy watches.

"What the hell's a Chia Pet?"

"This," Professor points into the bucket. "Plus pottery."

"Pottery?"

Professor sighs, goes rote in his explaining. "A Chia Pet consists of a hollow ceramic form, like a sheep or other furried animal. You would spread the gel consistency, made by mixing the chia seeds and water, on the wet pottery and it would sprout leaves to look like hair. Saturday Night Live did a parody commercial where bald men used it on their heads. It was called *Chia Head*."

"And why do you know so much about these products?"

"Lot of faculty Christmas parties in the eighties. Had a closet full of them." He lifts the oar out of the chia gel and lets the residual goo curdle down the blade. He appears satisfied with the viscosity. "Those and clappers."

"What's a clapper?"

"Are you *literally* twelve years old?"

"I tried to tell you—"

"Here." He hands Jimmy a ladle and a spatula. Points to the arm. "Start spreading this on him."

The pair spend the next few minutes spreading the chia gel.

(If you want more detail into how this process is carried out, just close your eyes and imagine you're rubbing a gritty hair gel all over a toolbox with a mannequin arm sticking out of it. Best I can do.)

"Now, we wait," Lytrall says, happy with the coverage.

"Wait?"

"Seeds have to sprout."

"How long."

"No time at all. Three days."

"Three days!"

"We'll be so busy gathering and watering supplies for this little adventure it will seem like seconds."

"What do you need?"

"Just one thing."

"Come on!"

"It's a big thing. Could take us a lot longer than three days."

"What?"

"I'm going to require the AI do something to me that will impose bloody certain death. Like dropping a ten-ton weight on my head—toes too at that weight I imagine... Plowing over me with an industrial snowblower... Blowing me up—"

¬Ǝ/Ǝ

Jimmy's back with the three bomb vests of those Zealots. He's looking over each. "What are you a *medium*?" he says to Lytrall.

Professor *does* take the medium. "Excellent." He bows at Jimmy. Jimmy bows back.

"Now we wait."

iii

Smash cut to...

We're in the middle of a field behind Lytrall's homestead. The professor's got the bomb vest on. Jimmy's got the detonator in his hand. AI arm sits sprouted on a table next to the two. Lytrall waves a little sensor over Jimmy. Sensor beeps and a light goes green. Jimmy looks like he wants answers.

"Baseline," Lytrall offers. "You're lit up like a Christmas tree. Pure biology." He waves the device over the leaf-covered AI. Same beep. Same green light.

The Teleporter and The Interventionist start out walking.

"You sure about this?" Jimmy asks.

"Not my first time proving the Gimmick™."

"On yourself?"

Silence.

Jimmy pats Lytrall on the shoulder.

In for a penny…

They stop at exactly one hundred yards out the arm. Jimmy looks at Lytrall with a tilting. Lytrall gestures assent. Jimmy flicks on the bomb vest.

"I blow up, that's a death blow," Professor reminds. Points at the arm. "He blows up, he killed himself killing me and now you know for sure."

"QED." And Jimmy starts walking back to the Chia AI™.

Professor shouts after him as he goes, "Though the Danger Ranger™ will beam you out, be sure to get clear of that arm as quickly as you can. No point in blowing anything up if you won't be here to see it."

Jimmy waves an *I got it* over his shoulder.

Why not close the last two-thirds of the hundred-yard gap by beaming?

¬Ǝ/Ǝ

He moves the detonator nearer the arm and the appendage initializes. Jimmy flinches.

"You know to wait for the *go-ahead* right buddy?"

Arm gives a thumbs up.

Jimmy sets the detonator down. Arm flips the safety lid off the detonator button.

The one of these two with a face looks satisfied.

¬Ǝ/Ǝ

He's behind some polycarbonate ballistic glass equidistant Lytrall and the arm at eighty-six-point-six yards back. All the players in this game form an equilateral triangle of mutually assured destruction.

"OK!" Jimmy shouts.

Lytrall waves. Takes his little fob in hand. Squints at the arm a hundred yards away. "Sorry if this all goes to plan old boy. You've been a wonderful appendage." He hits the fob.

Robot arm starts to wave its hand over the detonator button like its saying *alakazam, alakazoo...*

Lytrall puts his fingers in his ears, closes his eyes.

Arm finishes with the theatrics. Single finger on its single hand comes to a point. Digit depresses the detonator button and...

BOOM!

Frigidarme™ silently instantly turns to a hovering chia dust. Larger pieces fly off everywhere.

Lytrall loudly instantly turns to glow. Pieces of him fly off everywhere else.

Jimmy's knocked on his ass though he saw the whole thing.

"Holy fucking shit!" But before he can process any of what it was he saw...

The Professor comes strutting out of that glow like a peacock, parts fully reintegrated.

He's beelining it for Jimmy.

Two yards out and he extends his hands. Looks like your grandma when you're seeing her for the first time in a while —after a minute if ya got a decent gramma. He gonna hug and kiss Jimmy? Not quite, though he does take the man by the hands.

Expression on our hero's face suggests all's a little awkward.

Lytrall grins. "Time for that leap of faith my boy." Jimmy nods. "Take us home Teleporter."

Deep breath...

¬Ǝ

15

THE FUN BEGINS

Ǝ

They're back in the lab. They're fine. QED.
Nevertheless...

Jimmy's patting himself down like they do in the movies. Like that'll tell him if he's completely intact or something. *What if ya lost your hands then you'd never know if ya lost yer head?*

Lytrall's beaming. Successful test. "Well!" he says. "Now the fun begins."

"I have to take care of something first."

¬Ǝ

ii

It's Everest, south summit. Winds are extra cruel. Blow like the wish was to turn the wet in the air to razor blades. The men are in heavy furs, armed with something carbine-like. They're low, sneaking up on a figure in blaze orange at the very peak. Figure's in meditative position. Hands are spooned. Eyes are closed. Appears to be doing some serious contemplation which means there's no way to hear it coming. No way to hear the men about to...

"Fire!" shouts Custy as his furried Customs goons leap out of the snow and wind firing tranquilizer darts.

Several hit the orange figure. Figure keels over.

Custy runs lusty. Lusting over thoughts of all he's going to do to Jimmy when he gets his hands on him. Trudging up the last few feet to the summit, he tears his leather mitts off. Looks like he wants to strangle Jimmy and with bare hands for maximal joy.

"Gotcha ya son-of-a—"

But no joy. It's a couple fists full of straw is what Custy's got. He relaxes those fists, watches as the strands flow away from open palms.

His men amble up behind him.

"What?" he mutters at the gold spun to straw.

He starts tearing at the orange robe. All we have is a scarecrow with a paper mache Jimmy face. It's all straw inside save for... Custy reaches deeper into *Effigimmy*. He pulls out the Jar full of nanotrackers. He realizes immediately what he holds. He smashes the thing into the firn, looks up to the blustery sky...

"ADAMOWSKIIIIIII!!!!!!"

Eyes open nowhere near the south summit.

Jimmy grins.

iii

Seven-forty-five pee-em. Bart sits in her easy chair. In

her pajamas incidentally. Wants to be comfortable while she stews? She's thinking about giving Jimmy another five minutes. Third consecutive *five minutes* she'll have given him if she relents. She's thinking about it when...

Ǝ

"Jimmy?"

He reaches out to her.

¬Ǝ

Ǝ

They're at a neutral location, They're at the Kairn Center Concert Hall again. Empty. Doors are locked.

CRACK!

Bart's slugged him.

"Dammit you can't just do that Jimmy!"

"You wanted to talk," he says turning his Danger Ranger™ fob to green.

"On equal terms."

"You said anytime." Now he rubs his chin. "You're one to talk of such respect."

"You snatched me out of my life!"

"You were sitting in a chair!"

"What if a baby was sleeping in the other room?"

"You don't have—"

"Sister does."

Jimmy gets a pang. "I'd see," he insists.

"What if the phone was about to ring? An emergency? My parents. Just as you pulled me away!"

"I'd—"

"No! No you wouldn't Jimmy. Not for certain. Christ,

what if it was just something on the stove? Why does it have to be anything other than the lack of consideration?"

"You set me up!"

"You came to us. Stayed of your own free will." She's hating herself the second she says it.

"They would have killed y—" He catches himself. Wanting to say what he was about to seemed the most natural impulse in the world for him, still does. *Damn her for rendering these compassions null and void?*

She closes her eyes. "I'm sorry."

"I know. Heard ya already."

"So you *were* listening?"

"*I'm* sorry..." he trails off at the start of the apology.

"What?"

"Sorry..." he says through pursed lips. "...For the snatching."

"Forget it. Just don't do it again. It's wrong."

He nods. "*We need to talk?*"

"We do."

"It was more rhetorical. A reminding—"

"Jimmy!"

"Yes?"

She sits him down in one of the chairs of one of the over-linened tables. Napkin-wrapped place settings on lapkins on taupe table cloth on eggshell undercloth. Must be something going on here tonight. She stays standing. "I-I didn't do what I did because I wanted to help you." Jimmy looks around. Looks like he's about to— "No!" Bart defuses. "Don't go. There're no tricks. I never wanted to hurt you. I meant that."

"Then what?"

"*MonsterVision.*"

"What?"

"Listen. I just wanted to be able to live with you. Spend time with you without... For peace of mind..."

"Why are you being so bloody cryptic—"

"Goddamnit Jimmy I'm scared to death of you!" She's backed herself up a couple paces saying that. Admission's calmed her the slightest too. Now she has to reckon with it. "N—not *Jimmy the man*... Jimmy *The Teleporter*... Not *even* the teleportation so much—"

"The Gift."

She nods. "I mean, we all have fantasies. We imagine people in ways... With us in ways... Ways we'd never want them to know about. And yet... Yet you Jimmy! You've got a front-row seat to all our lives! I can't help a thought about a colleague, say, popping into my head but that's just my head... He doesn't know I've got a mind's eye view of the two of us... *In flagrante*."

...

Try-not-to-look-like-you're-thinking-'which-colleague?'
Try-not-to-look-like-you're-thinking-'which-colleague?'

...

"Jimmy?"

"*GYAAHH!*" He composes himself.

She looks funny at him a second. Continues, "I can't control an image popping into my head. You can't control your head popping into our bedrooms! Maybe."

"Are you saying you fucked me over because I make for a real good peeping tom?"

"No!" She starts pacing. "That was the top of the slippery slope. Got me thinking. Over-thinking. Christ Jimmy, you're like a *sorta* God on Earth. You watch us. You provide for us. You give and you take. You punish, Jimmy... What if you screwed up? Got angry? Even if you got mildly pissed at someone, you could spot him in your dreams and teleport him off a cliff. In your sleep for Christ's sake!" She sits. Pacing's taking the breath she needs. "Maybe someone I know. Someone anyone knows. Cares about. I was scared. I wanted you under control."

"Tracking me wouldn't have—"

"Does it sound like I was thinking it through Jimmy?" Her head goes down. "I wanted peace of mind. That's something you can't think yourself into."

He feels a second pang. He didn't ask for this yet how's she wrong? What would life have been like if he never had what he got? Never would have met her, that's what. She's not wrong but she wasn't right. But... He puts a hand on her shoulder.

She takes this comfort in her own. Her head stays low. "Believe me Jimmy, after the training wheels, this was the biggest mistake of my life."

"Training wheels?"

Gives herself permission to look up, "Just another thing to be sorry about."

She smiles one of those smiles that tests the state of reconciliation. *We Ok? I owe? You owe? What's next?* It'd be a smile-by-half if of joy, yet it's more than enough given the proposition's: *please tell me where we stand.*

He'll answer.

He rises, backs away. There's deliberation in his movements. She watches him, curious. He reaches into his pant pocket, pulls out a little piece of paper. "Do you have a pen?"

"In my pajamas?" But she furrows, makes a bit of a face. "Wait..." She pulls that dry-erase marker out of the breast pocket of her flannel top. "This work?"

Jimmy takes it. He jogs his memory a second then starts writing. "Here." He hands her the note.

"*Chia Seeds?*"

"Other side." She flips it. Looks confused. Jimmy explains. "That's the username and password for my fitness tracker. Connects to this." He holds up his wrist revealing his FatButt™. "When I do what I do, my heart rate slows tremendously. Like five beats a minute slow. Watch." He holds up his watch showing a graphic of an animated beating heart. *84 BPMs* is indicated under it. His eyes close. The rate begins to diminish quickly, already down to twenty-five beats per minute. "Your boss is listening to Fleetwood Mac real loud in his office." Four beats per minute. "*Rhiannon.*" Jimmy opens his eyes and the monitor indicates his heart rate is already climbing. It's at fifteen beats and rising. "Go ahead check," he says.

"With what?"

"You mind?"

"Sure."

¬∃/∃

He hands her her phone. She takes it, appreciative. "Sirli, call Boss."

Calling Boss.

Dial tone. Then...

"*Woman taken by the wind...* McRae here."

Bart's is a face of astonishment. Then... "Turn that music down you inconsiderate bastard!" She says this in a low disguising voice.

"What!" says the voice on the other end. "How the fuck did you... Goddamn it Bart! You're a real dummy if you don't know I got your little narrow ass on call display!"

"Nobody calls it *call display* anymore ya old butt!"

"Mother fu—"

She hangs up grinning.

Jimmy taps the note Bart's thumb's pinned to the screen

of her phone. "Log on and count the beats any time you want."

She looks at him in a way you'd almost swear is joyous.

"For peace of mind," he adds.

She leaps up, hugs him. He's responsive to it though with a strange caution. Perhaps not perceptible to her?

She pulls back a little. "Why now?"

"Now?"

"Why *now* did you decide to reach out?"

"I just wanted to... Just to make sure..."

"Yes?" she encourages.

¬∃

16

WHAT FUN?

Now the fun begins?

It's the red eye, cross-pacific flight. An A321's in dual engine failure, coasting. Going nowhere other than to bits in the midmorning of its last leg. Going to bits remarkably slow as it's coasting, remember, but there's nothing the pilots can do to increase thrust. They won't even make the shore.

Eyes open. "I'll just beam on board and take the passengers off one at a time."

Lytrall shakes his head. "You'd be teleporting onto a plane moving at five-hundred-eighty miles per hour. It would be like firing yourself into the fuselage from a cannon." Jimmy grabs at his temples. "What is it Jimmy?"

"The cries."

"Don't do anything rash."

"There are no cries."

"There were. Give me a sec—" Prof rushes to a panel of monitors. Looks like air traffic control because it is. *It's whatever The Professor wants it to be.* "See these?" He waves Jimmy over to see. Jimmy does. It's a collection of little green pixelated jetliners. Lytrall's pointing to each jetliner representation in a particular order, says, "There, there, there, there, there, there, and there. Gift a look at all of these based on the coordinates. Get an idea. Their fuselages are identical to the plane in trouble. Quickly!"

Eyes close. Then... "Ok. Got em."

"I'm going to line up the planes *by* coordinates *by* speed." He points at the first set of cords. "This plane is about to accelerate for take-off in Atlanta. You can jump on in thirty seconds and still withstand the inertia. However, it'll make you lurch." Jimmy nods, Lytrall continues. "This one will be at take-off speed in thirty, that'll be the second jump—"

"Wait! You sure about this?"

"If they aren't at the speeds I say they'll be in thirty seconds they'll fall out of the sky. Now listen. All this happens in thirty:" He recommences the pointing. "This plane will be ascending at an acceleration sufficient for the third jump. Then jump to this one," he points. "Then this one," points again. Keeps pointing. *Jump, jump, point, point.* "You'll be at speed and you can get to the plane in trouble." Jimmy nods. "Now for the rescue: I've got another plane flying at speed here." He points to a B77L indicated in red pixels. A *Fed Up*™ company cargo plane. Flying empty. "Move the passengers here." Jimmy nods. Lytrall taps a little timer on the terminal. "Ten seconds before first jump. " Jimmy nods. "Bear in mind, I've accounted for the slight loss of acceleration in World Three but you can't spend more than a half-second there." Jimmy nods. Lytrall puts both hands on the hero's shoulders. "Remember the order and you'll teleport up those eight planes like climbing a *flight* of stairs." He looks seriousness into Jimmy's eyes, then... "Mind the lurches. Go!"

¬Ǝ/Ǝ

Jimmy's on the first plane. He lurches. Before the passengers can see him and gasp and freak out...

¬Ǝ/Ǝ

Gets to the second plane. Lurches.

¬Ǝ/Ǝ

Gets to the third.

¬Ǝ/Ǝ

The fourth.

¬Ǝ/Ǝ

Fifth.

¬Ǝ/Ǝ

Sixth.

¬Ǝ/Ǝ

Seventh.

¬Ǝ/Ǝ

The plane in trouble! Made it!

Plane feels fine. Like it's moving through the air just fine. It isn't. It's coasting, remember. It will for at least a few minutes more. It was knowledge of the near-impossible twin engine rollback that caused the initial panic not *this*. This pointless calm is like some excruciating insult to these people. Jimmy looks around. No one's screaming or wailing, just as it was in The Gift. Loved ones are embracing. There're some prayers. A lot of tears. No panic. Too much time on their hands, they're having had everything cut so short.

A few notice Jimmy. If anything, they're only confused as to why some passenger's out of his seat. They have no concerns to warrant attending to our teleporter dropping by unannounced. Why would they? Plane holds over two hundred and lucky for everyone it's at a little less than half capacity. And that's including the six crew members.

Jimmy's been running triage. Women and children first? Justifying why women and men are to be separated in these circumstances aside, he doesn't have the time to be cordoning everyone off. Children should go first though, and not without their parents.

He's not marching up the aisles but Gifting himself a look at the passengers. **Only one child. An infant with a mother and father.**

¬∃/∃

A slight lurch. *Mind your time in World Three!* He's at the row the *Mom*, *Dad*, and *Baby* sit in. They regard him in a way imploring though in all due pity. Why wouldn't they?

"I can get you out of here." Jimmy reaches without taking hold of anyone.

"How?"

"You're just going to have to trust me. I can take you, Mom. Dad'll watch the baby, then I'll bring her then Dad."

"No!" The mother holds her baby closer. "I'm not leaving her." The father holds them both, just looking at Jimmy.

"The four of us will go at once," he offers.

"No."

Just reach out and take them Jimmy?

It's not right.

He doesn't have time for this. He breaks away from the family. Speaks to whoever'll listen. "Alright! Who wants off here? I can take ya, three at a time." They sit in silence, most ignoring him, a few shaking their heads.

Sit down! is heard from the front. Likely a flight attendant. Jimmy ignores the command.

"You have nothing to lose," he adds. Still silence. "You're going to die."

"You don't know that," says a passenger. Others gesture in agreement with her.

Jimmy rubs at his forehead, pinches the skin of his brow as though a massage. Not helping anything. What the hell's he supposed to do?

Just reach out and take them Jimmy?

No, it's not right. But...

"I'll go," says a *Man* sitting next to a *Woman* he's holding the hand of. Man's rising. "Come on honey," he says to her.

"No!" She pulls her hand free of his. She won't budge.

"I'm not dying in here," he says.

"You're not serious about going with him?"

"I'm serious about leaving. Either the guy's on the level or he's crazy hon." Man speaks to more than just his wife now. "And yet you all saw him appear out of nowhere a second ago. Something's happening here." Looks back to his wife. "Crazy or no, he's right about one thing, we've got nothing to lose." He reaches his hand out again. She refuses.

Jimmy looks at his watch like it'll tell him when it's *outta time o'clock.* Think Jimmy. Then... "Do you have a phone?" he tries.

"Phone?" Man asks, a little confused. "Yeah, sure."

Jimmy leans to the Woman. "I'll get him safely out of here and he'll prove to you he made it." Woman's incredulous. Jimmy takes hold of the Man. "Your going will convince her. You'll save her life. Nothing to lose remember? I save you so you can save her."

Man nods vigorously. Woman's still unconvinced. Jimmy closes his eyes, sees Lytrall pointing at the cargo plane coordinates. He gets it. Puts a hand on the Man's shoulder. Then...

¬∃/∃

Plane nine, Fed Up™. Jimmy and the Man lurch a little in the empty fuselage. "It's alright," Jimmy says. "We're ok."

"Oh boy," says the Man, a little confused. Then... "What a trip!" A bit of relief, but... "My wife!"

"I'll get her. Hand me that phone."

¬∃

∃

Jimmy's back on plane eight. Beamed in right next to the Woman. Before she can react, Jimmy's playing the Man's message to her. He's got the phone's volume cranked so as many passengers can hear as possible.

*Made it baby! Off flight *DC-427 and onto whatever this is.. Can't wait to see you!*

Last thing in the video is a pan around the empty fuselage the Man stands in.

Jimmy hands the Woman her husband's phone.

"Ready?" She looks like she wants to see that video one more *time* but..."We're running out of time," he urges.

She rises. Others rise out of their seats too.

Jimmy's hand goes up. "I can take three at a time." He turns around to face the parents with child. "Please." The mother shakes her head again. Jimmy turns away. "Ok. Two more!" He reaches out for the people closest who are rising. Then...

¬∃/∃

The three and Jimmy are on the cargo plain. All lurch where the Woman seems to do so right into her husband's arms. Then...

¬∃/∃

He's back with three more passengers.

¬∃/∃

Three more. Then...
¬Ǝ/Ǝ, ¬Ǝ/Ǝ, ¬Ǝ/Ǝ, ¬Ǝ/Ǝ,
¬Ǝ/Ǝ, ¬Ǝ/Ǝ, ¬Ǝ/Ǝ, ¬Ǝ/Ǝ,
¬Ǝ/Ǝ, ¬Ǝ/Ǝ, ¬Ǝ/Ǝ, ¬Ǝ/Ǝ,
¬Ǝ/Ǝ, ¬Ǝ/Ǝ, ¬Ǝ/Ǝ, ¬Ǝ/Ǝ
More and *more* and *more*... And...

Ǝ

The A321 experiences a sudden loss of altitude, jerks downward. It's losing its integrity though it's still on its glide path. No mountains luckily but the water will crunch the jetliner like a beer can under boot.

Jerk takes a few passengers an nth from panic. They start grabbing and pulling at those ahead of them. Their fear spreads. Induces anger too. All will coalesce to chaos unless...

SCREEECH!

Jimmy's drawing a bow along a violin someone's left in an overhead compartment. He gets the passengers' attention.

He looks at them, furious. "You all know me," he asserts. "Know what I do to get yer asses offa here! You all thinking you'll fight your way right into my arms, pawing clawing? You sit your selfish asses down or I won't hesitate to take you out of here and drop you into the Pacific.

¬Ǝ/Ǝ

He's launched into the face of the most aggressive of the panicked. Aggressor backs down. All others follow suit.

Jimmy recommences.

¬Ǝ/Ǝ, ¬Ǝ/Ǝ, ¬Ǝ/Ǝ, ¬Ǝ/Ǝ,

¬Ⅎ/Ⅎ, ¬Ⅎ/Ⅎ, ¬Ⅎ/Ⅎ, ¬Ⅎ/Ⅎ,
¬Ⅎ/Ⅎ, ¬Ⅎ/Ⅎ, ¬Ⅎ/Ⅎ, ¬Ⅎ/Ⅎ,
¬Ⅎ/Ⅎ, ¬Ⅎ/Ⅎ, ¬Ⅎ/Ⅎ, ¬Ⅎ/Ⅎ
More and *more* and *more...*

It's down to the *Pilot, Copilot*, and mother, father, and child.

Jimmy sits in the row behind the couple. Speaks at the back of them. "I know how you feel," he says. "Or, should clarify, I know how a person like me makes people feel. I know it's your baby's life you fear for and if it weren't for that precious life of hers the two of you'd've already taken that leap."

Parents take turns talking to Jimmy without facing him.

"What if we go and we get separated?"

"Won't happen," Jimmy promises. "Just hold on tight."

"I-I can't. Even if there's the slightest chance... Not with my baby."

"I won't let anything happen to her."

"You can't guarantee..."

"Ok," Jimmy says, standing. He sits himself across the aisle of the family this time. He buckles himself in.

"Wh—What are you doing?"

"Going down with you." Jimmy points up the aisle. "Pilots too."

"What do you mean?"

"If I take them out of here you die for certain. Can't have that. We're all going down with the ship."

"No. Don't."

"Then let's go."

Silence a second... "Why aren't you just taking us despite our protests?"

"Would be wrong."

"But..." Then more silence.

Jimmy turns. Intrigued. Ma, pa, even baby look poised not resigned. Curious. Could it be? "Are you permitting me to take the three of you without your permission?"

Silence. Then... Slight nodding from Mom and Dad. Jimmy rises.

He leans into the row of the family. He caresses the infant's chubby little cheek, takes her hand as she grips onto his index finger. "Mom, Dad, take hold of my arms." They latch on. "Don't worry. I promise we ain't going anywhere." *Here we go...*

But...

There's a loud boom at the rear of the plane. Instant nose dive and Jimmy's ripped away from the family, tossed backward down the aisle. Ma and Pa are held by their seatbelts. Baby's held tight by mama. Her hand's free of Jimmy's so she just puts the thumb of it back into her mouth.

THUD! His left shoulder snags the leg of one of the seats. Hurt him though it stopped the tumble. His adrenaline's still working away. He'll need some Icy Hot if he gets out of this but at least he's on the move, up again and struggling against a world of forces conspiring to stop him, though moving forward.

"Jimmy!" shouts Lytrall. "Whatever's happened up there the A321's moving too fast for the cargo plane. Must be in a nose dive!"

"No shit," Jimmy says stomping—really falling—toward the cockpit.

Jet pierces out of the lower stratosphere now.

RUMBLE! RUMBLE!

BEEP! BEEP! BEEP!

The cockpit instruments are lit up like Santa's village and screaming.

"What's happening?" Jimmy asks hanging through the cockpit door.

Pilots are surprisingly calm. "Lost our rear stabilizer," says Copilot. "Lack of thrust, matter of time."

"Is there anything you can—"

"Pray!" says Pilot.

RUMBLE! RUMBLE!

Jimmy looks around for the source of that rumble. It's probably due to the fact you're falling out of the sky Jimmy. Gets some better wits, "Are there any planes moving at this speed anywhere? Anywhere!" He asks this like it'll make perfect sense to the flyers.

Both pilots look back in some sort of gallows ridicule.

Jimmy looks dead serious.

Pilots start shaking their heads, but...

SMACK!

Copilot baps Pilot. "Vomit comet!" she says. Pilot grins.

RUMBLE! RUMBLE!

"What?" Jimmy asks, bracing himself a little more soundly.

"Reduced gravity aircraft. Simulates zero-gravity conditions by going into an intentional dive. Only possible thing in the sky that could move like us."

Jimmy hands Copilot a little card. Struggles against the shaking to get it into her hand.

"Can I use your radio? At this frequency?"

She hands Jimmy her headset as she keys in the values on the card. Gives a thumbs up as...

Dad grabs Jimmy by the shoulder wanting answers. Mom leans against the outer cockpit wall with baby. Jimmy puts up a *just-one-minute* finger though bows his head assuredly.

Plane's at near terminal velocity by the way.

"Broadsword calling Danny Boy!" shouts Jimmy into the mic. "Broadsword calling—"

"This is Danny Boy," says Lytrall's voice. "Go Broadsword."

Pilots listen to all this in confusion.

"Doc, you know of any reduced gravity aircraft anywhere? Traveling at our speeds?"

Silence. Jimmy feels his heart in his brains. Everyone does.

RUMBLE! RUMBLE!

CRACKLE! Goes the radio.

"Only one, Jimmy. And it's just entering zero gravity conditions. You've got twenty-seven seconds to board it but you're not going fast enough."

"You mean we've gotta go faster?" Jimmy focuses on the pilots. "Can you speed this thing up?"

Pilots respond just as you'd expect. "We're at twenty-five hundred feet!" says Copilot.

Jimmy implores on.

Pilot tilts his head, looks to be in wide-eyed resignation. *Whelp...* "Whatever you're gonna do you have thirty seconds." He flips a few more switches and...

WHOOP! WHOOP! WHOOP! BEEP! BEEP! BEEP!

Did the plane pick up speed? Who can tell under these circumstances.

"All the time I need. I think we're speeding up Doc. I'm going back to Gift mode."

"Alright Jimmy, here are the coordinates." Lytrall **points to the screen. Jimmy's got em. Lytrall adds, "The**

second you go into free fall you make that jump. You'll know the instant you start to float."

"Thanks Doc."

Jimmy motions for the pilots to move out of the cockpit. They start to climb.

"Thousand feet," warns Pilot as he rises.

Mom, Dad, Baby, and Pilots lean against the outer cockpit wall now. Jimmy balances in front of them.

"All of you take hold of me," he shouts. "Whatever you do don't break contact" Jimmy takes the infant by her tiny hand once more.

It's an impossibly long few seconds waiting to see if...

RUMBLE! RUMBLE!

...They levitate off the cockpit wall in the slightest and...

¬Ⅎ

SMASH! BOOM!

A321's the Pacific's now.

Ⅎ

The astronauts-in-training just stare as they float on in their vomit comet. Despite being in mid-freefall, they've managed to pick up a few passengers. They just stare at the motley crew, popped in out of nowhere. Gotta be a real strange sight to distract earthlings from the fact they're experiencing zero gravity for the first time. Motley crew are floating too of course. All but baby, safe in her mother's arms.

Coming out of zero-grav in five, four, three... hold onto something folks... one.

Jimmy pukes.

Right place for it.

Meanwhile, in the cockpit of the Fed Up™ cargo plane...

Right Seat Pilot's thumping at the instrument panel. "Sensor's gotta be fried again. Says were flying a full load."

"Fuse," says the *Left Seat Pilot*. "Better head back and change it out."

Righty unbuckles.

He opens the cockpit door. He looks to the cargo hold's worth of people just standing there looking back at him. One of the passengers waves. Righty bows cordially, reenters the cockpit.

"That was quick," says Lefty. Silence. "Well?"

Righty turns to him. "Did I ever tell you about my cousin Mooney? Guard at the jail?"

17

——————

HERO STUFF

"We need to talk Jimmy…"

Nope! Not who you'd think.

It's Custy. He's looking up into the ether like Jimmy's watching. Jimmy isn't.

"I've had immunity papers drawn up." He says this like he's trying to coax Jimmy out of the bedroom after a lover's tiff. He's saying it a bit too much like *I've made your favorite honey, naan Hawaiian pizza…* Little too anxious. Little too insistent. And no one likes Hawaiian pizza, faddish-naanish or otherwise. Jimmy isn't coming out of the bedroom.

"Come on you asshole!"

That's more like it, Custy. Treat him more like a dog to get in the car to go get emasculated.

ii

"He definitely wants you close Jimmy though not to talk." This time it *is* Bart doing the briefing. She's in her easy chair. "He's up to something and he's only got one trick up his sleeve: those Customs field agents of his he

194

keeps loaded for bear. Wants to get his hands on you so it'll be a nonlethal carry. That last assumption's mine. Everything else comes from a pretty decent source. Good talking Jimmy. Over and out." She says this with a grin.

She looks at the FatButt™ app on her phone, sees Jimmy's heart rate is normalizing.

iii

Custy's trying again...

This time Jimmy's listening.

"...Just to talk. That's it, no tricks." Custy spins in his chair. He reaches out and knocks on the wall behind him. Wall starts to wobble so he puts his palm out to stabilize it. "As you can see, it's just me in my office. Stop by won't ya?"

Ǝ

Jimmy's beamed up behind Custy, takes him by the shoulders...

¬Ǝ

The four walls of the makeshift office collapse outward in all directions as the confused agents behind them, bearing tranq guns, move in.

Ǝ

Custy's in a park. It's night so it's empty. It's dark too, therefore.

But...

Lights of the ball diamond burst on. Fed's spooked by this. He's looking all around for his men he knows aren't coming.

"You remember to hold your tongue in those meetings of yours yet you forget I can see right into the next room?" It's Jimmy's voice speaking from somewhere near.

Custy spins a few times. Stops to face the diamond's utility shed as though that's where Jimmy'd be if Jimmy couldn't be anywhere Jimmy pleases. "Kept it dark!" He puts a hand up to cut the diamond lights' glare.

"Dark's as telling as anything when it's not where it's supposed to be."

$\neg\exists/\exists$

A tap on his shoulder. Custy spins once more. It's Jimmy. Border man takes a last desperate look for his men...

"What do you want to talk about ya crusty old bastard?"

He gives up the ghost on his search if only for his touchiness. "It's Custy!"

"It's both!" Jimmy takes a few steps closer. "Well? Where're those papers?" He tries not to grin.

Agent reaches into his right pant pocket, real frantic about it. Keeps reaching. Jostles a little more then moves to the other. Looks like he knows he isn't gonna find what he's digging for like he isn't gonna find those men but he's too obstinate to give up. Looks like if he were masturbating there wouldn't be enough Viagra in the world. Would almost look like he were masturbating if it didn't look like he were trying to rip his own balls off. Give it up Custy. Then...

"Looking for this?" Jimmy reveals Custy's stun gun in hand.

Custy doesn't miss a beat, "You fuckin asshole you never said you could take pieces of us with you!"

"Never said I couldn't."

"You motherfuckin—"

¬Ⅎ

iv

Lytrall and Jimmy are conversing in the lab.

"So I says to the Prez' nephew…" Jimmy says. "I says, I don't know how you managed to swallow your headphones like that—guy had the left earbud coming out his mouth and the right earbud coming out his butthole, mind you—I said, don't know how ya did it, but I think I can help ya… *SHIT!*"

¬Ⅎ

Jimmy's beamed away. Lytrall waits.

Then…

¬Ⅎ

He's back, soaking wet.

"What happened?"

"Goddamn water!" Jimmy's wringing his sleeves out all over the lab floor."

"Jimmy!"

"Goddamn idiot kid was about to jump off his roof. Was flapping his arms like a bird. Just Gifted right into my head. Happens sometimes."

"Why are you wet?"

"I got to him mid-fall. Realized too late if I beamed us back onto the ground we'd hit it as hard as if we just kept falling. Had to land us in the backyard pool."

"Quick thinking."

"If I were so quick I would have used the trampoline…

Goddamn water." He flops around like a dog fresh out the lake. "Any ideas for catching the fallen without getting wet Doc?"

Professor goes to a laptop on the workbench. "One." He brings up some sort of CAD drawing of something. Just a couple of rectangles and figures. Looks like somebody took a leaf blower to a mathematician's birthday cake. "Been thinking about it ever since that airplane episode." He turns to Jimmy. "It'll take a bit more time." Protege's still just a drippin away. "At least the parents were happy?"

¬∃/∃

Jimmy's back with a Holiday Inn towel. Some maid's in for a surprise when she finds the nugget of silver he left for her.

"Not really," he says blotting at himself. "They accused me of *identity erasure*." Lytrall looks confused at this. Jimmy explains things not at all to someone lucky enough to have avoided most of the 23rd century so far. "They said, *our child identifies as an emu*."

Lytrall gestures all jittery like there's too much about this that's too stupid to address in any reasonable order. "B-But emus don't fly," he manages to spout. Jimmy shrugs. Professor's still at a loss. "That's crazy!"

"That's the suburbs."

v

"Source says he's got agents posted all over the city Jimmy. Gonna use a tracking device this time. They'll find you in no less than three minutes, depending. Over and out."

vi

We're back in that field behind Lytrall's. He's driving Jimmy to the far corner of it, toward a fenced-in area where the fence is covered in camo netting. Enclosure's got to be the size of half a city block.

"I was thinking something," he says driving through the enclosure gate. "If you're going to keep teleporting into the sky to snatch people out of that sky, why not do it from heights higher than four stories?"

They arrive.

Lytrall hits his fob and floodlights flood light all over the fenced-in mass.

"What's that?" Jimmy asks.

"What it is, in part—in a part you'll understand without having to study my schematics—is something that won't just keep you dry when you're saving the fallen, it'll keep you alive from impacts up to terminal velocity."

"You telling me I can snatch people from as high as I please?"

"And in all directions."

vii

The screams can be heard all the way down to the sidewalk. Bystanders look up and shudder at the sight of their issuances: a woman dangles from a helicopter hanging off the top floor of a skyscraper. Machine caught a skid on some electric cables and lost control. It toppled sideways over the edge of its landing pad, flinging the passenger out the door in the process. She managed to grab onto the door's handle as she was thrown, but that handle won't bear her weight much longer. In fact, it's about to...

199

SNAP!

It goes. She goes.

She screams and flails as she falls, her blouse catching in the wind and shimmering all along her. Would look beautiful if she weren't losing altitude so fast.

Then...

There's a tapping at her shoulder. A tapping? She tries turning but she isn't exactly able to twist her hips, kick out a heel, and pivot. The tapping hand turns her. Though half-stunned, she's still with-it enough to know what's before her's a man, smiling, falling apace.

"Wanna get outta here?" Jimmy says this pointing at the rapidly approaching ground.

She nods frantically.

"Was hoping you would."

He takes her hands and...

¬∃

Looks like a massive inflated rubber bladder spreading out across the whole of The Professor's fenced-in enclosure. Looks like rubber but it's really made of some sort of impossible Lytrall-Tech that completely neutralizes inertia at any velocity, at any angle—or something... The mass can manage this at any angle because it's an enclosure itself. It has a two-story high base and four four-story-high walls surrounding it at the same thickness as that base.

The mass just sits in the silence of the night. Almost majestic in its own way. All is silence until...

∃

Jimmy and the *previously-hanging-now-falling* woman

come barreling out of the sky about thirty feet above the faux-rubber room.

They smash into the bottom of the enclosure with a...

Nothing so spectacular!

By design!

The mass is soundproof in addition to being an anti-gravitational de-ionizing inertial neutralizer—or something... Let's call the mass an *INOS* which is pronounced like *PINOS* without the *P*.

Before the woman can get her bearings in that mush she's wrestling in...

¬Ǝ

Ǝ

Jimmy's brought her right back to the sidewalk of the building she fell from.

She looks at him like she knows he saved her life and that's impossible and that's all her shock'll let her understand at the moment. Then...

CREEYUNK! SNAP!

Helicopter above gives way. Starts to fall!

Gawking bystanders all scream and scramble. Not the woman though. She's just looking at Jimmy.

"Ma'am." Jimmy tips the invisible brim of an invisible hat of his, then...

¬Ǝ

Falling helicopter disappears in mid-air.

People on the street previously attending to the falling woman and marveling, then attending to the falling helicopter and screaming, now stare horizontal and marvel at nothing in particular. Then they shift their focus back to the woman-saved. She's still a bit shaken though she's getting her sense back.

When...

"Shit lady!" shouts one of the bystanders. "You know what just happened? You got ported!"

Jimmy pops his head into the side entrance of Lytrall's lab complex. Lytrall barely notices as he's too engrossed in putting the last few obsidian cubes onto the outer shell of the black hole.

"Got a use for a helicopter?" Jimmy asks.

Not looking away from his work, "Already got one in here somewhere."

"Alright, I'll take it back."

viii

Alarms blare. Sirens are heard in the distance. Three crooks burst out of the bank they've just robbed. They pile into a getaway car and the driver peels out into heavy traffic.

They're really moving. Running every red and weaving in and out of any lane the getaway driver takes to be the path of least resistance. He zips around objects in his way like they're standing still. Guy's calm about it all. Done it before. Does it with callous abandon though. Won't hesitate to smash through whatever he can smash through *and* stay mobile and he's heading toward a residential area.

Cops have managed to catch up and keep pace, slowing the thieves, but they can't get these scumbags off the road! A half-dozen blocks more and they're in a school zone. After that it's precious seconds before the crooks are blowing through a crosswalk full of grade schoolers.

"Gonna have to back off man!" *Passenger Side Cop* shouts.

"I got kids in that school!" *Driver Side Cop* makes a last desperate attempt to sideswipe the getaway car and angle it off the road. Getaway car shimmies a little though rights itself quick. Cop car does the opposite. Loses control in a skid. Brakes, but can't stop before slamming into a delivery truck. All involved will walk away but that was close. Then...

Ǝ

Jimmy's in the back seat of the cruiser.

"Can I try something fellas?"

Cops look over their shoulders. Look back at each other.

"No fuckin way!" they say in unison. "Did we just get ported!"

Jimmy tips an invisible brim.

"Hell yeah man! Let's do it! I got kids up there." Driver side guns it and peels out into traffic.

"Just pull up alongside," Jimmy says. He searches for a window button. None. "Can you open this?"

Passenger side cop hands over his nightstick. "Go for it dude."

SMASH!

Jimmy hangs out the window as the cruiser approaches the getaway car. Getaway's bumping off the remaining cops one after another. "Get close!" Jimmy shouts.

The getaway car's broken free of the last nudging cruiser and's picking up speed. Now for those precious seconds...

But...

The Teleporter's cruiser's come flying up the straightaway, angling in next to the crooks.

Kids are crossing just a block up as Driver Side Cop lays on the horn. All other cruisers diverge and slide to a stop along the curbs. *Passenger Side Thug* lifts himself out his window of the getaway, turns, aims his pistol across the roof. Jimmy bobs in and out of his sights.

"Ready?" Jimmy says to the cops.

"Ready!"

Teleporter reaches out for the getaway car.

Thug gets his aim.

"Buckle up!"

Thug's gun's cocked. Kids at the crosswalk stop and look up at the coming danger and freeze. Trigger's pulled... When...

¬∃

The two vehicles vanish as all the stolen cash and guns slide and bounce along the pavement up to the kids' toes.

WHOA! Look at that! say way too many of them as school staff and cops come running over to confiscate all the fun.

¬∃

Cars fly into the wall of Lytrall's li'l *INOS*. Wall caresses them all to a gentle stop.

"You're under arrest," say the cops to the now disarmed robbers as all wobble and stumble on the mushy mass trying to get to wherever they need to get to.

Jimmy's just sitting back in the comfort of the *INOS*. He tosses a nine-millimeter shell up in the air. Catches it coming down.

ix

The inertia-neutralizing mass once again sits in the silence of the night. Almost majestic in its own way. All is silence until...

¬Ǝ/Ǝ, ¬Ǝ/Ǝ, ¬Ǝ/Ǝ, ¬Ǝ/Ǝ, ¬Ǝ/Ǝ, ¬Ǝ/Ǝ, ¬Ǝ/Ǝ, ¬Ǝ/Ǝ, ¬Ǝ/Ǝ, ¬Ǝ/Ǝ,

¬Ǝ/Ǝ, ¬Ǝ/Ǝ, ¬Ǝ/Ǝ, ¬Ǝ/Ǝ, ¬Ǝ/Ǝ, ¬Ǝ/Ǝ, ¬Ǝ/Ǝ, ¬Ǝ/Ǝ, ¬Ǝ/Ǝ, ¬Ǝ/Ǝ,

¬Ǝ/Ǝ, ¬Ǝ/Ǝ, ¬Ǝ/Ǝ, ¬Ǝ/Ǝ, ¬Ǝ/Ǝ, ¬Ǝ/Ǝ, ¬Ǝ/Ǝ, ¬Ǝ/Ǝ, ¬Ǝ/Ǝ, ¬Ǝ/Ǝ,

¬Ǝ/Ǝ, ¬Ǝ/Ǝ, ¬Ǝ/Ǝ, ¬Ǝ/Ǝ, ¬Ǝ/Ǝ, ¬Ǝ/Ǝ, ¬Ǝ/Ǝ, ¬Ǝ/Ǝ, ¬Ǝ/Ǝ, ¬Ǝ/Ǝ,

¬Ǝ/Ǝ, ¬Ǝ/Ǝ, ¬Ǝ/Ǝ, ¬Ǝ/Ǝ, ¬Ǝ/Ǝ, ¬Ǝ/Ǝ, ¬Ǝ/Ǝ, ¬Ǝ/Ǝ, ¬Ǝ/Ǝ, ¬Ǝ/Ǝ,

...

Jimmy's dropping people left and right! It's raining men, women, and children. Good guys and bad guys! People of all shapes and sizes. From all over the world. He's catching crooks and saving innocents by the dozens. It's like a pepper shaker of people dumping itself all over that mysterious caressing rubber!

People stumble and bumble along the massive mushy platform looking for a way out. Innocents saved will be met with shuttles to take them as close to home as possible and the guilty caught will be met with prison vans to take them as close to justice as possible.

Lytrall greets those who made it to the gate of the surrounding fence. "Alright everyone. Civilians to the shuttles at your right. Crooks to the paddy wagons at your left. I can say *paddy wagon*. I'm Irish. Civilians to the right. Crooks to the left. Who do you think yer foolin buddy you're still in the prison issues you escaped in! That's better. Crooks to the left, civilians to the right..."

x

Custy's standing in his office pretending to be briefed by an agent who's really just attaching a tracking device to his lapel. Device is embedded in a *Where's the Beef* pin. Why Custy couldn't do this himself, who knows...

"Quickly idiot," Custy demands in a hush. He gets louder now and stupidly theatrical. "Well, yes... Thanks agent. That's an invaluable report you've got there." Agent gets a face like he's wondering *what the hell is this guy talking about?* as Custy continues. "Get the hell out now... Yes... Much appreciated. I have an important meeting..."

Agent leaves the office confused.

Custy looks up at nothing. "Well, as you can see Jimmy, it's just me in my *real* office this time—"

Ǝ/¬Ǝ

Ball diamond lights pop on again. Then...

"A whole car Jimmy? A whole son-of-a-bitchin car!"

"So what?" Jimmy shrugs.

"This has serious ramifications for importing and exporting!"

"*So? What?*"

Custy huffs and puffs in some sort of strange despair. Doesn't this Teleporter asshole give a damn about trade restrictions? It's a world out of order! "You said *only if you could lift it off the ground!*"

"Said no such thing. Said if I could lift it off the ground I could move it. Never said if I couldn't lift it, it couldn't be moved."

"You son of a bitch!" Custy starts scanning around in all directions.

"Where's the *Where's the Beef*?" Jimmy asks. Agent lifts his lapel up and away. Pin's gone. There's one last desperate spin almost like a pirouette as Custy searches on. "Don't worry," Jimmy assures. "Left it at your place. In your panic room." Border man's breathing heavy again. Looks like he's gonna faint this time. Jimmy smirks. "*Apropos.* Sure your guys were told to do whatever they had to to get to you?" Eyes close. "Pity about that Yama Twenty-Five Cup Cold Brew Coffee Tower of yours. Retails for seven-hundred and seventy-four dollars ninety-nine cents? Just knocked it right off the counter. Maybe you can save the frame... Nope! They stomped it!" Eyes open to a fuming Custy.

"You! You son of a..."

¬∃

"Bitch!"

∃/¬∃

A copy of *Introduction to Logic* lies on the ground. A post-it on the book reads, *See: 'Denying the Antecedent' pg. 23.*

"How the fuck am I gonna get outta here?" Custy shouts.

∃/¬∃

A child's bicycle lies next to the logic book.

xi

Another plane's going down. Twin engine flameout over the Andes. It's full. Way too many passengers to move. They're done for? No! Because...

Jimmy's flying through the sky. Somewhere near? Somewhere far? Doesn't matter! He's picking up speed! He's dressed in high-altitude-low-oxygen skydiving equipment minus the parachute. You dare-devil son-of-a-gun you!

"You're almost at speed Jimmy but you've got to correct your angle. Five degrees to what would be your *up.*"

Jimmy opens his arms to reveal some ripstop nylon wings. He moves his arms out and downward slightly. He rises.

"Alright, you got it! Now beam to that plane and take her home!"

Jimmy's right on target. He's floating along the top of that nose-diving fuselage heading right for a mountain two-hundred and fifty feet *over there.* Hero puts his hand down to the frosty aluminum and...

Inertia-Neutralizer absorbs the jetliner like a gentle caressing catcher's mitt. Jimmy, on the other hand, goes flying off it like a flicked fly—right into the wall of the enclosure. He's fine.

Passengers have disembarked, stumbling happy—if not confused—out the enclosure gate.

"Passengers to the right, crooks to the left. Big plane. Lotta passengers. Statistically speaking, some of you are criminals. Passengers to the right..."

A little kid can be heard shouting, *again!*

xii

"A goddamn jetliner Jimmy!"

There's a copy of *Logic for Dummies* at Custy's feet.

xiii

One more adventure...

They're not Zealots and they're not WAMN assholes. These guys are pros. Serious pros. They don't want attention and they don't want to die. They'd be happy living out the rest of their lives on a private beach somewhere after one last big score earning twenty percent.

Eyes open.

"Eighteen."

"Hostages?"

"Twenty-six. Seated. Hands and ankles bound."

"Where?"

"Hostages are all on the thirty-eighth flo—"

"Thought the Fox building only had thirty-five floors."

"Not the Fox building."

"Oh."

Three suspects armed with Walther P5s and MP5

submachine guns watch the doors at the ground floor. Six suspects sweep six floors apiece, all the way up to thirty-seven. They're armed the same. Six are with the hostages on thirty-eight. Also armed with P5s and MP5s. Three are in the vault room on thirty-nine.

"Armed?"

"Yes, holstered side arms. Not sure the make."

"What's wrong?"

"Something's off."

"Describe everything exactly as you see it."

All suspects are wearing what looks like some sort of holter monitor around their necks.

"EKG readout?"

"Yes."

"Hostages too?"

"No."

"Suspects are wired up for something. Anything else?"

Each of the hostages and suspects wear an armband around their right bicep. Has a green light. Flashes on and off periodically.

"According to any rhythm?"

"Doesn't look like... Wait..."

Each time any one of the four guards moves across his assigned corner, there's a corresponding flash.

"Three flashes? In quick succession?"

"Yeah."

"What do you see in those corners?"

Tripods. Have something like little solar panels on them.

"Motion detectors."

"What's it mean?"

"Not good. Any explosives?"

"None that I can see."

"Check any hollows: vents, suspended ceilings, elevator shafts."

Nothing.

"You're sure?"

"Checked every floor. Peeked through every crook and crawlspace," Jimmy says. Lytrall remains silent. He paces. "What are they wired up for?" Jimmy asks.

"You."

"What do you mean?"

"Hostage takers are wired up so if they're harmed the EKG falters. Then what? Boom most likely? Something really bad. However, that's standard protection against a cop breach. Hostage takers and hostages alike are wired up to those motion sensors so one body more or one body less means some other horrible outcome? The same as in the case of a breach? Not a cop in the world is trained to sneak hostages out one at a time. Not a cop in the world could. That's your MO Jimmy. They've rigged up some horrible fate for everyone involved so you can't just move everyone out. Now, what is that fate?"

"There's nothing in that building that shouldn't be in that building other than the hostage-takers."

"*In* the building? Check the roof."

Nothing. He keeps scanning. Some old satellite dishes. Just more... *NO!* **Rockets! Three!**

"*Rockets*? What do you see?"

Something like rockets. Looks like they're sticking out of massive cameras.

"Those are targeting systems Jimmy. What else?"

They're on tripods as well. That's about it.

"What's the shape of the missile?"

It's weird, like a big lawn dart with a smaller lawn dart coming out its top.

"Bunker busters," Lytrall snaps a finger like he's got it. Gets a look like he doesn't want it. "It's a spike missile system with bunker-buster warheads. Designed to penetrate reinforced concrete, steel, all of that stuff buried in the ground."

"Gimme a minute..."

"What are you seeing Jimmy?"

One of the suspect's laptops. On the vault floor. Has a parabolic shape on the screen. Could be a... Oh no...

"What?"

"A trajectory. A complete loop. Up and away and back into the top floor."

"Not *into* Jimmy, *through*. That's the failsafe. Make any kind of move and those three bunker busters fire. Everyone would be killed near-instantly and they're counting on you knowing that. That must be their leverage."

"I'll drop those missile systems into the Grand Canyon."

"Too risky. Chances are, you touch one you set them all off. Even setting foot on that roof could trigger them."

"I'd be quick."

"You'd be burned alive by their ignition."

"I'll—"

"What? Snatch three firing rockets out of the sky?"

"Then... What?"

"I-I can't imagine." Lytrall's expression's dire. "They've got us Jimmy. You can't touch that building without setting off those missiles."

"I mean... I don't want to start rationalizing. It's just, there are worse things than letting a few crooks get away with some bearer bonds."

"Jimmy, they're not walking out of there."

"What are you saying?"

"That missile system isn't just a way to ward off you and

the law. It's key to the meticulously planned accident they require to distract the police and escape."

"You're saying..."

"Yes. An old tactic that hasn't been employed since the mid-twenty-first century, from a book written in the late twentieth century. Hasseldorf's *Hostage Terrorist, Terrorist Hostage: A Study in Duality*. The first known application of the method involved strikingly similar circumstances to these. In nineteen-eighty-eight, a group of thieves posing as terrorists took over a—"

"I know of the Hasseldorf method and its inspiring real-life events Doc. The question is, what do we do to prevent its application now?"

Lytrall sits, slumps into the chair closest him. "I told you Jimmy, anything you try may set off that missile system. You can't touch that building."

A beat.

"That's not entirely true..."

Smash cut to...

The scene's a festival of cop-waiting and jurisdictional posturing. The most costly of all *waitings* and *posturings*. The skyscraper stands stoic and dignified nonetheless.

You'd never know by looking at it that the twenty-six tape-recorder company executives it holds are going to lose their lives furnishing eighteen terrorists-turned-grand-larceny-lovers with a hundred million dollars in bearer bonds.

You *can* tell from all the interagency coppers running around with their chickens cut off that *something* dire is going on inside. You can also tell that these chickens—these upholders of the *officious-non-solution*—will almost certainly only ensure good things for the bad in there and bad things for the good in there. Unless...

"Four assholes coming in the rear in standard two-by-two cover formation..." says a nerdy-looking hostage-taker monitoring the periphery of the skyscraper. He's watching a live camera feed featuring the east wall of the complex.

Ⅎ

"...Wait. Who the hell is that?"

"Who the hell are you?" says one of the four assholes in standard two-by-two cover formation eyeballing a Jimmy just standing up against that east wall.

Teleporter doesn't answer the asshole, just stares up at the building. He sees nothing but the most warped three-point perspective of a monolith not even imaginable in the gnarliest of surrealist art. His eyes hurt and he'd see more of this slab's detail Gifting it drunk than he would looking at it like this. Head lowers.

"I asked you who you were!" says that same asshole taking a single step out of that standard two-by-two cover formation. "Answer me!"

It'd be a good idea to acknowledge the four assholes about now. They're getting a little antsy. Jimmy obliges reason. He turns to face them and his lips form a soulless smile of some perfect combination of defiance and contrition. One of those *sorry guys, but I gotta do what I gotta do* smiles of lips never separating. At this, the assholes move in in no particular formation, though in all due confusion.

Jimmy puts his palm to the building.

"Don't touch that! That's not yours!"
Then…

¬Ⅎ

Jimmy and the building are gone. Jimmy's taken every-thing with him but the hostages now *not* suspended in mid-air just plummeting from five hundred feet up. Down they come as…

Ⅎ/¬Ⅎ, Ⅎ/¬Ⅎ, Ⅎ/¬Ⅎ, Ⅎ/¬Ⅎ

Jimmy's moved all the assholes clear of the vacant lot as the hostages continue falling… And screaming… Then…

Ⅎ

Jimmy's back again. He's not alone. He's brought the whole of Lytrall's Inertia-Neutralizer. He couldn't bring the hostages to the rubber mat so he brought the rubber mat to the hostages! Whatever works Jimmy boy.

All twenty-six hostages smash into the bottom of that mat with a…

Nothing so spectacular! Again!

They're fine.

xiv

"A goddamn son-of-a-bitchin building Jimmy!"

¬Ⅎ

18

MAN OF THE PEOPLE

Once again, the current administration's unprecedented move in pardoning the main-most involved in the Kairn Center conspiracy has left many looking for answers. Others, however, feel the pardon long overdue.

We're with Senator Fletcher caught by Ottawa press in the halls of parliament. They're not exactly grilling him just playing a game of it. Playing at holding the powerful to account. To account for a growing authoritarian image a little too close to commensurate with a fully-matured authoritarian reality... A reality shockingly close to rendering the worst of commensurability claims true. What's that mean? Means they're putting Fletcher on the spot—*his mark?*—so he appears slightly helpless in all of the press' complete and utter accommodation. Just a little dance to cause viewers at home an hallucination of checks and balances. Just a little dance to insure the same for all involved in the footwork even?

And *ACTION!*

"W-Well," says Fletcher trying to fumfer in just the right measure, "I've always maintained my PA's innocence. Kenneth Figurace is a good man whose biggest mistake was being too trusting of a system where there will always be those looking to do it harm from without. This was my mistake too. However, we are now properly vetting any new hires at my office as well as all others within parliament. This won't happen again." Fletcher says this staring into a camera he must believe is broadcasting to the greatest number of people.

But! shouts a reporter up front a little louder than the rest. *There were recordings of Figurace planning the attack.*

"Deep fakes ladies and gentlemen. Never authenticated and you know very well how very talented but very nefarious the people who post misinformation like this tend to be. Misinformation abounds, not to mention disinformation, not to mention malinformation, not to mention misoinformation and pseudo-information and extra-crispy-information and, well, all the other forms of information at this point."

"You really think you're fooling anyone?" says a reporter in the back going off-book. He's speaking loud enough for everyone to hear if not loud enough to out himself.

GLARE! from Fletcher. Then... "Like many, I think it's completely reasonable sounding and not at all absurd that the vast majority of us elected officials have abruptly and out of nowhere taken to trying to convince everyone in the world that the scariest goddamn thing in the whole goddamn world is, of all things, *information*. Not at all pathetic and unconvincing..."

None appear convinced.

"Look," Fletcher continues, "there are brutal totalitarian

regimes and then there are hastily uttered statements that are true that I claim are false because I don't like hearing them and I think I'm fooling anyone. Historically, there's been Hitler and unpleasant language. And I'm not sure which is worse quite frankly. Not at all pathetic and unconvincing..."

But—

"And... *AND!*" Fletcher insists. "Should any of this awful awful misinformation end up being substantiated, as misinformation usually is, it's all a conspiracy theory."

"Because it *is* a conspiracy." Reporter in the back again... "Figurace conspired to kidnap The Prez' nephew."

Fletcher glares once more. Does it in the reporter's general direction—tries finding him but the reporter's gone silent. Then...

BUT! BUT! go the other reporters.

"Ladies and gentlemen," Fletcher recommences. He waves his hands like he's trying to get them to settle. "Kenneth Figurace was scapegoated in my opinion, plain and simple. A man made to take the fall so there'd be someone influential to blame in order to ameliorate the people always demanding these events feature some powerful kingpin. They needed to scapegoat someone at the top is all."

"Some would say, *second-from-the-top...*"

GLARE! GLARE! GLARE! Senator barrels on nonetheless. "*Ahem...* However, sometimes a cigar is just a cigar and a group of thoughtless revolutionaries with only the most tenuous of ties to our government who manage to nearly pull off an insurrection or something similar..." He pauses to catch his breath. "...Are just that cigar." *What!* "These are radicals who got lucky."

"But Libby was a part of *your* administration and he was caught putting The Prez' nephew in a chokehold."

Fletcher's gonna need some visine he keeps bulging them eyes out of his head at the truth like this. He ignores the reporter altogether this time. Then...

Will you be once again working with Kenneth Figurace?

"Hmmm, sadly no. As much as I would like that, Kenneth has decided to stay out of the public eye. And for very good reason." Fletcher reaches for a door handle behind him and lucky enough for him one is there... To a supply closet. Home audiences can see the mops-in-buckets on the floor and jugs of chemicals on the shelves. "Well..." he says as though something important is going on in that closet. "Ladies and gentlemen, I thank you for your time—"

BLIP!

Lytrall's hit his fob pausing the streaming news item. "What's Fletcher got on The Prez?"

"Nothing," Jimmy assures matter of factly.

"Come on! Letting the guy who came for his family go? He's started wars for less."

"He's started wars against *outsiders* for less, the old fool. Who's he gonna go to war with now, the legislative branch? Nah. He and Fletcher thought they'd put Figurace on ice and look like they'd pulled the rotten tooth. Too bad for them the public didn't buy it. It's Fletch they want on a hook. That'll really damage the machine so Prez figures he pardons the government players in all this, on his authority alone, and enough of the people will think it never involved the government at all, just a bunch of asshole revolution-aries ingratiated themselves into a system *far too trusting* for its own good."

"That strategy sounds incredibly stupid."

"It's only stupid if the people aren't."

"And..."

"I don't think they are, not in large enough part. But Prez

only needs to fool enough people more are calling for his censure than are calling for Fletcher's head."

"Could work."

"And if enough buy it, Prez and Fletcher are permitted the already increased gate-keeping of their petty little club. The same career politicians getting reelected forever and ever what with 'terrorists' infiltrating government bureaucracies and all."

"You Gift all this?"

"Yes, but it's also just bland old Amerikan politics."

"Right. You Gift what Figurace's up to?"

"Nowhere you'd expect him to be. Nowhere public. Not that I can see."

"If he's seeking any kind of retribution against anyone after Libby, it'll definitely be you."

"I'll see him coming long before he sees me." Jimmy says this with a confidence new to Lytrall. New to Jimmy, quite frankly.

Professor has a look of slight concern where, if it were over Jimmy's hubris, it could easily be mistaken for Figurace getting the drop. "Still, I wish we knew where Figurace was."

"I know where Fletcher is right now." Jimmy says this suggestive as can be.

"You do what I think you're thinking of doing and you'll be painting a target on your back so bright the powerful'll give every permission in the world to Custy to do whatever he has to do to put you in a hole and burry you and walk away and leave you a duty invoice for the dirt."

"Won't catch me." Jimmy points to the Danger Ranger™.

"You underestimate a man's ability to tease out another's weaknesses, especially when the man's left groping in a dark that hurts. Introduce a man like Custy to as many vulnerabilities as you have Jimmy, and you only grant him a knowledge of all the vulnerabilities there are."

"We'll burn that bridge when we get to it."

"You're bored is all. You've gotten a taste for righting wrongs where just the specter of you is now the deterrent. You've got nothing to do."

"Plenty of white collar crime out there..."

"Jimmy!"

"*LISTEN!*"

The Teleporter damn-near roars this.

Lytrall waits for what's deeper.

Hero's insistent now, assured. Nothing errant. "I get that you've clocked in me some misplaced confidence. And I know it's misplaced. I also know you've got this... This near-autistic approach to every goddamn problem where you act as though if the cause of some undesirable outcome ceases to be then so too do the lingering effects of that outcome. Like because the mechanisms of those visions, because we stopped them, the memory must be gone as well. It's not." Lytrall knows Jimmy ain't done. Jimmy *ain't* done. "About now I've learned to deal with every single wretched epiphenomenon of those memories save the anger, so *at* this point it's either the anger or the misplaced confidence and it's the confidence that allows me to be the closest thing I can be to rational and because I'm as close to pure rationalism as I'm ever going to be—and that's a damn sight closer than the ninety-nine—the rationalist in me understands those callous sons-of-bitches deserve to pay for what they did to *those* people in *those* visions that fucked me up so bad. My rage tells me to punish them so I turn it off and my derivations tell me to punish em more. Disjunctive elimination. You *know* what that means."

Lytrall knows what that means.

¬∃

ii

Fletcher's sitting at twelve o'clock in *his* of the office suite. Maybe the other hours are vacant, maybe not. Probably not at midday. No cause for concern either way as what Jimmy's got planned for him will only take a second.

It's a very special kind of ignorance that Fletch sits in. Men like him don't understand Jimmy yet they fear him. A better way of phrasing it might be, *men like him don't understand Jimmy SO they fear him.* Ignorance is their sufficient condition. In this case it's wise. In this case Fletcher's wearing the standard security measure all people in his position have been fitted with. A little tracer wristband set to alert his guards should he press the little button on it *or* should he experience a drastic shift in biometrics *or* should the wristband become separated from him in any way. Men like Fletcher don't understand Jimmy so they don't understand that he can just...

∃/¬∃

Snatch the thing away anytime he wants and because he's left it in World Three, where time don't pass, it'll never send the intended information to the security detail out in the hall.

Fletcher glances to where something feels off, missing. Notices that bare wrist as...

∃

Jimmy's on him. Wrenches him out of his seat and puts a hand to his mouth as though Fletcher isn't too petrified to whisper anything more than...

"What are you going to do?"

¬∃

Figurace's a patsy. Fletcher's the rat, see!

Is one of the chants.

Figurace blew, Fletcher knew!

Is another—*and* one appearing on a few signs.

Fletcher resign... From the planet!

Lock him up!

I guess political bullshit is the one shit that don't roll uphill!

And that's three more slogans issued by the protestors—in print and voice.

They protest on the main lawn of parliament.

There are more slogans that more or less make the same point—and are more or less clever. There are fewer protestors today than there were yesterday. The Prez' plan appears to have worked. Remaining protestors are peaceful and that doesn't mean *mostly*. They're peaceful, simpliciter. Though, as we can clearly see, that doesn't mean they're contented.

These men and women are the vestige, the compliment really. The counterparts of those who only raise their voices when the harm done is too great or, in their eyes, of a partisan nature favorable to their *part*. The bulk of those voices—of whom the people here today are only a mere vestige, the compliment—have left. Gone home due their grotesque faith in roughly half the men and women who occupy the center block of the complex in which those of the vestige remain. Faith in them to do what? They've never thought that far ahead. Faith in uneventful occupancy maybe? It's only uneventful because the occupants can make the *illegal* legal with a pen. The *guilty* pardoned by the same. And maybe that's precisely the way this grotesquery brings peace of mind? Identify the *legitimate* with the *moral* like the worst of our fools have always done?

Either way...

The broke-down machine of the conservatorship oligarchy has a new coat of paint and all but the vestige can once more breathe the delusion of its renewal. Faith restored.

The deluded never wanted better. They wanted a scapegoat outside of their machine. Like Fletcher and Prez knew they would.

Not those of the vestige though. They want justice.

Seems like it was a billion generations ago something like this happened—not for the first time, but—for the first time it was knowledge. Happened back when it was the shock of the realization of the corruption of a cherished institution that drove the vestige. Today it's the anger of that corruption metastasized, where everybody sees it and none but the vestige do anything about it and even then, what are they *the few* even doing?

What would these people do if they ever got their hands on the subject of their discontent?

Then...

Ǝ/¬Ǝ

Fletcher's smack in the middle of the petitioners.

He's spooked though he has some sense of survival in him. Career politicians tend to. He puts his head down to blend in, only lifting it periodically to look for a way out. It's

Fletcher striking a cautious balance in the hopes of achieving a viable end. Something completely foreign to him.

He can't strike that balance.

He can't blend in.

Not in that suit of his.

Holy shit!

You seeing what I'm seeing.

It's him!

The crowd forms a tight circle around the senator. He gestures at them as though they're mistaken, mouthing *no*, shaking his head. And yet they're not mistaken and he's not going to convince them and he knows it. He stumbles around like some sort of pathetic species for whom, when it's time to die, spends the last few moments of its life searching for a place to do that dying... What? Comfortably? He looks like that but if he had his wits he'd very much want to live. But he looks like that. He stumbles into a wall of them as though there's any grace left and they'll simply part. There is, though maybe he's gotta earn it?

He appears short to them. Older than television suggests.

He reaches out to who's closest. *Please* he says as any grip fails and he falls to the ground curling into himself.

They hover over him.

We know who put you here. You've got far greater problems than we could ever cause for you.

The protestors disperse.

Then...

Ǝ

Jimmy sits the broken senator back into his desk chair. Guy slumps. Jimmy sits himself in the guest chair facing him.

"People like you," The Teleporter begins, "you set in motion events sending anybody *but* people like you into a world of cruelty and despair. Remember, what I did today I can do any time I please. Can do it worse. You got off easy."

¬Ǝ

iii

It's not Simone Simmons reporting. Maybe she really did retire to start her own YouTube? Best of luck to her if she did. It's just some generic talking-head now. Her replacement.

It's *Generic Talking-Head* reporting,

Although it appears absolutely no one has mixed feelings about the recent resignation of Laurentia Senator Flaurice Fletcher, the same certainly can't be said of the events many believe precipitated his sudden departure...

"Fletcher's a bum and he's guilty of all of that what happened with the Prez' nephew and even if he ain't, shit's still gotta roll uphill, but dropping a politician into a crowd of everyday people's just plain cruel and unusual."

"You can't just expect the leaders of a democracy to walk among the people. The whole of our democracy would collapse! The public hates its leaders! What-a-ya mean 'in a democracy, the people are the leaders?' No no. That's where you're wrong. This is a representative democracy. You can't expect our representa-

tives to just walk among the people. The people hate their repre-sentatives. 'How can one person represent another if the purported representative is hated?' See... We... We actually live in a... A representative republic! Yeah, that's it. Does that get me off the hook?"

"I thought it was funny. I think The Teleporter should drop our PM into small town Laurentia next. Let that pencil neck get a taste of the will of the people out there!"

And it isn't just Flaurice Fletcher and the average 'Amerikan on the street' who think The Teleporter may have gone too far. Elected officials all over the country have been resigning en masse, sighting the safety issues inherent in unplanned interac-tions with constituents free of adequate security and speech writers. More on this as it develops. This is Generic Talking-Head, reporting.

Lytrall's reading a newspaper like it's a hundred years ago. They still publish those things? "You've set off a bit of a chain reaction here Jimmy. Minister of Agriculture just resigned."

"Damn, I thought he was one of the good ones."

Professor raises an eyebrow at this. "Maybe he is?"

"Not if he defies the will of the people."

"What makes you think the will of the people's a right-eous will? For that matter, what makes you think a leader-beloved is a righteous leader? Drop Kim Jong Un into a crowd of those he rules over. They'll bow to him."

¬ヨ

Jimmy's blipped away.

3

He's back.

"You're right."

Lytrall chuckles. "There are two types of political bodies Jimmy, those that get in the way of the people just living their lives and those that get in the way of the people getting in the way of the people. A democracy is a much larger political body but it's still a political body. It's gotten in the way of the former and it's gotten in the way of the latter. Power is power." A beat. "Stifle it all."

Jimmy raises an eyebrow. "The latter?"

"Stifle the former, there won't be a need for the latter. The latter is self-annihilating on its successes."

19

AND JUST WHEN YOU THOUGHT
YOU WERE IN EQUILIBRIUM...

We go now live to the national headquarters of US Customs...

I t's Custy at his desk in address mode. Emboldened as hell. Hands folded in that unnatural way that makes you think the makeup artist did it between the powder or the prop master did it between deciding on the Newton balls, the inbox, or one of those brass bankers lamps with the translucent green tops. Maybe it was the network mortician because Custy doesn't just look stiff, he looks embalmed. Pancake powder pallor with rosy candy apple cheekbones. Maybe he ain't feeling well? Ring that little coffin bell? Anyway, there he sits, cameras all around him as the various crew members scramble away just in time for him to begin his address.

And *ACTION!*

"Good people of these United States of Amerika, the Department of Customs, as promised, has maintained the closest surveillance of the mysterious figure known colloquially as *The Teleporter*. Within the past few months, unmistakable evidence has established the fact that a gross accumulation of contraband—goods illegal in terms of both their substance and status, the latter meaning improperly taxed and/or duty-paid—has amassed within the city limits of West Brandon. The presence of these goods can be for a purpose none other than increasing bartering capabilities among freely willing agents across the Western Hemisphere... Without giving the government its sweet sweet duty. Need I remind you all of the various statutes and regulations found within our wonderful—"

Alright! Enough of that! We'll fast-forward. Custy's answer to that last question of his is *yes* because he goes on discussing those statutes for a good twenty-two minutes. Then he talks about a car he had in his twenties with an aluminum alloy chassis where the aluminum was imported and the manufacturer failed to declare it and Custy wrote his congressman and who really cares... Then he rants about how duty-free shops are nothing more than an anti-Amerikan plot by hippies and trotskyites (?). Then he goes back to the statutes for a few more minutes... However, it's the last bit of his address that's the most relevant to the tale. We'll be getting to that last bit any second. Just gotta slog through a little more of...

"*If it moves, tax it. If it keeps moving, regulate it. And if it stops moving, subsidize it. A verrrrry* wise prescription that I was shocked to learn was in the process of being derided by a *verrrrry* misguided hippie president!" Custy puts a hand to his brow all a sudden, peering. "What? Wrap it up? Oh hell!" He shuffles through his papers to get to the last of them. He peels a little post-it note off the last and reads it while stuck to his index finger. He looks into the camera now. "Ahem! The Prez' Administration wishes for me to provide the following information:" Custy rattles all of what follows off in a rote perfunctory manner, "The Teleporter's real name is Jimmy Adamowski. He lives in West Brandon most of the time. He doesn't just have the ability to snatch you or your loved ones out of thin air and take them anywhere he pleases, like drop you into a volcano... Can even do that to your house if he wanted... He can also see anywhere on the planet in order to watch out for where he's going... Like to not teleport off a cliff... This means he can see you anywhere you go, even on the toilet... He's probably watching you and your loved ones right now... On the toilet... No point trying to hide... He's a very dangerous man. *Blah-dee-blah*" Custy leans into the camera with a shit-eating grin. "Ha! Dangerous?" He pinches his index and thumb together. "My guys are *this* close to hunting that dirty smuggler down!" He stands up and the camera crops out his head and he thinks he's speaking directly into it. "You hear that Jimmy? Ya stinky bastard! I'm coming for you and when I get my hands on you I'm gonna teleport your head from your neck! Now, where was I—"

Test Pattern.

Lytrall looks to Jimmy. Jimmy looks to Lytrall.

"This could be trouble."

ii

Smash-cut to...

Posters have gone up all over Amerika with the slogan,

Now you see him, now you don't. But he sees you.

Posters got Jimmy's face on them too, in extreme foreground, a computer rendering though it's a good rendering. He's real menacing-looking.

iii

Professor and Jimmy watch a report about a new type of activist on the block. Appear to be partly made up of *WAMN*. *WAMN's* everywhere there's a potential for mayhem. Any port in the radical storm... Groups have been protesting outside various Government buildings all over Amerika. Key to their agenda is the ability to utilize Jimmy's powers to ease the mundanity of their lives. Real selfish assholes.

"Why shouldn't The Teleporter serve me? What-a-ya mean because I'm a selfish asshole? Fine, then The Teleporter should serve people in vulnerable groups... Serve em everything I want... To me. Then I'LL help the vulnerable groups. Yeah... that's it. That's the trick! The Teleporter needs to pay his fair share!"

"Why should I... Why should a person in a vulnerable group have to drive forty-five minutes to work every day both ways? The Teleporter needs to pay his fair share!"

"I... That is... People in vulnerable groups could work from home and no one'd ever know. Just beam me... I mean people in vulnerable groups into an empty toilet stall or something, then I'll punch in... Whataya mean 'is that a euphemism?'... Then I'll punch in and he'll just beam me right back home. The Teleporter needs to pay his fair share!"

"Won't somebody please think of the adult's we treat like children! The Teleporter needs to pay his fair share!"

"Look, all I'm sayin is, my ex-wife... I mean people in vulnerable groups' ex-wives have no right to that Vette. We just beam into her garage and beam it out. Lickety-split. The Teleporter needs to pay his fair share!"

"What-a-ya mean 'vulnerable group' is a nonsensical term?"

"Sunken treasure! The Teleporter needs to salvage his fair share!"

"Ya know, I could... I could *just*—"
"Jimmy you'd be moving people all day long and they'd just keep piling on more demands for more of your services."
"But if they're vulnerable..."
"There's nobody vulnerable! That Cult's just using people society tends to sympathize with to fool you into thinking you're helping the downtrodden when you're really only serving those selfish cretins!"
"Right Doc."
The report continues. We're back on Generic Talking-Head yammering on,

But other of Adamowski's detractors aren't so embracing of his powers...

"Guy like that could be lurking anywhere... My house. My kids' rooms. Guy can just snatch them away. If I... I-I want whoever's got a gun to shoot him if they see him. Shoot him on sight. What? I don't care if there're legalities involved. Shoot. Him. Dead. What? I don't care if there are legalities even in me saying it. Kill him where you see him or it'll be your kids next!"

"I say we start a neighborhood watch and take care of ourselves. Teleporter wants to intervene in our neighborhood, guess what, we'll get your ass on trespassing. And please give us a reason to use 'self-defense'."

"This mother-fucker wants to use his 'Gifts' on me, he'll get a look at my Jose Canseco bat up his ass! Open yer eyes and yer buttcrack hole Jimmy!"

"We gotta keep watch of this."

"You think they'll mob up and come at me swinging Doc?"

"*Gouging* by the sound of things... Though I'm thinking less about the fearful and more about the selfish. These people say *fair share* like they could define either word. Fair share is a simple concept and these people don't *want* to understand it:

- You pay and they don't sell, that's not fair.
- You sell and they don't pay, that's not fair.

Everything else is fair in love and barter. It takes a real miscreant to have so much, contribute so little, snatch up whatever else is within arm's reach, then whine about too little falling *within* that reach. They could hurt you if the right people ever convinced them to turn militant."

Jimmy's initiating the first gesture of assent when...

When asked about the potential for terrorist actions, federal investigators had this to say...

It's McRae addressing the press but it's the fact Bart's standing behind him with a couple other agents that's got Jimmy so exercised. His look changes from serious to ridiculous. Real goof-off-ee goof-ball.

Lytrall's concerned.

Hero's bane.

iv

And then they go too far...

The press swarm The Widow. She's just trying to get to her car to leave her place of work.

Mrs. Renda! Mrs. Renda!

Your husband is said to be the first victim of The Teleporter! Do you want retribution?

Mrs. Renda! Mrs. Renda!

Some are saying if Adamowski hadn't taken your husband, rescue workers would have gotten to him in time.

Mrs. Renda! Mrs. Renda!

Is it true Adamowski has been paying you hush money to not blow the whistle on his attack on your husband?

Mrs. Renda! Mrs. Renda!

She stops in the crowd in order to speak. They stop along with her and their mics, cameras, and other recording devices are shoved in her face real presumptuous.

"J-Jimmy's a hero. He saved Bobby's life."

They erupt in interrogation again. They're trying for something incriminating again. They circle around her tighter.

But how can you be so sure?

Even so, the invasion of privacy!

"Please, let my husband rest in peace—"

But your and your husband's rights!

It goes on and on as the muckraker cyclone spins faster and tighter around the woman.

On and on until...

Ǝ/¬Ǝ

The pair are back in The Widow's kitchen. She looks none-too-pleased.

"Jimmy, you shouldn't have done that."

"I didn't want to make it worse for you. Robert's memory—"

"No!" she asserts. "No Jimmy. Never." She puts her palm to his cheek. "It's not me you need to worry about. What will those vultures do now that they know you're swooping in to steal their stories?" Jimmy feels selfish in his altruism here. He's done nothing to suit himself yet her concern for him, at a time like this, considering what they're doing to her and her family, tells him he can never do enough. "I can hear it now," she says, "*Jimmy Adamowski: enemy of the free press.* Oh Jimmy, you really shouldn't—"

Can never do enough but trying starts now?

"Yes. I should have." He reaches out to her. She takes his hands in hers. "Let me take this all. So you and Bobby can have peace, so everyone who could ever say, *I've crossed paths with Jimmy Adamowski* can be free of those jackals. They want their foils, someone to shine a light on The Teleporter, who better than the man himself?" He shakes those hands of hers he holds. "They won't bother you again."

v

He leans into the podium. A nest of microphones look like fingers trying to tickle at his chin.

It's a large facility in which he speaks. Oddly enough, it's the Kairn Center Concert Hall. He didn't choose it. Maybe it's choosing him? Like the hotel in *The Shining* or something?

He speaks,

"I would like to read a prepared statement if I may, and then I will try to answer as many of your questions as I can." He jostles some papers. "My name is Jimmy Adamowski and I am The Teleporter. If you will permit me to demonstrate..."

¬Ǝ

He's vanished from where he speaks. They're some gasps.

A door opens left of the stage and Jimmy walks in. He returns to the podium and returns to his statement.

"I am indeed The Teleporter. In addition to possessing the ability to move myself distances great and small instantaneously, I can move objects other than myself—potentially massive in size—those same distances. In addition to teleportation, I have an ability come to be called *The Gift*. The Gift allows me to see and hear anywhere I've been or know the location of. This latter ability seems to be of greatest concern to most. I understand your apprehensions. I wish to be absolutely transparent and I wish to allay your concerns.

"Understand two things, the limits of my powers *per se* and the limits I impose on my powers for my scruples. As for the former, I can't watch you if I don't know where you are. I'm neither omnipotent nor omniscient. I can't watch you in your sleep as I can't see in the dark nor manipulate your environment to turn on the lights. I can only observe what you are able to observe. Even less, since I can't smell or touch.

"That may not seem like much solace. However, understand, I only watch or teleport people without permission if it's to protect the innocent who they're hurting. These are the aforementioned *imposed* limitations.

"I feel as though things can be made clearer if I just move on to answering your questions. So, if there are—"

You said you only teleport victimizers, shouts a reporter. *But you save people's lives all the time, victim of an aggressor or not.*

"Not without their permission."

Why should we believe you when you say you're not watching us? asks another of the reporters.

"Nobody's watching you, you're cable news." A bit of scattered laughter. A lot of resentment. "In all due honesty, I don't watch you, in the main, because you're not that interesting. You're not that interesting when you're not getting in the way of everyday people just trying to live their lives. However, now that this suits your gossip-mongering, it seems getting in the way of everyday people's all you do. And that meddling, ladies and gentlemen, that's my line. Many of you, many in this room today, have crossed it."

But the public has a right to know—

"I'm going to stop you right there. Argue the ethics of your profession all you want, you won't make a successful case to sustain a hypocrisy for yourselves will you? Whatever you think you're entitled to do to others to get your story I'll do to you by half. Whatever you think you're entitled to by virtue of your profession we are all entitled to by the same right. If you don't like that, you should hate yourselves. Hate this:" He taps at the tips of the microphones at his chin. "That's my line: get in the way of the people just trying to live their lives and that's when I'll be watching you. Watch them, I watch you. I think that's fair."

But you watch elected officials...

"And criminals and terrorists," Jimmy adds. "Just like I said, I watch those who disrupt the lives of others."

Is that another joke?

"I wish—"

Then...

"Hey, Teleporter!"

A cameraman who turns out to be no cameraman at all pulls a handgun from the cassette slot of his camera.

"Gift this!"

He points it at Jimmy and...

BANG!

BEEP! BEEP!

vi

"This is the kind of behavior you get when people are allowed to go around spouting violent rhetoric all the time..."

"Ya ask me, I think The Teleporter paid the guy to shoot at him. To get our sympathies."

Lytrall mutes the video monitor. Turns to Jimmy. "This is getting worse and worse."

"At least they'll come to me now Doc, not... not... *Nahhhh...*"

But Jimmy can't get the point across. Can't cuz he's looking at the muted video monitor over The Professor's shoulder. Looking ridiculously...

Hero's bane.

"Yes, the women in your life Jimmy." Lytrall doesn't have to turn to know Bart's featured in the news Jimmy's watching—can tell by Jimmy's doof-in-the-face. "Hero's bane Jimmy. You have people out to get you and they know they can't touch you. So they'll get to you by getting to Agent Bartholomew."

"*Already have...*" Jimmy says it like he's swooning.

"Jimmy!" Lytrall turns off the monitor.

"Hey!"

"You hearing me? They'll come after her."

"Already have! Feds all over already know we worked together. Far as they're concerned, she betrayed me and now it's complicated."

"*It's complicated?* You sound like a thirty-seven-year-old divorcee running to the internet after a one night stand!"

"She just provides me with information from time to time."

"You're infatuated with her."

"Am not!"

"Are too. And you have more than just bureaucrats and the press to worry about now. That gunman's proven that. Your enemies will figure it out and use her and they'll figure it real easy because you're infatuated with her."

"I'm n—"

"Humor me then Jimmy." Lytrall takes out his phone. "Gift yourself a look at her right now."

"Come on..."

"You come on."

"Fine."

Eyes close.

FLASH!

Eyes open to a picture of Jimmy's stupid face.

"Look at that stupid face!" Prof takes out his fob. He pushes the button and a four-by-four grid of pictures appears where that news report was streaming. Pictures are of Jimmy making the same dopy face. "Those are just yesterday's," Lytrall says. "And I only spent a total of eighty-five minutes with you."

"My god, is that what I look like?"

"You better get a handle on this."

"She can take care of any whacko with a VCR gun."

"Custy?"

"Far as he knows, she betrayed me. On the outs."

"When those bots were in you they tracked you to her place. Twice."

"Forgot about that…"

"And he knows about her role in reacquiring that pack of yours."

"That too…"

"Any time the two of you interact it's like you can't help betraying yourselves to the feds. It's like you leave finger-prints all over each other… Get that look off your face!"

'What do I do?"

"First and foremost, get that damn look off your face! Now get control of its cause. Get back into the meditation. Temple's a good place to be these days anyway. Anyone who wants you bad enough finds out about that hold she has on you, they'll snatch her up in a second. And she can't just teleport away." Jimmy's shaking his head. Lytrall reminds, "They got her once. They got her once and they knew how much of a hold she had on you then. They find out every-thing's forgiven and you're swooning all the more—despite her betrayal—they'll know the leverage is all the stronger. They *got* her once." Heart on Jimmy's sleeve sinks a little. Prof catches. He puts a hand on protégé's shoulder. "But know this, you can protect her. *We* can protect her. But you have to bring her in."

"Here?"

"No. They can't know about me either. And, if she knows you, and I know you, then if she knows me, then they can get to any one of us through any one of us. Transitivity. Bring her in on the scheme's all. Our circle of tricks. You go get stoic, then make her the offer."

Jimmy tilts his head. "Right doc."

"And I'll lay low right here."

"When have you ever not?"

"I'm going to lay low here *with* impunity."

"But you're invulnerable."

"Yeah, so let's tell the whole world about it? *Toll Lytrall needs to pay his fair share!*"

"Right... Hey Doc, you never asked if I could trust her even after what she did. Come to think of it, ya never questioned her intentions a second."

"No. I didn't."

20

THE FED WHO CAME
IN FROM THE COLD

Bart reaches for her key. Just getting home. A note's taped to her door. Note reads,

'∃?'

She takes out her phone, turns on the FatButt™ app. Jimmy's pulse rate is in the normal range though falling. Falling fast.

She looks up at nothing. Gestures in the affirmative.

∃

"Thanks for checking first," she smiles.

"No prob."

He's wearing a ball cap and he's back to favoring a beard. It's near-half ZZ Topped and he only yesterday learned of a world filled with *Kill-Jimmys* and *Gimme-Jimmys* and all the other greedy White&Contrite™—and White&Contrite™ adjacent—types lurking in the dark recesses of the urban. Places like universities and modern art museums.

Bart turns back to the door. Starts jostling with the lock. Then...

"Oh damnit!"

"What is it?" he asks trying to peek around her to see.

"It's this damn deadbolt," she says over her shoulder. "Been sticking for months and I'm pretty sure I just stripped the cylinder."

"Mind if I give it a try?"

"Have at it." She backs away waving her hands in a *there-it-is* motion at the key in the keyhole.

"No, I meant..." He taps the note on the door.

"Oh!" Bart chuckles. "Go right ahead."

¬∃

She can hear the cylinder turning and the deadbolt go *CLICK!*

Door opens. Jimmy's all abeam. "Come on in!" He swoops his arm inward. "Don't mind the mess."

She smacks him on the shoulder as he lets himself further into her place. She smiles but he can't see it. Heart rate's normal.

"Ha! You're worried about me?" she laughs. "You should be worried about *you* Santa Claus." She gestures like she's going to give a tug on his beard *only* to toss her head back and scoff more. "I saw three of those *he can see you* posters on my way into work yesterday. Know how many I saw today?"

"How many?"

"Don't know. There were so many *Jimmy* protestors outside our branch office I had to work from a satellite."

"Brats wanting my imports and exports, not wanting to tithe for it, might get Customs off my back and onto theirs."

She leans forward in her chair. Footrest is tucked in so the chair rocks as she leans. Looks serious at Jimmy a second. Then... "Remember in Jaws? How Mrs. Kintner put out that three-thousand dollar bounty on the shark and all those carpetbaggers swarmed to Amity Island to collect it?"

"Yeah."

"Did the locals just hang it up and stop fishing? Did Brody go after either the locals or those carpetbagger poachers for trying? Or, did he just fish right along with em?"

"You think Custy's Brody?"

"No."

"Quint?"

"No."

"The president?"

"Do I think Custy's the president?"

"No, is The Prez Quint."

She frowns.

"Ben Gardner?"

"Jimmy, it doesn't matter who anyone is. What matters is, people with an all-consuming obsession don't just give up on the object of that obsession because there's competition. They don't give up pursuing that object because there're similarly appealing quarry all around all a sudden. They up the ante. They go after everybody and they go to extremes. That's *my* inference." Jimmy tips his head like he's trying to see over glasses not worn. Bart explains, "My contact at Customs went dark but that doesn't mean you're off the hook. Quite the opposite. There are just far more serious consequences for getting caught leaking Jimmy details. Custy's escalating things. *My* inference again."

"Well darn..."

"*Well* indeed," she says, letting her words linger a little in a reckoning. "They want you not me. Can't get to you through me either. Fool you twice..."

"It's different now."

"How?"

"There's a... An... A more intense drive... In me..."

But Bart ain't no dummy. Ain't blind either. She sees on the phone on her lap that Jimmy's heart rate's over a hundred. "You mean you like me you really like me?"

"I wouldn't put it that way."

"How would you describe it then?"

"Oh you described it just fine. I just wouldn't describe it in those words. You don't got the perm for it."

"Ha! Ass! I'm not upending my life on the off chance someone divines a list of your favorite people. I carry a gun."

"Carry a stubbornness too."

"You sound like my mom."

"And dad don't agree?"

"Gets it the same from my mom. And she's not wrong and he's no hypocrite."

Jimmy smiles a fading smile at this like maybe he won't let himself get too comfortable in this setting. "Look," he reinitiates. "I'm not asking you to go into hiding. Just let me help you defuse the situation sufficiently so serious precautions will be unnecessary. Let's take it off the table."

"What do you have in mind?"

ii

It's McRae's office. Bart's made him a proposition and he's on the warpath.

"You just wanna give these half-children everything they ask for?"

"What they *say* they want—"

"Oh that'll definitely put a smile on their faces, only there's one problem agent! One missing piece of the puzzle!

They want their own personal drudge in your friend Adamowski and nobody's seen him in weeks!"

Ǝ

Jimmy's teleported into the chair next to Bart. McRae doesn't miss a beat. "And *you* mother-fucker..." Says it like Jimmy's been in the room all along. "I'd love to have *words* with you but this is agency business."

"I asked him to join us boss."

"Oh, so you just took it upon yourself to not even do my job but *not even* the job of the goddamn Director?" He turns to Jimmy. "And speaking of jobs ya little shit, you're doing a real good job stirring up those spoiled little half-assholes."

Jimmy's counting on his fingers. Half-children, half-assholes makes a whole alright... "Half-holes?"

McRae keeps on at Jimmy like the math ain't nothing. "Lot of greedy lazy people exploiting a lot of poor struggling people to get to you. Thinkin you owe them. Making our lives a living hell."

"They're not terrorists. Yet. What business are they of yours?"

"That's the fuckin problem magic man. Hardest people in the world to police are those we're not allowed to."

"Don't let anyone ever tell you you ain't Eff-Bee-Eye."

"You know what I mean! It's a critical mass of em just a cunt's tooth away from terrorism, cultism, whateverism and we can't do a damn thing!"

"I can."

"Alright, just what do you have in mind convict?"

"I'm no convict."

"Not a jury in the world say otherwise I get you to sit still to take your medicine. What the hell do you have in mind!"

"We give em what they want. Exactly what they say they want."

"What Jimmy means, boss, is give them *exactly* what they say they want."

"Oh I get it! Little Jimmy Robin Hood is gonna ease the burden of the downtrodden. One tiny little thing though. Giving these protestors what they demand means giving a world of people *but* them what they need. Only gonna piss em off more!"

"Give them credit then. Give the babies a bottle of something just as sweet."

"Sweeter," Jimmy adds.

"Give them a high they won't believe. Where the only thing they'll know for sure is if they ask for even a single thing more, the good goes to dust and so does their credit. Make them drunk on their own prestige."

McRae leans back grinning like he's still mad as hell yet knows a learning lesson when he sees it. But there's just one piece missing as he likes to say... "I hear you Bartholomew, but there's just one piece missing." He points at Jimmy. "Why's this joker even need the help of the Eff-Bee-Eye? Never did before."

"To keep all things fair in the world."

"Well I'll just wave my magic wand!"

"Wave it at *Natural Resources* then boss. Get Jimmy a list of Amerikans on social assistance while you're at it."

iii

A Charitable Montage...

A stock boy looks like *this is gonna be his ass* as he paces his way along the cereal aisle. Empty. Every shelf devoid of any kind of breakfast good. He stocked them himself just a half an hour ago! On he trudges up that linoleum swath, those empty shelves riding up his peripherals vanishing-point style. But... What's that? Is that a bale of Shredded Wheat up there? He moves faster to it.

It's not Shredded Wheat. It's not even off-brand. It's raw gold but he doesn't know that. It's not cereal that's for sure. He strains to pick it up like it's a medicine ball stuffed into a softball.

"What the hell is this?"

Cut to:

Children in a small if homey apartment are munching on some Cap n' Crunch, happy as anything. Behind them is a row of cereal boxes on the counter with all and only the sugary ones with tops torn open.

Cut to:

Groceries are disappearing off of shelves all over Amerika. Always replaced with gold, platinum, silver. Diamonds, rubies, sapphires.

Countertops all over Amerika are filling up with the freshest and healthiest of foods—and some of the good stuff too.

Cut to:

Countertops overflowing with the juiciest San Marzano tomatoes you've ever seen, while...

Tomato Farmer and Hand are jumping for joy though not as high as usual as the fortunes in their pockets ain't light.

Cut to:

A mother enters her kitchen holding her baby in her arms. Baby's hungry and the bottle's empty. She drops the empty bottle into the sink. She's exasperated. The mother cries.

She opens her cupboard like this isn't the tenth time this morning she's fooled herself she can just will away empty shelves with her mind.

You do this when you struggle.

Only this time, it works.

Cupboard's stocked full of formula. Mother slams the cupboard door then slowly pulls it open again. Her eyes are closed. She pops them open. Formula's still there. The mother cries.

Cut to:

One of the few senators to not flee politics in fear enters his office. There's a note on his desk. Note reads,

You didn't resign so the people still have faith in you. Getting out of their way is the

only way to repay them. Don't, and I'll be back to do more 'lobbying'!

 Yours,
 Jimmy

Senator picks up the phone.

Cut to:

A young man in torn bib overalls stands at the back aisle of a corner convenience store. Overalls aren't dirty just torn. Either he's worked in them though not for long—and not for a while—or he's always just used them to keep warm. He reaches out for some bourbon in a plastic twenty-six-ounce bottle. Label has a bird on it as so many do.

As he's pulling it off the shelf...

Ǝ/¬Ǝ

He has a copy of *Penultimate Draft* in his hand—voucher card actually. Little note attached to the voucher says 'write it'. Bottle's been put back on the shelf for him. Young man puts the voucher in his pocket and re-reaches for the bottle...

Ǝ/¬Ǝ

It's a MacBook Pro this time.

 No excuses.

Re-re-reaches...

Ǝ/¬Ǝ

It's a smartphone and card with phone pin and QR pattern. Man unlocks the phone and scans the pattern. An investment account has been started in his name. It's a portfolio worth one million dollars in equity.

Consider it something like a genius grant.

Re-re-re-reaches...
A bottle of champagne.

Don't drink to feel better. Drink to feel even better. Drink when you have a reason to.

Young man looks a little exasperated. In a good way. He's given up on giving up.

Cut to:
It's the news.

Despite the price of gold and silver plummeting, the economy has never been stronger. Analysts are chalking this up to the recent ratification of the Twenty-Eighth Amendment, legislation that guarantees: <u>should a relationship of any kind, of any number of participants, be legal when money DOESN'T change hands (even de facto legal), then there can be no law restricting this relationship when money DOES change hands</u>. Analysts say these new protections are what account for the recent—rapid—expansion in the entrepreneurial sector.

Critics fear the amendment will 'make every car a taxi, every kitchen a restaurant, and every bedroom a brothel.' while supporters are hopeful the amendment will 'make every car a

*taxi, every kitchen a restaurant, and every bedroom a brothel.'
Not surprisingly, the dividing line between detractor and
supporter has elected officials, Corporations, Unions, and their
collective lobbyists on one side, and talented people on the
other.*

*In other financial news, the drop in prices of precious metals
doesn't seem to be a cause for concern for investors as they've set
their sights on a different commodity: fine art. The source of
these recently auctioned paintings: various drug cartels around
the globe. Channel Number Five News had a chance to speak
with a cartel representative about the recent rash of 'thefts'. He
had this to say,*

It's a man disguised by silhouette and a digitally altered
voice that makes him sound like Elizabeth Holmes.

"I mean, we were just so psyched to be ported you know."

Cut to:
Another portfolio.

Build it.

Cut to:
Another portfolio.

Paint it.

Cut to:

Another portfolio.

Dance it.

Cut to:

Another portfolio.

Time for that proof of concept.

Cut to:

Another portfolio.

Time for that grand opening.

Cut to:

Buy. Buy. Buy. Sell. Sell. Sell. Dream. Dream. Dream.

Cut to:

It's the news again.

With record employment and minimal commutes, Amerika has truly turned a corner. Although, not all agree it's the 'new morn-

ing' economists are predicting...

"People in vulnerable groups are not helped by more freedom, opportunities, and wealth. They're helped by forced adherence to my... THEIR values!"

"Capitalism is slavery! What? I don't care about record happiness and upward mobility, what about environmental justice? What? I don't care if upward mobility necessitates efficiency and that necessitates minimizing pollutants... I just wanted to work from home!"

"No, I don't think I'm being essentialist by calling people who are no longer vulnerable 'vulnerable'. Because I don't call people 'vulnerable'. I call them 'people in vulnerable groups'. I don't give humans human properties, I give those properties to nonhuman things like groups. What? Of course it's dehumanizing, that's the whole point of collectivism, which is my primary means of foisting my values onto others! For the greater good! Whatever that is!"

"I just wanted to work from home!"

"Whahhhh!"

"Death to Jimmy Adamowski!"

End of montage

iv

"Well that didn't work exactly the way I said it wouldn't work convict! Now the Gimme-Jimmys and the Kill-Jimmys have joined forces. These people don't just want prestige. They want goods and services for free, forever, while they revel in that prestige. And they want those services rendered by The Teleporter!"

"I'm not a convict."

21

DELIVERY

A figure stands in a wood backlit by torchlight. We can't see his face, yet we know it's a man as he speaks and from him issues a man's voice. The torches behind cast his shadow in our direction. They're held in the hands of masked men and women forming a crescent. They appear well-disciplined as though their primary function is to serve this figure. If it's one torch for one disciple it's a multitude too great to subitize—not by the quick glimpses we're given anyway. There are too many to account for in-whole but it can be seen of any smaller subset at once, they're all masked and in dark shawls.

"I know better than anyone of his menace." This, the figure issues to an even greater multitude at his front. Those of the front possess no torches and so appear only as a mass of shadow streaked periodically by the figure's backlight. They listen in silence. He speaks as though coaxing. "I know better than anyone, given my time to seek my answers— time thrust on me—what truly constitutes him, so what he is truly capable of. It's too late for me though not for you to bask in him and I do say *bask* as there is more to take than any have thus far taken. Far more to take than any one of you alone could know. Without my guidance to give—which you may now receive—you could never have known. No longer. Rejoice!" The multitude he implores are disciples too? Would-be disciples? The little less of the dark obscuring them, because torches flicker at their front unlike at their leader's back, reveal no masks. "Those of you before me, first understand: yours is now the group-vulnerable!" The crowd would cheer but they're still a little lethargic from a life of being them... "You've always given of yourselves, in your self-aggrandizing slogans of yourselves, and he's only ever taken. Taken from you! He's deprived you of his gifts at every pass, yes, but he's taken from you what is more precious. He's deprived you of your foils.

"By making their lives this *better,* as so many of the misguided put it, you've been doubly deprived. *Better! Better! Better*: simply the disastrous notion that self-determination, freedom, opportunity, peace, harmony, mutual-earned-respect and so many more of these bigotries determine so much more beneficial a social function! How is this *better* than a tiny handful of people like yourselves benefitting disproportionately *while* changing nothing *while* patting yourselves on the back for your lofty rhetoric *while* fooling no one but yourselves *while* attempting to vilify and conde-scend your way to a world where none of the countless who merit more than you collect on this merit for the hopeless-ness you've instilled in them or fear of the world's revile-ments *while* you do all this solely to free yourselves of any challenge to your having just a little bit more? More and More!

"He took all this from you.

"More.

"He took from you your equally precious group-level

statistics. What informs those *more* capable than you of their being *less* capable than you. What determines you and only you—their benevolent ally—the ordained who ought decide their best interests for them! The ordained who ought *enforce* these best interests! He took from you your audacity to insist to your betters, in all your cock-sure presumption, *you're of an oppressed class.* He took from you your temerity, when told, *but I make three hundred thousand dollars a year,* to follow up with the absurd proposition, *but you really only make forty-five thousand dollars a year because that's the group average and that's the group you're in.* My desperate, defeated, true-believers, he even took from you the gall to walk away from all the stupidity you've spewed before your betters *before* they can say to you, *that's not how averages work!*

"You can't say *Stop! We're talking about people at a group level!* because that level is now itself one of affluence! He stole from you your only manipulation left and now you look upon me pathetic and neutered... However, there is still a hope!

"Those of you before me who want him dead are right to fear him though wrong to devalue him to the extent that his death is preferable to his life *only* in servitude. Those of you before me who desire his servitude are right to value him as you do though wrong to wish to waste his talents on such trivialities.

"It's too late for me, what with my being his *first* ever and *worst* ever victim..."

The use of *victim* activates the torch-bearing disciples. They move to narrow the ends of their crescent to form a near-closed circle with our demagogue at the center. The near-closing illuminates the figure just enough to see... It's Figurace!

"...It's too late for me," Figurace continues. "As I was his first, I had no one like me to guide me to the truth of the love I ought have embraced, never hate. It's too late for me as I became so quickly mired in a hatred of *The Man Who Walks Without Step*. I hold nothing but animus now, yes, though I can guide *you* to a love of him necessary to bask in him. I am your best guide as I know him yet I do not, cannot, know the same love you seek *but* that blinds in its seeking *and so* will keep you, not me, out of reach. I can reach but not touch. You can touch but not reach. Let me, in my hate, reach for you. If you are ready to truly bask in The Man Who Walks Without Step, to see him pay his fair share, give yourselves over to my teachings, no matter the mystery in them.

"You will be set free. You will finally have what you desire most. You will finally be able to work from home.

"If you are not ready, you may leave at any time as soon as you've been killed."

The leader and his masked disciples observe the crowd. None move.

"Wonderful!"

Figurace claps his hands together then motions to his torch bearers. They break into pairs. One of each pair takes the torch of the other to light the other's way. The torchless begin distributing dark hooded shawls and black cloth masks to the new recruits.

"After our sacrifice," Figurace says, "they will deliver him on a platter!"

ii

The pair go over all documents on the *Jimmy Cult* McRae was willing to provide. They do this at Bart's place.

They both sit crisscross on her living room rug, stack of papers between them.

"Cult's been quiet for a month," Bart says looking at a recent stack of hot sheets from various precincts around Amerika East.

"That's good."

"Not quiet from the Kool-Aid quiet."

"That's bad." He strokes at his beard like maybe he'll divine his enemies' intentions by the gesture.

Bart tilts her head at this. "Speaking of *months*. Your beard's gotta be a month's longer than yesterday. How much time are you spending in that limbo?"

"I can most easily quiet my mind in there. Speaking of quiet, the—"

"Wait!" She stops him. "You can't just segue to a topic you pulled out of your butt just so you can segue to it. It has to arise naturally in the conversation! What you just did's a cheat and, speaking of cheating, stop cheating!"

"*Oooh!*" He winces. Starts twisting and turning like he's trying to reach behind himself.

"What is it?"

"My back!" She looks on in concern when... "Speaking of *my back*, get the hell off it!" She swats him. "What does *quiet* mean for these cultists?" He re-inquires.

"Hell if I know. When I knew these assholes they were terrorists for hire. Can you Gift them?"

"Needle in a haystack. I have a friend who might be able to track them down. Guy sees more than I can sometimes."

"I don't believe it."

"I'd prove it to you, but he's real secretive about methods."

"No, I meant I don't believe you when you say you have friends." She tilts her head, simpers.

"I have you…" He wishes he hadn't said that.

Bart's simper turns to an awkward smile. Significant of the question: *how receptive ought I be to this?* Her hand moves the slightest bit toward his when…

"Yer close enough!" He adds this levity trying to defuse the tension. He wishes he hadn't done that even more.

She swats him playfully again. "Lunch time," she says, insistent.

He agrees. "What are you in the mood for?"

"Boston Royal Pizza."

Jimmy's eyes roll up and to the left at this—at a contemplative loss.

"Dad," Bart begins her explanation. "Dad used to take my sister, mom, and me there all the time."

"I'll go. What do you want?"

"Can't. Not a single one left in Amerika. Not a single one in all the world except for Miami Florida, Old America."

"I'll go. What do you want?"

She chuckles. "Forget who I'm talking to sometimes. I want their namesake, *The Boston Royal.*"

¬ℶ

He's ducked out, but…

ℶ

"They don't deliver do they?" She throws a pillow at him. "That's not why they're called *throw* pillows," he says though shouldn't've. She groans. "A walk to the door'd do me great for some exercise," he tries again though shouldn't've,

She throws another pillow.

¬ℶ

Goes right through him.

Ⅎ

He's back. Thirty minutes or less. He's got a stack of pizzas gotta be a dozen high.

"What!"

"I forgot your order. Was already halfway there..."

"And what is *halfway* to the blink of an eye?"

"Not the distance I go that matters only how far. Thought it best to get one of everything." He sets the stack of boxes on the coffee table next to the *rug office*. Bart rises.

There's *just* enough incredulity in her as she moves to those pizzas. "You remembered to go to the only location in the world of a *Boston Royal Pizza* yet forgot I wanted *The Boston Royal* Pizza? Name didn't jog your memory?"

"I'm sure it's in there somewhere," he assures as she flips the lid of the top box. She beams at the contents. He enjoys this. "Oh look! The very first one!"

She beams at *him*.

They've gorged themselves almost to the point of a Roman incident. They lie on the living room rug now, papers on the couch. They lie in opposite directions though their solar plexi are in alignment. Elbow to elbow is another way of putting it.

"Why are we lying this way?"

"Their food kinda just makes you lie where you fall."

"No, I mean why are we lying this way when we have a feed lot's worth of dairy moving through our colons..."

"I'm going to pretend you didn't say that, ladies man."

"I'm going to pretend I wasn't dead serious..."

She snorts. Sits herself up on her elbow. Looks at this mystery weirdo with all due intrigue.

"Jimmy Adamowski?"

"Yeah?" he obliges as he props himself up as well.

"Tell me your life's story." She says this serious, tongue in cheek, and coy all at the same time. Jimmy looks somber, somber, and somber all at the same time. Bart gets what she's caused. "I'm sorry..."

"No no," he says. "I just... I don't really have one."

"Everyone has a life's story."

"Not me. I've always just sort of wandered around. Resources came easy enough, until they didn't, then I'd just lay low. Then wander again. Had some personal stuff that took me too long to deal with but I've handled it... I think. That's it really. Life just sorta started into the second act."

"There's gotta be more to it than that." She stares obliquely at him just a second. Appears a helpful question's incoming. "What's your first memory?"

"First memory?"

"Yeah, or an early one, like one of my first memories is of watching *Ghostbusters* on our TV using this strange device my dad brought home. A VCR."

Jimmy chuckles. Closes his eyes. He's not Gifting.

It's a flash of a three-month-old fetus in an amber fluid-filled pouch. The child's about the size of a chicken's egg. Human though, with a little face and everything. The fetus is attached to the amber pouch via a standard umbilical cord. Attached to the pouch are synthetic tubules. Looks like surgical tubing but it's almost certainly something more sophisticated. Tubules feed the amber placenta. All of this is itself suspended in a secondary bladder of unknown constitution.

Another flash! Child's eight months old now. All materials surrounding the infant have increased in size proportionally. Almost as though naturally, without any human intervention. Like the synthetic placenta is growing.

A final flash! My god!

Jimmy's come full-grown! He wrestles in the fluid of that amber pouch, itself grown to accommodate him. He bursts out of what had held him, spilling the Virtual Amniotic Fluid from what was his home. He fights out of the secondary bladder now. It's so much stronger though his panic—his first-ever emotion—drives him. Bladder tears.

He tumbles out and across the laboratory floor as lights flood him. Scream at him. He blinks profusely. Everything is a blur.

Security and some techs have rushed in, immediately halted and overtaken by what their expressions suggest is a real grotesquery.

Jimmy hears the commotion—can barely see. He looks around frantic nonetheless. He senses no escape. Makes out the globular sagging outline of the burst dual chamber. He crawls for it, grabs for home but a utility cart sits between. He's reached through the middle tier containing a wireframe basket. He feels at it, latches onto the contents within. **It's a file folder. Says *J. Adamowski* but he can't read it just yet, not with his eyes in their present condition.** He intuits this nonetheless. He holds it to his chest feeling some strange comfort.

The guards and techs have lined the side of the room from which they entered. They block the exit.

One of the guards inches forward, reaches down for the torn umbilical cord hanging from Jimmy's belly.

Don't touch him! shouts a tech.

Jimmy crawls to the corner, leans against it, shaking. He

lets the amniotic fluid take him sliding into fetal position. He lays shivering as the lab employees approach. He feels a strange sinking feeling like of something pending. Something he can't control. Something he can hone?

He decides to give in to what's coming...

¬∃

"That was it," he says. "My first memory, and to this day, the clearest."

The pair are still on the floor, only lying facing the same direction now. They look up at the ceiling.

"When did this 'birth' take place?" Bart asks.

"A dozen years ago."

"So..." She doesn't want to say it considering the gravity of Jimmy's admission though the inference has been drawn and the urge has overtaken her... "...You're twelve!"

"I had the body and mind of a full-grown man—"

"Full grown man who hadn't gone through puberty."

"I told you I was fully grown!"

"So when did you go through puberty?"

"I didn't have to—"

"Ha!"

"Look," he says insistently. "I've probably lived three years at least in that limbo so—"

"So you're not even old enough to drive!" She laughs. He tugs at his beard at her. "Peach fuzz!" she rebuts.

"I'm going to stop now."

"I'm sorry."

But...

Her levity has put him at ease. She's put him at ease. Feels like passage, huh? The last piece of the puzzle? He no longer need fear sending himself to oblivion or hurting the people he moves. That's all gone. He need only seek a calm absent but-for his origins? The knowledge is illusive, always has been, though this fact causes him apprehension now, *not* pain. *Never* pain. Slight apprehension, if anything at all.

"Maybe peace..." she says having watched agitation turn to stillness to this apprehension, "Maybe peace, Jimmy, is attainable though it's a process *not* the flipping of a switch? You're free of so much only now you want that knowledge. Your curiosity isn't torture though? Is it?"

He shakes his head. Stillness returns. He closes his eyes.

"You're more at peace now than you've ever been yet you've a little further to go?"

He sleeps.

iii

Her phone alarm is going off. She reaches for it across Jimmy like the gesture's the most natural thing in the world. She realizes she's been asleep in his arms the better of the afternoon. Like the most natural thing in the world. Did he notice? Did he initiate the embrace?

She taps at her phone, having forgotten why the alarm's even...

"Damn!"

"What is it?" he says popping awake.

"I have to meet my grandma in ten minutes and you tele-ported me here from work."

"I'll take you." He reaches his hands out as though they'll leave as they came.

She shakes her head. "Can't, I have to drive her to her appointments."

"How old's your grandma?"

"Ninety-two."

"I'll drive you two."

Bart's intrigued by this. And not just at Jimmy's helpful insistence. "No teleporting?"

"She's ninety-two Bart."

"Right." Another realization. "You have a car?"

"*That* I can teleport over." A little suspicion. He gets it. "*Yours.* I'll beam it right to your parking spot. Just give me the all-clear." He stands up and reaches out to Bart to give her a lift before the lift.

She rises, trying her best to get her bearings after a gorge and a nap that just didn't cut it. They move for the door.

A bit of bearing now, a warmth. The pizza? "Jimmy?"

"Yeah?"

"You don't just help people when it's *easy* do you?"

"This is easy." He says this as effortlessly as he leaves to go get grandma.

She smiles. She feels warmer. The pizza?

Another realization...

"Jimmy!" she calls after him. "Any chance you can do something about that gnarly beard? She's ninety-two!"

22

BAND-AID SOLUTION

OOM!

Their first bomb went off in a men's room in a shopping mall. We could make a joke about bombs worse than that going off in there all the time but that wouldn't be true because nobody other than Jimmy's been *using* those bathrooms and he has the lab and the temple now.

To work in!

—He still uses the desert for the other—

Needless to say, no one was hurt.

The location of the bombing wasn't an accident and the cultists promised a second would go off in a much more populated area. A park they said. Or an airport. Or an arena. Or an office space of a business with a director dumb enough to get himself roped into a twenty-five-year lease. He'd have everybody who works for him *sleep* in that office if he could. He'd have the traveling salesmen never leave that office if he could—less mileage that way. He'd have the people he fired punch in and wait for their unemployment checks while drinking before noon in that office if he could. He'd have the window washers wash the outside windows on the inside of that office if he could—if only those damn metaphysicians would hurry up and invent *the one-sided pane!* Gotta get his money's worth. Point is, the place will be full of innocent people *and* their director.

Jimmy-Cult's not dark anymore but they're still underground. Figurace's got them working like a fine-oiled machine. The vicious little middle-agers have promised to carry out acts of semi-predictable violence every two weeks for two months. Then it'll be no pattern, in perpetuity, if the federal government doesn't deliver Jimmy up *as slave* on Figgy's platter.

Since the demands involve shipping and delivery, naturally, US Customs has been tasked with the investigation.

Jimmy realizes the weight of the Cult's promise.

Lytrall realizes the weight of something else. "The easiest thing in the world for the government now would be to kill you the instant you're spotted and present your corpse to the Cult. To show them their actions are futile: *The Teleporter is dead. Your mission has failed.* Have you observed anything of the Fed's plans?"

"They've all taken to using that headgear. Can't hear a damn thing."

"You might want to swipe some files, if your ethic will allow it."

"Oh it will. Yet it's no good."

"Encryption? I might be able to break it."

"Not this. They read with some sort of specially calibrated eyewear, activated by continuous retina scan."

"By the time I unlock that, if I can unlock that, they'll have you."

"Yeah..."

"Well, at least Custy hasn't been given carte blanche to do whatever he has to to take you down..."

"Har har. Don't worry about Custy."

"I'm more worried about that gleam in your eye."

ii

"Custy's orders are for any federal agent to detain you on sight, alive or dead."

"And if you detain me alive? Then what?"

"Kill you so you can't just teleport away. That's my inference. Explicitly, we've all been issued tranquilizers." She shows Jimmy the thing in its holster. He looks at it like looking into a floodlight with the sun at its back. "What?" she asks, curious.

"Just making sure the safety's on."

She frowns. "Jimmy..."

There's a bit of pain in his expression. "What'd they say would happen if you refuse Custy's orders?"

"They *said* summary dismissal. What they'll actually do... You don't want to know."

"I do know. Saw you in that cage remember?" She reaches out to him. He flinches, recoils. "I'm going underground too," he adds. "As you agents like to say." She wilts a little at this, like something's slipping away. He fails to notice. "We can't meet here anymore. Custy only knows about us in a minimal capacity or he'd have pressed you. He finds out any more, he'll hurt you. We'll communicate the usual way."

She holds up her index finger and thumb near-pressed

together. "And I was so close to calling *this* our *usual way*." Pinching fingers become part of an open palm sweeping across her living room. "I'm almost starting to think you've stopped trusting me Jimmy..." Her voice breaks a little saying this.

He doesn't hesitate now. He reaches out to her. He pulls her toward him and embraces her. She moves into this embrace the entire of its founding. No resistance. Like it's the most natural progression in the world. He holds her head to his chest a second then pulls back, caressing her cheek. He's looking her in the eyes, reassuring her.

She leans back in. Kisses him. Plants a serious deep one on him like she means it.

There's no affect in him. He's buried stronger senti-ments... He pushes away. "No."

"Why?"

"I can't. It's wrong."

She's grasping for what that means, but what else could it be? "Because *I set you up*?" She scoffs this in that kind of irony that hides exasperation—desperation?

"Yes. Only, for what it set in motion *not* because there isn't a trust."

"But forgiveness?"

He bows in assent.

She's confused even more by this. He's forgiven her, then why? She doesn't get it. He came to her for *his* endearments after all. Or so he said. Is this some cruel trick? Retribution? "Then haven't I at least earned an answer? Why your reticence?"

"You hadn't. Not yet. Hadn't yet earned the trust required for this betrayal."

"*Hadn't? For This?*"

"I've taken an oath," he admits.

"An oath?"

"Of Priesthood."

"You're not a Priest?" Jimmy's silent. Bart gets *something*. "Those monks?" Jimmy's silent. "No! You're not!" She examines him a second like she's trying to see the holy in him. Then... "No you're not! You can't be that kinda goddamn Priest Jimmy, you're Polish!"

"Ukrainian."

"*Adamowski*'s Polish"

"My family assumed a Polish name when they fled persecution."

"You don't have a family!" But she stifles. Hates herself a little for her haste. "That's not what I meant." she reaches out.

He backs away again. "I have the story."

"You have a mother—"

"They see my teleportation as sacred. I'm a *reincarnative figure*."

"Reincarnative? Like a god?"

"Not a god. A messenger. An embodiment of the rebirth concept. The temple has one prophecy, the only temple that permits of such a thing. One temple of prophecies, one prophecy. *Three times a figure will emerge, able to choose his rebirth at will, in multitudes.* This is a symbol of a time of renewal. Three for all time. I'm number two. That comes with certain privileges and exceptions."

"Do you believe it?"

"There are stranger things."

A beat.

"You're not a goddamn Priest Jimmy! You're j-just... You've been using m—"

¬Ǝ

(Like pulling off a band-aid only what the hell's been healed?)

iii

Could be worse company but Lytrall's no Bart. Couldn't be much worse really as it's been near two weeks that he hasn't seen her beyond The Gift and it's been the same *near* two weeks he's been cloistered up with The Professor on his homestead.

They've certainly been getting on each others' nerves. But in better times who knows? Mentor and mentee on a beach somewhere and they'd be having a hell of a time? He'd want Bart there though. They're frustrated as that near-two-weeks also means the Jimmy-Cult is preparing to strike. They're running out of time.

Cult operates with expert secrecy. Needle in a bloody haystack. No footprint. Gotta be something but what? Not even The Professor's figured anything useful.

Jimmy's emptied his pack. Third time today. He's flipping through his photos of that little yellow house. Aim is to distract himself from all that's consuming him. However, a focus on *any* peace brings the focus around to *her* peace: the peace in his past that's only a reminder of her absence. Pure paradox. On he flips. He flips and he flips and he...

"What's with you and that pack?" Lytrall asks.

Jimmy frowns. Professor sneaking up on him like this was jarring but something else is eating at him too? "It's my only connection to my past. It's all I have of the beginning. My memory of escaping that lab."

"Lab?"

"I told ya already. My first memory is of escaping a laboratory doing some sort of experiment on me."

"Ha," Lytrall chuckles. "That's weird."

"Weird? That's my origin!"

"So?"

"So? It explains everything."

"Especially your *weird* fixation with what, fluids? Like the fluids in that big sack or something else that was a unique feature of that lab?"

"Water, mostly... How did you—"

"And let me guess, you carry with you some artifact you took from the laboratory you fled? Likely a *secret* laboratory? You took something that's enough of a clue of your origin you fixate on it? Not so telling it gives you any real answers or a starting point?"

"A file folder, with my name on it."

"And there's a bunch of pictures of a little yellow house and a sonogram of a baby at three months gestation."

Jimmy's staggered. "How do you know this?"

"Because that's not your file that was your mother's. Her case file. You were part of an experiment Jimmy. *Rapid gestation*. Intended to be a boutique service for parents who couldn't be bothered with the time required for nature to take its course. The sonogram's of you. The house is where they told your mother she'd live in return for her participation in the experiment."

"You were there?"

"I'm everywhere these grotesqueries take place. I was responsible for one myself. Got out of control. I try to stop them now. Call it penitence. Help the victims when I can't."

Jimmy stands. "Tell me everything!"

Lytrall sits. "Consider three questions Jimmy. *First*, I

know they lied to your mother about that house. How do I know? You were one of three Jimmy. Three. Then they pulled the plug. All died except you and all the mothers had those same photos in their files. They weren't all going to live together yet they were all promised the same little yellow house? They were lied to. *Second's* what was that lab doing anyway? Like I said: intending to suit wealthy couples with instant offspring. Grow an infant to term in little over a weekend. That's that sack you were in. It's called a VAC, *virtual amniotic chamber*. The first two died because they were harvested too early. Had to be three months old at a minimum."

"Harvested?"

"As awful as it sounds. For the conceptus to remain viable, from mother to VAC, it had to stay *in utero*. This could only be achieved via hysterectomy."

"Good Christ."

"Hence the promise of a home and a life... These women, your mother, they weren't just volunteering a baby, they were volunteering their motherhood.

"Lab thought they'd hit it with you Jimmy. Everything going to plan. You were viable, surviving, developing. You went from three months to seven—in gestation terms—in a day. Then came the night. You didn't stop at nine months as was the plan nor did the rate of development remain constant. You went from a seven-month-old to an adult in the span of that single night! You were something around a twenty-two-year-old in body and mind. A man as any other having lived a couple decades, only there were no memories. That was twelve years ago."

"What's the third question?"

"Jimmy..."

"The third!"

"Alright Jimmy, it's this: Who gives a good goddamn about the story of Jimmy The Teleporter? I know I don't."

Jimmy erupts. "This is important to me!"

Lytrall doesn't move. Looks straight ahead.

"Asshole!" Jimmy shouts in his ear. He backs away. "I always thought that *callous son of a bitch* side was just an act. Now I—"

"The real question, Jimmy, is your mother."

Jimmy shuts up.

"The real question's your mother but you know this. That's all that really matters and yet you consume yourself with a mystery that's no mystery at all. You're a miracle beyond the miracles under God's purview—the miracle of life—you're something in addition, something requiring a human touch and accident. There's no mystery in that. Nothing like you has ever been in nature so you're not natural. Short of God branching out, you were contrived. Where else but a lab? That's the answer to the story of how you came to be *Jimmy The Teleporter* and that's as trite a story as could be! The real question is: how'd you come to be God's little James? Jimmy before that lab?" Teleporter's still shut right the hell up. "You hide from the real question but you know this. Who is she? Is she alive or dead? Did she volunteer or were you ripped away from her? Now you know she volunteered and that only frightens you more because now you know this: if she volunteered did she just give you up or did she intend to raise you in that little house? What possible circumstances could have made her do what she did? Is she alive? Where is she? Did she love you? *Does* she love you? That's the last torture of Jimmy Adamowski." Mentor stands. He looks Jimmy right in Jimmy's eyes. Jimmy turns away, sits. Lytrall puts a hand on his shoulder. "It's your last. I know it. I've always known it.

I've always been at a loss with this... With what I can't just fix by flip of switch." Hand squeezes. Jimmy turns back to The Mentor like he's looking for something more. Something he doesn't deserve from the man reaching out, when... "We'll solve that mystery, Jimmy. In time."

"Yeah?"

"Yeah."

"You think she's alive?"

Lytrall considers this a second, smiles. "I do. She was very young when she had you. And Christ Jimmy, you're only twelve!"

Jimmy laughs. But... "One last thing Doc..." Lytrall's receptive at this. "Where do we start?"

He looks thoughtful a second anew, then... "That wasn't your file, Jimmy. It was your mom's."

"Yes?"

"That was her name not yours. You might want to start by searching for Adamowski women with the first initial *J*."

Jimmy leaps up at this. Beams. He pats The Professor on the back like he's drumming his gratitude into him. He's about to rush off. But...

"Almost forgot my past." He grabs his pack and his stuff. "*Mom's* past!"

Lytrall smiles at this again. "*Cherchez la knickknacks.*"

"*Shur*-what?"

"Follow the Knickknacks Jimmy. Your heirlooms. They've never led you astray."

"Right Doc!" Jimmy bolts again.

Professor's smile fades a little. "Follow the NikNaks."

iv

Miss you, hopefully you're making some headway?

v

"There're your terrorists." Lytrall's pointing at what amounts to a touchscreen mapping app on one of his terminals. Hundreds of little pinkish-orange pins feature across Amerika.

Jimmy's zooming in with the pinch of his fingers, individuates a cluster. He closes his eyes. Gifts himself a look right into a small group of forty-five-year-old dummies in surgical masks and hoodies. "Holy hell!" he exclaims. "You map all their brains or something?"

"No. I just tracked NikNak activity."

"NikNaks?"

"Short-form streaming video content. You see, users—"

"No, I know *what* a NikNak is. How do you catch these guys with them?"

"Only kids watch NikNaks and *WAMN*. *WAMN* is completely off-grid when in-complex. However, once in the field, the first thing they do is scramble for the internet, for their NikNaks. I just monitor excessive NikNak usage on Blackberries."

"Blackberries?"

"No one under forty uses a BlackBerry. Anyone using a BlackBerry to watch a NikNak is over forty therefore. Anyone over forty watching a NikNak is WAMN. Process of elimination."

"Ha! So we got em?"

"Got em when they come out into the light. Like I said, completely off-grid when in their hideouts. However, this'll allow us to stop em before they cause any—"

¬Ǝ

"Mayhem."

Near-instantly the masked weirdo fogeys start dropping into the *INOS*. Remember that? Been a while. The *Inertial-Neutralizer Or Something...*

They're falling as fast as Lytrall can track them. Faster than he can get the relevant authorities to the *INOS* Jimmy's using. Doesn't matter though. *WAMN* runs they *run* to their NikNaks and Jimmy brings them right back. Brings them right back with all their weapons and explosives and plans which are more than incriminating. Plans talk of their targets but also of their love for that leader of theirs. The irony of appeasing Figurace so Jimmy be delivered on a platter while it's Jimmy delivering the appeasers *the same*. Never will they go off book and that's not Figurace's concern anyway, as rule one of their tome is: don't name the leader.

Their end is Figurace and Figurace's end is something you'd have to ask him. Though he sure as shit doesn't want Jimmy delivered so Jimmy'll help *WAMN* assholes work from home. Probably wants something petty and predictable like bloody revenge. Point is, WAMN assholes are happy to incriminate themselves for their cause because they seek the ends of that cause like soft little middle-aged terminators.

Jimmy keeps delivering those terrorists along with their weapons, explosives, and plans *only* not before making a copy of those incriminating documents for he and Lytrall's use.

vi

Should be over soon...

It's written on that little whiteboard but Bart's not—
"Jimmy!"

He snaps back to the task at hand.

"A cult of personality only they won't talk about the boss." Lytrall says this looking over his share of the documents-duplicated. "Must be really eating at them too since they love the guy so much. *Oh Great Leader* this and *Oh great Leader* that..."

"I just don't understand how we can get them the second they go online yet it happens nowhere near any kind of headquarters—"

"Unless this was part of their—" Lytrall stifles. Flips through the last three pages of his stack again like maybe he didn't see what he thought he saw.

"What is it?"

"Jimmy, I don't want you to worry—"

But Jimmy grabs at the papers in Lytrall's hands. He manages to snag the last. It's a charcoal rendering of the professor. "Doc..." he says in self-incrimination. "I should have been more careful."

"They're doing exactly what I said they would. Sit a second Jimmy."

Jimmy pulls a stool up to the draft table they've been using. "Ok..."

He hands Jimmy the other two pages. "Try to keep your focus."

Jimmy starts reading. The professor carefully, quietly, hits his fob.

"Female, early thirties, federal agent..." As Jimmy reads he goes pale. *"...Narrowed down to The Bureau or Marshall's office."* He looks up at Lytrall. *"Adamowski's closest confidant. Possible romantic ties..."*

He's about to beam away when...

BALAINK!

The professor's locked him out.

"I can't Jimmy. This might be what they're counting on." But Jimmy isn't hearing it. He rushes to the terminal. He's trying to remember the lock-out override. Lytrall reasons, "If they're doing what they're doing to get next to you, making themselves visible to me to plant this information, they may just be fishing..." Jimmy's tapping at the terminal blindly. "...Waiting for you to rush to her to fill in that missing piece of their puzzle...." *Tap Tap Tap...* "...Or, maybe that's not their plan only now you know they're searching for people close to you and they obviously didn't just dream up these details..." *Tap Tap Tap...* "...They've gathered them without getting so close they can grab her. You only increase their chances if you go..." *Tap Tap Tap...* "...Either scenario, doing what you intend puts her at a greater risk than..."

Jimmy stops. "What?"

"Everything else."

Jimmy's anything but noncommittal in his obstinance. "They may already have her!" *Tap Tap Tap...*

Lytrall grabs out for Jimmy's hand-tapping.

¬Ǝ/Ǝ

Jimmy dodges. Reach goes right through.

Lytrall gives in. Tries more talk. "When did you see her last?"

"Yesterday." He's still trying everything on that terminal.

"And, has she ever failed to return to her apartment by this time of day?"

"Yes."

"And you can't look where she goes when she does this?"

"Yes."

"Then you need to wait. She'll return. Even if they've gotten to her, she's a competent agent Jimmy. Just wait." His messing with the terminal slows. "You'll only hurt her and yourself. Close your eyes."

Jimmy does.

"Do you see her?"

"No, the chair's... No! She's home! She's there. Must have just got in the door. I see her."

"Any distress?"

"Yes, only not from... It's something else."

Lytrall hits his fob. "You're free now Jimmy. You know what you have to do."

She's looking at the tracker app. Looking at Jimmy's heart rate. She's excited to see he's Gifting. Hopeful. She's about to look up at nothing when... Heart rate goes to zero.

All stats go to zero.

Her eyes close tight squeezing tears.

Jimmy hands the tracker over. "I can't be anywhere right now."

Lytrall starts a nod only his head stays down there. He's not so lacking in empathy.

¬∃

World Three.

vii

Seven o'clock. She's there. Watching that app. Always at seven. She hasn't given up on him. He's given up on her? He did it for her. Not really given up. It's because he won't give up. Right? Where's that peace? That culmination. The last of it was supposed to come with her. He'd find her, with her. She'd be by his side. That's what he thought.

She looks up at nothing. "You've stopped the attacks Jimmy only he's not removing the kill order. I'd never hurt you. I don't know if this is because... I just want..."

viii

Seven o'clock. "Just to know..."

ix

Seven o'clock. "Please..."

x

Seven o'clock. "Any sign at all..."

xi

Seven o'clock. "Just tell me you never want to see me again if that's it. Just that, if that's what it is. Please..."

xii

Seven o'clock. "Measure for measure. I made a promise."

xiv

Seven o'clock. "I..."

But she stops herself.

She rises to him and he opens his arms. She moves into him with her palms clasped together at her chest. He holds her as best he can so she doesn't fall. She looks up and he cradles her face in his hands, minding himself so moving through her is a rarity, so he doesn't break the illusion of substance. It feels real for just a second before...

She tears right through him. Her arms move outward and upward as she reaches her hands to her crown. She rears backward against those hands, closes her eyes, shudders spinning away. "I Can't..." She takes hold of that little whiteboard.

"Not like this..." She starts writing, quick, hastily. "I can't anymore..."

Where's her peace?

She tosses the board onto the chair. "I'll show you Jimmy. After all I've done for you." She moves swift, in heavy steps. He can hear their fading.

Of course he'd never follow...

He just stares at that little missive,

I'll show you.

23

WAITING

McRae's office.

"I wish there was some other way little sister. Customs officials got you dead-to-rights fraternizing with Jimmy long after the order went through."

"Long after the order was moot, you mean? Jimmy-Cult's stopped in its tracks."

"Badge, agent."

She starts reaching, stops. "You know what?" she says at McRae putting the acid on him. "This is just so perfect. I was this close..." she pinches her index finger and thumb near-together. Little daylight gets between. "*This* close... Then you go and shut me out too."

"Just what's that supposed to mean?"

"Means maybe I'm ready to deliver him up on a platter just not to you anymore."

"You better pray that's some kinda brain infection doing your talking for you. Better pray because that's our only out in keepin obstruction off your ass!"

"They ain't got the manpower to stop me from stoppin them." She rises.

"You sit your narrow keister back down right this—"

She's out the door.

McRae looks like a stick of lit dynamite's gone and swallowed its own fuse.

He picks up his phone like protocol's up his ass. Hesitates. Sets the handset back on its cradle and... Picks it up again and *SMASH! SMASH!* slams the earpiece end into the receiver of the cradle a couple times. Sets the handset back down, real ginger.

ii

A month has passed.

Nothing on the Cult. No NikNak blips no bombs no anything. Custy's kill order's still in place despite no Cult to appease. This just government efficiency again or government pettiness? There's been no word on Bart and Jimmy couldn't care less about anything else but his dear friend. She's vanished.

He's still been doing what he does. He's stopping crime despite the rarity it's become. He's saving the odd life here and there though peril's minimized too—so's the despair. Custy's kill order's feckless thanks to The Danger Ranger™ so there's no problem with Jimmy being Jimmy. Where's the calm? Visions are quieted. Dreams are neutered...

He holds his fitness tracker in his hand. Cult's gone cold. Custy's on a psychopath warpath yet what can he do? Customs has less pull than that Cult.

Hell with it?

Hell with it!

He holds up his wrist, puts the tracker to it and pulls the

end of the strap over his scaphoid. He's about to thread the scaphoid end through the bottom eyelet when...

"Jimmy!" shouts Lytrall. "We got Cult activity."

Teleporter rushes to the terminal map. He clocks the location. Eyes close.

"This doesn't make any sense."

"What is it?"

Just some old lady on a park bench.

"She's gotta be using a Blackberry?"

"She is, only she's just some sweet old lady."

"Well it's almost certainly some sort of—"

¬Ⅎ

"Trap."

The *Sweet Old Lady* sits contented as can be just watching her phone. Contented as can be as Jimmy comes slinking around the bench and sits himself next to her. He glances over to confirm The Gift wasn't lying. NikNaks! On a Blackberry!

"Ma'am?" he musters. She looks to him. "Are you really enjoying—"

"My! You must be Jimmy!"

He starts looking around—tries for furtive but there's a hint of twitchy. The Old Lady's a little concerned. He calms to calm her.

"T-That's right ma'am. My name's Jimmy. How did you—"

"I was just sitting here and this nice person handed me this thing." She wiggles the phone. "He asked me if I'd do him a favor and let the shows play until a friend of his named *Jimmy* came to get it. Said you'd have a beard."

"That's me."

She hands him the Blackberry. "Here you are dear."

Jimmy thanks the woman as she lifts herself off the bench with her cane. *Bye now*, she says waving.

Jimmy waves at The Sweet Old Lady's back. Then... A vibration.

Jimmy?

He's about to respond, but...

Jimmy?

Watch this...

It's a video.

He hits the play button on the little thumbnail in the thread.

It's a man with his back to us in foreground and a woman sitting across from him in midground. It's a restaurant only *which* and *where* who can tell? It's just some *al fresco* dining scene. The woman is leaning, retrieving something, so she can't be identified. Then she speaks and her voice is unmistakable. Jimmy instantly feels infatuative fire rip at his soul. The voice soothes while the words make him want to die.

"You and I have a mutual acquaintance." Bart says this rising from under the table. She hands a picture of Jimmy to the man across from her—guy with his back to us. "Thorn in both our sides, better. We really should talk."

This drives our hero nuts. Doesn't know what to do. What's happening?

And then...

Bart looks into the camera. "If you're quick Jimmy..." She writes something on a napkin. Holds it up. Coordinates.

Eyes close.

The man still has his back to us but so too does Bart. They've left the table. The man is veering at an angle to our left, moving casually. Bart is not. She's moving at a diverging angle to our right and swift.

Now for the dilemma: follow Bart or follow her accomplice. Follow the seat of reason or follow the heart? At least he's rational enough to know the difference. He's gotta identify the accomplice but...

He warps...

It's Figa-fuckin-race! Grinning like he knows Jimmy's gonna give in to his all-consuming motivations to attend to her. To hold on and never let her go! No! She's betraying you again you dope! Is she? Figurace walks even slower, taunting Jimmy. He tips the invisible brim of an invisible hat. Taunting times ten!

Fuck off Figurace!

Jimmy warps back to where he last saw Bart. Only her coat on the ground now. Memory Jimmy, something you haven't had to rely on in... *Ever.* Just been peeping your way to the facts your whole life. What was she wearing under that coat? Cream! That super soft cream cashmere sweater her grandma gave her. You know because she put it on that day you took her to see her.

He's warping and panning and scanning... When... That's it. The sweater!

She's reaching for a car door when...

¬Ⅎ

Ǝ

Jimmy takes her by the wrist. Spins her. *Her?*

A Cultist! A spinning grinning Cultist! Younger of the bunch, still... Old! And a decoy! A bloody goddamn decoy!

"You can take *me* Jimmy," *Decoy* mocks. "Beam me out of here. Call me your consolation prize."

Jimmy lets her go with a slight shove. He spins for one last desperate search for Bart but the Cultist's not finished.

"She's not done with you yet Jimmy. And in case you get some bright idea to snatch me up and torture me to tell you anything, you get nothing. I'm gonna walk out of here and you just hold onto that phone. Await further instructions as us hostage takers like to say." She runs off now.

Jimmy doesn't just let her go, he's happy to.

He looks at that phone, adrenaline managing to keep beating a heart-ripped-in-two ripping to shreds.

iii

"I just don't get what she could be thinking Doc. I just don't fucking get it!" Jimmy's pacing the complex, phone in hand.

The professor puts an arm out, halting him. Talks... "Jimmy, I can't tell you there's no possibility this is part of some second betrayal. Or part of a much more elaborate first betrayal. I can't tell you she's only doing her job just using you in the process. That it's justified because you've certainly used her. I can't tell you what she's doing isn't the grandest of gestures to prove herself to you and win your heart..." The Professor pauses a second. "In fairness, that last one's redundant as we both know where your heart lays, yet she doesn't know that. Probably believes the opposite after your distancing yourself from her like you did.

"So, of all of this, I can't say any of it is true and I can't say any of it is false. I can only tell you this: you're going to watch that phone and I'll bring you a charger from the stone ages so you don't freak out when in all your obsession you let the battery die and throughout all of this, in the end, you're just going to have to grin and bear it all. It's the only way you'll get the answers you're looking for."

"I just... I-I wish there was some World Three I could crawl into where time stood still on the inside. To get this over with."

"No you don't Jimmy. You don't want to lose a second with her if things are on the up-n-up. Even if they're not. You don't want to lose a second with anyone past present or future who'd add the same meaning to your life. You don't. So you're going to wait. You're going to wait and feel a torture a tenth of anything you've ever felt in your life and thank her for helping you find this peace at least. Just. Wait."

Deep breath.

Jimmy looks to his mentor, stone.

"No."

¬Ǝ

24

BETWEEN A (THIRD) ROCK
AND A HARD PLACE...

He sits. Calm. Crisscross applesauce and palms spooning. Blackberry sits in those spooned palms. His orange robe flows in that unearthly warmth.

Then...

Phone vibrates.

Eyes open.

Eyes close.

He's Gifting a look at the exact coordinates texted. It's a video monitor in an empty room. Currently off—

On now!

It's Bart, she doesn't seem to be aware she's on camera. She's arguing heatedly with Figurace. Seems like business. Kind that really tears Jimmy's guts out. They're in what you would almost swear is foliage only the periphery's too dark to confirm. A few of Figgy's disciples hang about, masked and hooded.

Keep it calm Jimmy boy...

"They're not ready for the final play!" Bart urges.

"I disagree," Figurace says.

"I won't let you blow this whole fuckin operation, politician!"

"I'm a bureaucrat my dear. Don't you ever insult me like that again. Now, as someone in my position, who knows the power of a bargain in addition to the benefit of obtaining the object of that bargain, I feel I need ask, what exactly is your leverage here?"

"My leverage *here* is the same failsafe I brought on board when you welcomed me into this flock of shitbirds: you rush this and I'll tell our mark where he can find you, me, this whole damn operation."

"Yeah?"

"Oh, yeah."

"Me first."

Figurace motions and his goons reach out and grab hold of Bart. One of them puts a strip of duct tape to her mouth wrapping it all the way around her head.

Figurace turns to face the camera, face Jimmy. "I know you're watching. Keep watching. Keep figuring." He assesses the surroundings. "Not gonna show? Oh that's right, you need an address."

Jimmy's calmed incongruous to everything. Calmed more. Hands still spoon. He watches as the disciples put a bomb vest on Bart.

"Stand by Jimmy boy. This won't work without you."

ii

He sits. Calm. Crisscross applesauce and palms spooning. Blackberry sits in those spooned palms. His orange robe flows in that unearthly warmth.

Then...

Phone vibrates again.

Eyes open.

Eyes close.

¬∃

He's teleported into the dark. Dark save for a cyan panel underfoot. Area smells of pine.

Then...

There's a *CREEYANK!* sound and the panel turns crimson.

"Oh hell..."

"That's right Jimmy..."

Stadium lights burst on illuminating them all: The Teleporter, Figurace, his three disciples, and Bart wired to that vest. It smelled like pine because they're in the Cult's forest compound. Who knows where it is relative to anything else. Jimmy only knows by the coordinates given and he more intuited where to beam from those coords than knows of their location on any map.

Bart's been seated in a chair bound and still gagged and Jimmy faces her at a distance just far enough to be nonlethal if that vest goes. She and Jimmy are surrounded by the same polycarbonate ballistics glass he stood behind watching Lytrall explode. Only, in this case, the glass makes up a fence about fifteen feet high, forming an enclosure a little smaller than a hockey rink. Figurace and the three disciples are behind the glass of course. Figurace's walking around to Jimmy's side.

"...You've teleported right onto a pressure-sensitive trigger. You move from that panel and... Well... You know what that trigger will trigger."

But Jimmy's not taking his eyes off Bart. Not taking his eyes off hers to be precise. They've welled in the moments before all this. She's not sobbing or crying at him now though. She appears to be imploring him.

"No. No teleporting for you Jimmy." Figurace says this in an irony too thick to be effective *but-for* the coercive elements he's ensured. He lets himself into the pen that holds the two. He notices Jimmy watching Bart intently. He promptly steps between, staying outside the range of lethality of that vest as well. He stands toe-to-top-of-that-crimson-pressure-panel with Jimmy. Jimmy stares right through him to her. Figurace doesn't track this focus.

"The way this is all going to work," Fig begins, "is I'm going to fit you out with a timer and a set of coordinates. Coordinates are on this post-it." He holds up the note. It's stuck to the tip of his finger. Written on it are longitudinal and latitudinal values next to the words *150 feet under*. "Nothing you haven't seen a billion times before. The timer on the other hand, is in this." In his other hand he holds up a familiar-looking syringe with a familiar-looking fluid. It's the glow that's the giveaway. "Now, I know you've seen this before if only once. However, I bet it stuck. I also know you can get that mentor of yours to clear you of the nanobots in this syringe and that's kinda the point Jimmy. These bots are designed to self-annihilate not replicate. You can beam away from them. You can scan em to dust, *or* you can just let them wind down to a quantity of zero over time. Regardless of the means, as soon as they drop below critical mass value, the timer's up and *BOOM!* Your girl's giblets. You're gonna want to just let these bots wind down to nothing, naturally. That way you'll get yourself forty-five whole seconds worth of her remaining in one piece."

Jimmy entertains but Jimmy don't flinch. Jimmy he don't move an inch. He entertains out of the use in not arousing any volatility, but he keeps his direction on her. "What would you have me do in that time?"

"Nothing so difficult. You're gonna *do* The Prez."

Don't flinch. "No dinner first? Foreplay? What am I gonna do with the other thirty-five seconds?"

"Yeah I heard you could be a real fucker in these situations. You're gonna *kill* The Prez."

"How?"

"You figure it out Teleporter. You got all the tricks. Drop him off the Statue of Liberty's head or something. Teleport him onto the 401. Hell, bring him here and *I'll* finish him off."

"Why?"

"If he'd just given me my war…"

"You're that petty?"

"I'm that political," he corrects. "But it's a two birds one stone scenario here. What do you think happens when somebody kills a president? You think it's law and order and checks and balances and *habeas corpus* and the upholding of any aspect of the constitution?" Jimmy's hands spoon. Figurace smirks. "Of course not. It's bedlam. The establishment is out for blood and they'll get it. That's in your John Wilkes Boothe Lee Harvey scenarios." A bit of beating around the bush now… Then… "What do you think happens should an overpowered freak like you kill a president?"

He don't flinch here either though close. Nothing will ever be the same. That's the bureaucrat's design. Jimmy don't flinch but his top hand moves under the bottom in that spoon. His sights stay on her. Precisely for the reason that nothing will ever be the same. That's the design. "You've got everything so carefully planned, what about this? How the hell do I find the guy in just forty-five seconds?"

"You've already found him." Figurace wiggles the post-it note still stuck to his finger. "He'll be in this fixed location. A fifteen-by-fifteen foot box a hundred-fifty feet underground."

"Do I even need to ask how you'll get him into that bunker? Or, does it have something to do with the fact all but three of your bonehead disciples are around?"

"Clever. A few shootings, some bombings, hijackings. That's an international incident and that'll send the Prez deep down into the earth."

"Why would they do these things for you? All they've ever wanted was free shit and a ride."

"Oh, they think they're getting that ride. Think you're coming to save them at the last. Before any harm befalls them. Because I told them you're coming and: They. Believe. Every. Thing. I. Say."

"He's setting you up." Jimmy yells over to the goons. "You know I can't get to all your friends in time."

Goons get a little restless.

Figgy turns to them. "What did I tell you I would do for you? I said I would do the impossible: I'd bring you The Teleporter in a state of powerlessness. A powerlessness only I can reverse. I said I could do the impossible and did just that so surely I can do what's next-to-impossible and have him save *you*." A beat. "Or have you lost all faith?"

Disciples back down. Defused. No point in Jimmy trying that—

"No point in you trying that again Jimmy. You're a dirty trickster to them. I'm their god now."

"So what now your eminence?"

"We wait. In twenty-five minutes the first attacks will begin and by forty-five the president will be safely tucked away. I shoot you up and you're free to leave. Only, move quick or your girlfriend will move quicker. In every direction at once!" And then a shit-eating grin comes across Figgy's face. "So, we'll bide our time! However, while we do —while *you* wait to go off to do all this to save her—I want you to answer me a question." He gestures limply at Bart. "What makes you think she's ever stopped fearing you? What makes you think that little game of counting heartbeats could ever really allay her?" Hands change in spoon. Figgy chuckles like a fop. "Oh yes, she told us all about you and her. Think she wasn't reaching for that phone late at night, looking to make sure you're not about to murder her whole world in your dreams? Destroy everything that's ever mattered to her? I know I'd never be able to turn it off... We all fear you you goddamn freak but only I can control you!" He hunkers, plays like he's going to smash that red panel under Jimmy's feet. Jimmy don't dance yet Figgy acts like the toying with him's working despite it all. He slams his palm downward stopping it a couple inches from the red, rises abrupt, scoffs. "Only I've ever stopped you! Only I can allay their fears. Hers. *For peace of mind...* She knew this all along?"

Jimmy reaches for a stoicism. Reaches. Nothing will ever be the same...

Figurace moves to give him the clearest view of her. View's the same for Bart as it is for Jimmy. She starts wrenching. Furiously. *No!* but The Teleporter looks right through.

"How can you ever trust her again?" Figurace chides. "You *know* what she's capable of."

Doesn't matter...

"What was that?"

"Doesn't. Matter. Either. Way." He says this flat, no real discernible tone. "I understand." He's not saying this to Figurace but to Bart and Bart's activated by it. She stops communicating by movement a moment though she implores on. Her eyes are fire like she's trying real hard at something. But...

Jimmy kneels. He interlocks his fingers at the nape of his neck, brings his elbows as close together as they will with his head as fulcrum and woven fingers as governor. Makes it look like that's what's dragging him down but his lowering's a matter of exasperation and gravity. Figurace watches in lust as clasped fingers break free. Jimmy grants himself a look while the rest of him *after* visage stays kneeling as though in supplication. He looks into the ether. Looks up at nothing. Expressionless. "Doesn't matter either way..."

She starts moving again as much as her bonds will let her. Screams as loud as her gag will let her the same.

Jimmy just shakes his head and adds, "None of it." Takes a second. Prepares to say his last words of his world as he knows it. Words are for her. He flashes a look at her and not *through* and she catches it. "You know..." he says to a girl now as still as though of World Three. Kept. Like this culmination drives her to attend to nothing outside The Teleporter's suffering nihilisms. She's focused on his last testament. Waiting in her deathbed reversal of demeanor.

While...

Figurace revels in the torture play.

Then...

"Ripley Jeanette Bartholomew..." He's never Gifted more deeply into another as her. "There was a time when I thought you worth moving the heavens and the earth for."

He cocks his head forty-five degrees, puts his right palm onto the pressure panel.

Fingers ball into a fist.

Knuckles flat to the red.

"Best I can do now..."

He grins.

"...Is Earth."

¬∃

25

THE WHOLE WORLD, JIMMY!

Jimmy's teleported the world away.

He's teleported the whole world away from Figurace.

Figurace floats in dead space. Just he and that bomb vest-unexploded.

Takes him a second to figure out his plight and even then, what can he figure with absolute-zero kicking every inch of him in the ass? He gasps and spins. He steams. Lack of pressure boils his blood. Will he die? Some physicists believe, corroborated by some physicians, a person in dead space, without any protective gear of any kind, can survive with minimal harm for roughly the exact amount of time Jimmy's gonna make Figurace sweat. (Or steam...)

Ǝ

The Earth's back. Figgy's collapsed on the ground catching his breath almost exactly where he stood before Jimmy ripped the whole planet out from under him. Fig's lying on that blue panel now. *CREEYANK!* Sorry... Red panel.

Bart's out of the vest but also her bonds. She stands behind the ballistics glass a little dazed.

Where is that vest anyway? Well…

Lytrall walks to the top of that red pressure panel. Sits right there on the ground in front of it. He observes Figurace a moment then gestures for the hyperventilating bureaucrat to sit up and face him.

"Might as well be comfortable," he says to Figgy. Figgy can see the bomb vest. Sees the red under him too. Sees the explosion in his mind's eye. He starts to scramble to get up. "Whoa whoa, easy," says Lytrall. "Sit." He tugs at the lapel of the vest. The aide does as he's told. "Why?" Lytrall asks.

"Bloody revenge."

"Thought so."

"Why are *you* wearing that vest?" Figgy asks.

"Oh, that'll take a bit of convincing," The Professor assures. "Best get to it." He hands Figurace a lighter.

Where's Jimmy anyway? Where's that skyscraper he moved that time for that matter?

Bart was just staring confusedly at that studious-looking guy sitting so comfortable in her bomb vest but now that she's got her wits, she starts to take in the scene. She's getting a little frantic when…

"You're still here."

She knows that voice.

Ǝ

She turns. Relief.

He faces her, unflinching.

She flinches. "I—I know there's nothing I can say to convince—"

He takes her hand in his. "I wasn't lying when I said I understood."

"There's more to it—"

He gently opens her palm. He drops the badge into it.

A tear rolls down her cheek. "Pick Hank's pocket for this?" she manages to chuckle out.

"No." Jimmy wrys.

We're in McRae's office. He's shutting his door. He's turning to his desk when...

"You." he says to the figure behind it.

"Heard about your latest undercover op," Jimmy says.

"But... The kill order?" she reminds.

"Oh it wasn't me who talked to your boss..."

We're back in McRae's office just after the closing of that door. "You."

"Got a proposition for you," Lytrall says.

"I sent a proxy. Made him an offer he couldn't refuse..."

Lytrall's holding up a nano-syringe and the only device he has for flushing out the bots in it. McRae's intrigued.

Bart has a look like she's proud of Jimmy.

Jimmy has a look like he's proud of Bart.

Shit! That burns! Says Figurace off in the distance.

"You did *show me* after all…" he says.

"Yes, but Jimmy that wasn't it."

He raises an eyebrow. "McRae spoke of your desire to help. To make amends."

"True and true, but those two things aren't connected. This is what I wanted to show you." She takes a folded paper out of her inside breast pocket. Hands it to him.

He unfolds. It's a copy of a naturalization certificate. The form's nature is immaterial. It's the name on it that matters. Written on it is, *Adamowski, Jaryna.*

"*Jaryna?*" he says.

"She's still alive Jimmy."

"J-Jaryna… M—" But he can't quite…

"Yes," she assures him.

"Jaryna!"

He wants to collapse in his joy. His eyes well. He wraps his arms around Bart who's more than happy to reciprocate. He doesn't want to let go. But…

"Jimmy?" she asks.

"Yeah?"

"My boss has orders. We all do. How'd you—"

"Damn!" Hug loosens. He pulls back a little. "I'm on the clock! I gotta go!"

"Then you better."

He hugs her tightest once more then breaks away. "I owe you!" he shouts as he goes.

"We're even," she shouts after.

Now Mr. Figurace, how about you tell me of that first attack?

McRae stands next to a Red Dawn style detention center: a massive chain-link fence around an *INOS*. He waits with Custy and a bunch more Customs agents.

"This better be worth it McRae."

"Worth it for our salvation…"

"What was that?" says Custy, crusty.

"I made a promise."

"I'm the one who makes the promises. You're the one who keeps them."

"How about I promise you this: if Jimmy don't deliver and we end up having to follow through with your order—or, say your snake-ass decides to screw Jimmy on the deal anyway—I'll personally make you pull that trigger you officious little coward. I owe him that much."

"How dare—"

SMACK!

McRae's smashed Custy with a haymaker. Custy's on his ass out cold.

"Owe Bart too."

Suit One goes *Holy Shit!*

Other agents surround McRae to detain him.

"Look!" says Suit One.

Agents let go of McRae at the sight.

Figurace's three goons drop into the cage from above. Then…

Ǝ/¬Ǝ

One of the Cultists…

Ǝ/¬Ǝ

Another…

Ǝ/¬Ǝ… Ǝ/¬Ǝ… Ǝ/¬Ǝ… More and more and more!

Lytrall puts a hand on Figurace's shoulder. "Any more?" he asks. Figurace shakes his head. "Good." Lytrall looks up at nothing. "We're done here Jimmy."

Ǝ/¬Ǝ

Bart's gone.

Ǝ/¬Ǝ, Ǝ/¬Ǝ

Figurace's gone.

Figurace's gone?

KABOOM?

No!

Lytrall's been moved in Figurace's place on that panel.

"I guess I'll just walk back?" He takes a step off when...

BOOM!

Then...

Ǝ/¬Ǝ

Reintegrated-Lytrall's gone.

ii

INOS containment unit is full up with the Cultists. Jimmy got em all.

Custy's agents hold McRae in custody as...

Ǝ/¬Ǝ

McRae's gone. His cuffs fall to the ground.

Jimmy and McRae stand toe to toe. Bossman smirks, takes out that device Lytrall gave him and clears Jimmy of the Nanobots.

Jimmy smirks back. "You know I could have snatched that away from you at any time."

"I know."

"Custy still wanna kill me?"

"Of course convict."

"You gonna let him?"

"If he can do it with my handcuffs on. I'm taking Custy into custody."

"On what charges?" Jimmy asks. McRae give's him a *you serious?* head tilt. Jimmy looks disappointed. "Don't let anyone ever tell you you ain't Eff-Bee-Eye..."

Smirk widens[1]. "Made a real mistake going after Bart in front of that dogged son of a bitch raised her..."

Hero looks impressed. "Don't let anyone ever tell you you *is* Eff-Bee-Eye..."

"Just get me back to my agents so I can detain that skunk before they do."

Jimmy puts his hands on McRae's shoulders. "Oooh, you workin out boss?"

"Fuck you convict!"

¬∃

McRae indeed slaps the cuffs on a crusty Custy of Customs just barely come to. Custy's in custody.

"Throw him in that pen with the other Cultists and chill him out a little."

Jimmy turns to Bart and barely whispers *cuff crusty Customs Custy and put him with the culty cultists in custody?*

Bart grins. Lytrall laughs.

"Ya like that one?" Jimmy says to his mentor.

"Nah. I'm just tired and exploded."

Then...

---

1. Serious smirk-off taking place... Lotta smirkin off goin on here...

"I want you bad Jimmy boy!"

It's Suit Two looking for that *this-ain't-over*-style revenge. He moves swift for Jimmy. Jimmy gets in front of Bart and Lytrall, shielding them. He readies himself for attack as the agent pounds toward.

"This asshole too," says McRae looping his arm around Suit Two halting him like a toddler running into traffic. "Does Custy's wet work."

Cuffs are put on and Suit Two's detained alongside his boss.

Then...

"Jimmy Adamowski! I want you bad, man!" It's Libby! Forgot about that douchebag! He's marching towards Jimmy. He's bald!

"You made my life a living hell!" Libby cries.

"You were pardoned after six months ya shit!"

Libby fumes. "Worst thing to ever happen to me is the worst thing that *can* ever happen to me."

"Keep talking that way and I'll take your own personal hell up a notch."

"Any time man! I want you bad!"

"What a ya say then Jack? You want a shot at the title?" Jimmy removes and drops his monk robe onto the ground. Drops his Jets jersey too. He stands shirtless in his gong fu ku.

"Don't mind if I do!" Libby lusts.

Bart turns to the Customs agents and her fellow Eff-Bee-Eye to keep them from trying to stop this. They all just stare on in anticipation. She shrugs. Turns back to Jimmy and Libby squaring off.

Get him Jimmy! cheers Suit One.

Then...

HOOF!

Jimmy kicks Libby in the solar plexus and takes all the wind and consciousness out of him. Libby's out cold on the ground.

"Awww!" groan all the agents at the anticlimactic result.

"I told you all, I'm a Kung Fu Priest. Remember?"

No you're not!

"Whatever..." Jimmy crouches down to pick up his clothes.

Lytrall walks up to comfort him? "You fought one hell of an unfair fight there Jimmy. He's a senatorial aide and you're a martial arts master who can move planets with his mind."

"Whatever..."

But...

Just as the cuffs are going on, Libby regains consciousness, breaks free. Jimmy looks up from his crouching position to check on the commotion. Libby's grabbed one of the Customs agents' side arms. He's aiming it at our hero.

"Hey Jimmy!" Libby shouts cocking the gun. "I'm not gonna shoot you between the balls. I'm gonna shoot you between the eyes!"

BANG!

The bullet is flying right for between Jimmy's eyes as he crouches in the grass in front of Lytrall. Danger Ranger™ engage!

BEEP! BEEP!

¬Ⅎ

Jimmy's gone! It's just Lytrall standing a couple feet behind where our crouching Jimmy used to be!

SPLOOTCH!

Oh my god! Libby shot Professor Lytrall between the balls!

But...

The feedback!

SPLORTCH!

Oh my god! Libby's blown his own balls off somehow!

Holy shit! Suit One cries out in joy!

Ⅎ

Jimmy's back!

Yay Jimmy! shouts Suit One.

You know what? I've had just about enough of you! Custy barks at Suit One. *You're fired!*

Fuck you I quit! says One. *I'm a Jimmy man now!*

Jimmy and Lytrall look at each other confused.

Suit One flips off Custy as he backs away. He turns to Suit Two, "Oh, and Barry, I've been fucking your wife. Don't believe me? Go ahead and call my phone. I won't answer because I'll be fuckin your wife!"

Lytrall shakes his head at all this, taps Jimmy on the shoulder. "I'm going home."

Jimmy nods as Lytrall takes off. Doesn't watch the professor go as he's watching Bart debriefing McRae. He starts walking toward her. Lytrall walks away in the opposite direction, half-grinning.

McRae's facing Jimmy so sees him coming. Bart's not facing Jimmy so doesn't. "This can wait till tomorrow," he says. "See you at ten *eh-em* little sister."

She looks at her half-grinning boss in some confusion just as there's a tapping at her shoulder. She spins to latch onto Jimmy.

"Wanna get outta here?" he says to her.

"Thought you'd never ask!"

¬Ⅎ

26

———

DO-OVER

Jimmy's back at the monastery. He's with Bart. Special privileges. They sit on the front steps and talk in near-perfect contentment *as well* as contemplation *as well* as that unearthly warmth. They've spoken of Jimmy's debt to the temple—of his debt to her too.

It's only *near-perfect* contentment as Jimmy's in some mild lament. Talk of he and Bart's debts has sparked an awareness of the strange circumstances of their bond.

"Do you realize our whole relationship was founded on lies? Both yours and mine? Noble I imagine, though no less lies."

"And it didn't get much better did it?"

"A world-class bad start."

"Wish we could have a do-over."

A beat. An insight.

Then...

Here comes that perfect contentment...

"Can I show you something?" Jimmy asks, his hands extending.

Bart takes those hands in hers.

¬⅂

⅂

It's the concert hall where they met.

"What did you want to show me?"

Jimmy holds up a *just one minute* finger. He slaps that fake mustache onto his face and... "Hi, I'm Jimmy Adamowski. I'm a teleporter and a sadist. I'd love to hear your life's story starting with what your name is."

She laughs—obliges. "Sure... *Jimmy* is it? How about over dinner?"

"Wonderful. I'll get your name then Agent Bartholomew!"

She kisses him on the cheek.

"Need a lift home?" he asks.

There's a little deliberation but not much. "You know what, I think I'll walk. Need to rehearse that story of mine." Then...

"Who's in there?" A key is turning in the hall door.

She latches onto Jimmy in a way becoming custom. "That said, you can get me out of *here* instead of leaving me like the last time. Fast!"

¬⅂

ii

⅂

Jimmy's back at the temple. Forgot his pack.

"Can travel a million miles in no time, still gonna be late

for dinner."

He's reaching down for it when…

SCHWIPP!

A tranquilizer dart hits him in the neck!

Monks rush to get between him and the feds attacking.

As Jimmy loses consciousness he sees many monks incapacitated and those not, only fighting a losing battle. Just as he goes under, Custy emerges waving Lytrall's fob. Green LED is off.

iii

He awakes to sensory disorientation torture. He's lying on the floor. The top half of his head's encased in a device sending sound and light information at him in extreme intensity. He can't tell what's real. Are the strobing auras a product of a migraine induced or the torture itself? Are the grinding, shrieking, and pounding sounds of an intrinsic nightmare also? From outside? He can't ask such questions. He can't catch his wits in the calamitous overload. He's certainly not teleporting anywhere as there's no Gift under this.

Custy enters. Not that Jimmy would notice. Not at first, but as the agent starts talking, the images Jimmy can see and hear distort just enough to form shape and speech. Custy looms among the contrived aura and screeches of the torture. *Get him up* the agent demands in a distorted robotic whine as far as Jimmy can hear. Fed stooges lift The Teleporter barely at all before Custy hoofs him in the stomach crumbling him back to one.

Jimmy manages to plant a right palm on linoleum and prop himself up a little. He says the words *you got him you got no one*. Custy and the Feds hear it clear as day yet Jimmy has no idea of the articulation. He doesn't even know if his mouth is moving. He just repeats it over and over hoping he's heard.

Custy lifts his face in a fast grip. "I hear ya Jimmy. Got em all. Lytrall..." He throws the fob at him. "The girl..." He throws Bart's badge. "Hell, even the ol monk..." He throws a medallion that only Jimmy and the monk could know about.

No one.

Custy starts pulling at his lapels and hopping. Reveling as so many have at a Jimmy-trapped. As he did once himself, foolishly. "...I'm gonna make you beg Teleporter. I'm gonna make you beg for whatever I want you to beg me for for as long as I desire and *death* is just ninety-eight on my top one-hundred list of all-time things you're gonna be begging me for by the time I'm done with you! I'm gonna make you beg and I'm gonna use the mystery of their fates to keep you gropin and graspin teleporter man. Do it Jimmy! Beg me Jimmy you're already on the floor.

Jimmy rises to a kneeling position. Hands waving, grasping for any information in that ether. This is that groping.

Groping gradually turns to the beginnings of the begging posture Custy's lusting over.

But...

Just as hands are about to clasp together in supplication... Index fingers wag. *No no no* you disgraced off-the-books bureaucrat. Who let you out anyway? Then, appendages lower. Defiance? Of course. His right palm goes to the floor. Fingers rattle and prattle along it like he's playing chopsticks a second.

Still can't Gift.

"What you doin down there Jimmy? Lookin for this..." Custy stomps Lytrall's all-purpose fob to pieces. He's about to gloat, but...

Lackey barges into the interrogation room, frantic.

"What?" Custy shouts at him.

"The girl, her father!"

"Bart?"

"Guy's shooting his way in here. Two others with him. Some John-Wayne-looking mother-fucker and a glowing guy with tasers. Three-man wrecking crew!" Lackey puts a finger to his earpiece. "All those fuckin monks too boss! Kung fu hullabaloo!" Lackey runs for his life.

Custy frowns. "Party's over." He turns back to his quarry. "And what a party it would have been Jimmy." He whistles and Suit Two enters—not that Jimmy'd know.

Suit Two pulls out a Desert Eagle Mark I .357 magnum.

"Time to die, Teleporter," says Custy.

"Told you this wasn't over asshole," says Suit Two. Pistol barrel goes under Jimmy's chin.

Jimmy's fingers are still prattling on the floor.

Custy's still curious. "What the hell you doin down there?"

Prattling intensifies.

No more casual curiosity. Custy moves in and takes Suit Two's gun. Puts it to Jimmy's heart. Two moves around behind and holds onto where Jimmy's shoulder meets his neck.

"Tell us what the fuck you're up to ya bastard!"

Prattling stops,

Jimmy grins, mocks in Custy's voice, "*The whole goddamn universe, Jimmy?*"

Custy's eyes go wide. Jimmy snatches the agent's right wrist up in his left hand—index finger slips between Eagle's hammer and primer. Custy struggles yet Jimmy's grip's impossible. Two jumps in, tries wrenching at that vice as grip only tightens.

In all this The Teleporter's right palm has stayed flat to the floor, but...

Fingers ball into a fist,

Knuckles flat to the red.

"Hold on tight..."

EPILOGUE